OF GATES AND TYPHOONS

Also By Camilla Tracy

Of Threads and Oceans

Of Flowers and Cyclones

Of Blood and Tides

Soxkendi: A Family of Dragons

Of Spools and Billows

Of Gates and Typhoons

Join my animal loving community and learn about my newest book releases by clicking below or scanning the QR code:

https://geni.us/CamillaTracynewsletter

CAMILLA TRACY

OF
GATES
AND
TYPHOONS

THREADS OF MAGIC
BOOK 5

Camilla Tracy

Published by Pudel Threads Publishing

First Printing 2024

Tracy, Camilla, author

Of Gates and Typhoons: Book 5 in Threads of Magic

ISBN (paperback) 978-1-7381915-8-1

eISBN 978-1-7381915-7-4

B&N ISNBN 978-1-7381915-9-8

Under a Federal Liberal government, Library and Archives Canada no longer provides Cataloguing in Publication (CIP) data for independently published books.

Technical Credits:

Cover Image: MiblArt

Editor: Bobbi Beatty of Silver Scroll Services, Calgary, Alberta

Proofreader: Lorna Stuber - Editor, Proofreader, Writer, Okotoks, Alberta

Created with Atticus

to my forever friends

CHAPTER ONE

T HALI RUBBED HER EYES. Where the first of Bulstan's gates usually stood, there was nothing. "Veer starboard!" she yelled. The crew flurried to bring the ship careening to turn away from the invisible wall.

"Drop anchor!" Lobb yelled.

As the anchor yanked them to a halt, Thali used her magic to search the area. All she found was a barrier. Where Bulstan should have been was only an invisible, magic wall. She turned and whispered her findings to Isaia beside her.

"Like when we encountered the leviathan a few years ago?" Isaia asked.

Thali nodded. "Hoist the anchor, and sail gently," she said. She left Lobb, her second in command, at the helm and ran to the edge of the bow. She reached out with her magical threads, trying to touch the barrier. Maybe she could find a way to dismantle it.

Elric followed her and stood just behind her. "What do you think happened?"

"I don't know," Thali said. Her heart dropped to her stomach at the thought of something happening to Tariq, Bree, and Mupto.

They pulled the anchor back and approached the invisible wall slowly. Alexius edged up to her other side.

Any ideas? Thali asked Alexius along the magical thread in their minds.

We'll know more when we get closer. It doesn't look offensive, Alexius said.

What does it look like?

Protective.

As they continued approaching slowly, Thali felt the magical wall push in as the bow eased gently onward. She stepped forward, wanting to see if her hands could pierce the wall. A cool softness enveloped her. She closed her eyes as it passed over her face. Then she opened them again, only to see Bulstan, just as it always was, right where it had always been.

The ship came to a sudden halt.

"Thali, do you see anything?" Elric asked.

She turned and saw the soft shimmer of a pearlescent wall between her and Elric as he pressed his hand against it.

Alexius gently pushed through the wall to join her. "It appears only you and I can go through the wall."

Elric continued trying but could not push through.

"And me," Nasir said. He popped through next to Alexius. Thali watched as Derk, Amali, and Stefan—her ever-present guards—tried but also failed to push through.

"So only people of Bulstan and dragons can enter?" Thali asked. Nasir and Alexius shrugged. She looked down. They were still several feet away from the edge of the lock that allowed ships into Bulstan. There was no one in sight. Usually someone was there to herald their arrival, to start opening the gates.

"We need to be careful," Alexius said. He stepped back through the invisible wall, but Nasir waited for Thali. She looked out at Bulstan once more, and she could sense people ahead—Tariq was there, she was sure of it—but it seemed strange that all the people seemed to be concentrated in one place, as if everyone on the island was in that one space.

Thali stepped through the wall, and Nasir followed closely behind her.

"It appears only Thali, me, and Nasir can cross the wall," Alexius said to the rest of the ship.

Thali was surprised that Alexius had raised his voice until she saw her mother and father's ship had pulled up beside them.

Elric furrowed his brow. "So Bulstan is here."

Alexius nodded.

Thali saw Elric's jaw clench, but instead of saying anything, he dove off the side of the ship. She was so surprised, she blinked three times before she followed, dropping her heaviest weapons on the deck first. Thali reached out to a few dolphins nearby and noted a whale also nearby. No sharks though.

She swam after Elric. He was swimming along the barrier, raising his hand periodically to see if he could go through. He was a fair swimmer, but not as good as Thali, so she caught up to him in no time. She heard two more splashes and wondered which of the guards had followed them in even as she felt Elric's frustration. She followed him at a leisurely pace, but when he saw her pull even with him, he doubled his efforts to pull ahead. Thali decided to remain slightly behind so he wouldn't exhaust himself.

They were several yards away from the ship when Elric finally stopped. He tested the barrier again. Nothing.

He treaded water and turned around, looking a little sheepish.

Thali asked the nearby whale if he could surface so they could rest on him. Moments later, she felt the whale under her feet, like a massive island rising out of the water. Elric looked panicked for a second before understanding showed in his eyes and he sat cross-legged across from Thali on the large surface. The whale was even larger than the ship, and they were comfortable upon the peaceful creature's back. Thali gently reached for Elric's hands. He grasped hers and gave a squeeze.

She waited for him to speak. She shivered a little, so she wrapped them in a warm bubble with her magic.

"I feel so incredibly inadequate," Elric said. "I can't help you with any of the magic stuff. I'm not even as good a fighter as you, I'm not a sailor, and I can't watch your back when you go into Bulstan."

"None of that is your fault. Well, maybe the warrior part." She grinned mischievously at his offended look. "I'm just kidding! I have my mother, remember," Thali said. She squeezed his hands again and smiled.

He returned the smile and said, "I know it's childish, but that ship is full of *my* people. You asked them to sail toward an invisible wall just now, and they did so without question. *I* couldn't even get my own parents to believe that real creatures, ones you can *see*, are attacking our people and that danger is coming. I've studied my whole life to lead these people, to lead a kingdom, and seeing you outperform me every single time ..." He shook his head. "Tells me maybe I'm not cut out to be a ruler."

"Hey. No one knew magical animals were going to pop back into our world. And it's my fault my brother is coming for us. If anything, you should cast me out so he won't come knocking on Adanek's door."

"Never."

"Well then, we do this together. Yes, this part is a little more me than you. But you'll have to play your part too, the part where you'll shine. We just have different roles to play at different times, and we're kind of in my home territory: the ocean, Bulstan, the animals, and magical creatures," Thali said, gripping his hands.

"You're right, as usual," Elric said.

"I know it's not easy, and you're taking all of this really well. I forget sometimes that this isn't normal for you. At first, revealing my magic and talking about magical creatures was like suddenly wearing my underwear out in public, but now ... now it takes much less effort to be me. But then I forget that other people have probably never even imagined all this. Can I do anything to help you?"

"No, it's on me to get used to this. I know you're capable and strong. I also know I have to focus on my own responsibilities and let you take care of yours. You have to go to Bulstan with Nasir and Alexius, I know. But depending on what you find, can you at least let us know before you leave through some magical gate or disappear for who knows how long again?" Elric asked. He opened his mouth again, but then closed it, smiling wryly instead.

"What?" Thali asked.

"I was just thinking that we used to bump into each other, but now it feels like you're always leaving me behind."

Thali couldn't reply because of the lump stuck in her throat.

CHAPTER TWO

I T TOOK LONGER THAN Thali would have liked to get the small boat on the ocean and herself, Nasir, and Alexius into it.

"If you'd let me fly, this would be a lot faster," Alexius had whispered.

"There's no need for you to scare my family's crew just yet. We'll fly as soon as we're past the barrier. They won't be able to see then," Thali had said.

Once they rowed the little boat through the barrier—Thali holding her breath as the cool softness brushed her face—they anchored the boat and secured the oars to the edge of the first lock. Then Alexius jumped up and popped into dragon form. He stretched open his claws and gently offered one for Thali and Nasir to climb into.

Thali stuck her head between his knuckles as they flew over the gates and toward the palace. "You're taking this all quite well," she said to Nasir.

"This is a new experience, but everything is these days. Besides, I'm happy to be home. And happy to have such a fast mode of transportation." Despite his words, Nasir gripped the scales so tight that his knuckles were white.

Thali focused on her connection with Tariq and found them not in the palace but in a meadow.

Thali?! Tariq yelled in her head.

Why the squid turds is there a barrier around Bulstan?! Thali yelled back.

There's a barrier? Are you here? Is that why you feel so close? What happened?

Almost to you, she replied and blinked as they approached a clearing flanked by two large stone monoliths and surrounded by rows and rows of guards posted in circles around the gate. Someone was floating between the two monoliths.

Alexius is flying us in, so please don't shoot him, Thali said as the crowd looked up. She heard Tariq shouting orders, and the guards didn't move. As Alexius flew closer, Thali saw the inner circle of guards were Bulstan's royal guards.

She directed Alexius to the gate, and when they landed, he popped back into human form. As Thali and Nasir hopped onto the grass, Thali looked around at everyone gathered in the clearing. Tents had been erected along the clearing's perimeter near the trees.

"Ah, Thali, welcome," Tariq said. He squashed her in a hug and then Bree did the same.

"Three days ago, my father went for a walk and didn't come back. When we sent out search parties, we found him here," Tariq said.

Thali looked over at the wall of guards. Between them, she could barely see the person floating between the monoliths. While she couldn't see Mupto's face, he was extravagantly dressed, just as Mupto would have been—even for a walk.

Alexius followed the trio as they approached the floating figure. The guards surrounding the figure moved to let them through.

King Mupto lay hovering in the air, eyes closed, directly in front of the pillars that marked the gate's location. Thali used her magic, and sure enough, she saw threads from King Mupto connecting to the gate, flowing both to and from it.

"He's protecting the gate," Alexius said.

"We guessed as much," Tariq said.

"The guardians of the gate can connect with the gate, using only their will to strengthen the barrier between this world and the world their gate connects to," Alexius said.

"Sounds about right for my father," Tariq said. He put an arm around Thali's shoulder and gave her a squeeze.

Thali knew Tariq was stressed, but she was glad her friend was still here. *So, are you now the king?* she asked.

"Well, I've been running things, with Ambrene. But we've been waiting for something to happen." He turned to Alexius. "Do you happen to know, Alexius, what will happen next?"

Alexius's expression was grave. "This confirms someone is trying to open another gate. The gates draw power from each other as much as from their own world. If your father has done this, then it means the gate called to him. It means that it needed more power. Someone's already opened a second gate, and my guess is they'll try to open a third."

"Will it be this one, do you think?"

"Once a guardian connects to it, it strengthens. Right now, this is likely the strongest gate. Once the other three open though, it will be easier for this one to be opened," Alexius said.

They were quiet for a moment as the information sank in. Thali nodded. "We know there's a gate in Cerisa, and a gate somewhere in the Far North. We'll have to decide which one we can save because we can't make it to both."

Alexius said, "I think the Far North is too far away to get to quickly, and I also think it might be too late to save the second gate." Then he raised his chin and sniffed. "Does it stink to anyone else?"

Thali sniffed the air. She thought it was strange Alexius would interrupt such a serious conversation. She couldn't smell anything though. "What do you smell?"

"Wet fur," Alexius said. His eyes went wide, and he scanned the area.

"Oh, I think I know who you mean. Come. Follow me," Tariq said, then led them to one of the large, lavish, gold-seamed tents lining the perimeter.

When they walked in, Thali couldn't believe they were outdoors—in a tent. Fluffy, colorful carpets covered the ground, and low, ornate tables occupied one side, a taller table covered with maps filling the middle. To the rear were three curtains.

"Tobias, I'm sorry to bother you, but we have some friends we'd like you to meet," Tariq said. He turned to Thali.

But before Thali could ask or even open her mouth, her eyes went wide when a bear pushed aside the curtain and walked out. *No, wait,* she thought, *it's not a bear*. It was a human-bear. It had a bear's head and a human's body. He was hairier than anyone she'd ever seen, but Thali finally remembered her manners. She stuck her hand out. "Hello, Tobias, it's nice to meet you."

Tobias sniffed and then growled. His eyes narrowed as he looked around, ignoring Thali's hand—which she snatched back.

"It's generally considered polite to bow to royalty," Alexius snarled, and his voice came out ice cold.

"I bow to no one. I belong to no country nor kingdom," Tobias said.

"Actually, Tobias is a friend of Bulstan, and we do not ask our honored guests to bow." Bree swept in between them and smiled, diffusing the situation.

Amazing, right? Tariq asked Thali.

I've never met a species quite like him.

You'll have to forgive his manners. He's been a hermit for centuries.

Now there's a story.

Later, promise. Tariq turned to Tobias. "Tobias, this is another honored guest of Bulstan, Princess Routhalia of Adanek, Baroness of Bulstan."

Thali choked. "I'm a baroness?"

"Bree liked the alliteration." Tariq shrugged.

Tobias and Alexius continued to stare at each other, though the tension didn't escalate.

"Tobias is from Vancel." Bree nodded at the bear-man. "Tobias, do you know our friend Alexius?"

"This is our first official meeting, though all know of the royal dragon family. Our kind was given the wasteland of Vancel to roam because of them," Tobias growled.

"Mongrels have to go somewhere," Alexius snarled.

"Alexius!" Thali's eyes widened as she turned to him. She'd never known him to be that rude. *What is your problem?*

There's a reason they were sent to Vancel to live alone. They were criminals, terrorizing towns and taking whatever they wanted from innocent people.

This specific ... bear-man, or in general?

Their ancestors.

Then you need to let it go. If Tobias is Tariq and Bree's guest, he's our friend. He could help.

Hmph. Fine.

Thali turned and smiled at Tobias, who had just watched them silently.

"You are blood-oathed?" Tobias asked.

Thali swallowed. "I'm not sure how everyone can tell, but yes."

"A dragon, a royal dragon, blood-oathed himself to you, a human?" Tobias asked.

"Looks that way, doesn't it?" Thali was starting to side with Alexius.

Tobias threw his great bear head back and laughed. "What makes you so special?"

"All right, I must be failing as a host because we have no food or refreshments. Let us all sit down together for a meal, shall we?" Tariq asked.

Thali pulled her lips into a thin line and glanced at Bree. Her friend nodded at Tariq, so Thali stared at Alexius until he finally nodded. Tobias and Alexius watched each other as they circled the table before sitting down at the same time, incredibly slowly. Alexius sat next to Thali, Tariq on her other side, and Bree between him and Tobias. The opposite side of the square table remained empty.

Refreshments were brought out, and Thali was happy to sit with mint tea and nibble on her favorite Bulstani honey-and-nut snacks while she kept an eye on Tobias.

Tariq broke the tense silence. "So, to recap, there are four gates, and the gate at Star Island is already open. We know the others are in Cerisa, the Far North, and here. We also know this one is the most protected and least likely to open—or at least should be the last to open."

"So do we go to Cerisa or the North then?" Thali asked, watching Tobias and Alexius finally relax, drink their tea, and turn their attention to their hosts.

"Both are huge areas. Does anyone know where the gates are?" Tariq asked.

Thali shook her head. Alexius shook his head. Tobias only raised his eyebrows.

Tariq turned to Alexius. "Do you know where they each lead at least?"

Alexius shook his head again. Tobias's expression didn't change, and Alexius glanced at him before saying, "The second gate is said to be the weakest, which means it's likely already open or about to be. Do we know of anything that would negate that?"

Tariq and Thali looked at each other thoughtfully.

But then Bree spoke up. "The North is lightly populated. They would have a harder time holding the gate."

Alexius nodded. "Then we should go to Cerisa and assume that the North's gate is already open, whether it is or not," Alexius said.

"How will we know for sure that the North's gate has been opened, besides your assertion that that's why my father is protecting our gate?" Tariq asked.

"You'll start to see different creatures in our world. Perhaps more creatures in the oceans or in the air," Alexius said. He pressed his lips together as if holding something back.

"You must have some knowledge of the different worlds then?" Tariq asked. He didn't glance at Tobias, telling Thali her best friend had known his gate led to Vancel.

"No one knows for sure, but it is rumored that one connects to an underwater world, one to an avian world, and one to a hybrid world," Alexius said.

"Exactly how many magical worlds are there?" Tariq asked.

Alexius's eyebrows shot up. "We can't be sure, but I know of a dozen. My brother used to study the different worlds, and he thought there were over fifty."

Xerus? Thali asked.

Yes, he thought there were many, many more even, with strange life forms, Alexus replied.

"So, you're going to Cerisa?" Tariq asked as he turned to Bree though he spoke to Thali. *Do you think there's any way I can convince Bree to let me go with you?*

No, you need to stay here. You're king now. Bulstan needs you. Bree needs you, Thali replied. She was glad Tariq was whispering in her mind now. It caused her head to ache less and ring less. *What's up with Tobias?*

It turns out my people had invited him to teach us how to fight, but then after a few generations, something happened to make him feel unwelcome. He then went to live in isolation in Bulstan for three generations. You remember that tapestry map hanging in my dad's office? There's a two-legged bear on it. So I guess we've always known, but not known? My father almost threw all of us in jail for finding Tobias, but now ...

That's a lot, Tariq.

I know. But we're managing. I don't know if I should rule as my father did or as I see fit.

Is there a difference?

My father wanted to stay defensive. I want to go on the offense.

"If you two are going to continue with your private conversation, can the rest of us leave?" Tobias asked.

Tariq and Thali looked over at him.

"It's really obvious when you're doing it, Tariq. It's less so when Thali and Alexius do it, but you can't really focus on more than one thing at a time." Bree smiled gently and put a hand on his arm.

Thali saw the scar on Bree's arm from the injury she'd sustained from the bird-lizard's attack. *Alexius, can we fix Bree's scar?*

Does she want it fixed?

I don't know. But it reminds me only of pain.

It might remind her of strength.

Thali nodded ever so slightly. She made a mental note to ask Bree later.

Nasir coughed then. Thali turned to him, and he drew an arc with his finger.

"Right, the barrier. When we arrived, Bulstan had disappeared. My mother and father and the rest of my crew could not pass. Only me, Nasir, and Alexius could enter," Thali said.

"It's likely Alexius could only pass because of your blood oath to him. You said you're a lady of this land, yes?" Tobias asked.

Thali nodded. Before Tobias could add something insulting, she turned to Tariq and forged ahead. "Did you create it on purpose? If so, why?"

"I activated it," Tobias said.

"What? Why?" Tariq turned to him.

"You assume that those who want to open the gate will do it from Vancel's side. However, they could also open it from this world. If no one can find us, no one can open it. And I added protective barriers to prevent anyone who does not belong to Bulstan from entering." Tobias shredded his napkin to ribbons with a claw as he spoke.

Thali was impressed that his control was great enough that he hadn't scratched the table at all. *How much do you trust Tobias, Tariq?*

I trust him. He's been here for centuries. He could have taken over Bulstan if he'd wanted to. You saw the napkin. I think his skills as a warrior are far superior even to ours.

Thali glanced at Alexius. *I know you don't like him, but does Tobias pose a real threat to Tariq and Bree?*

I don't like them, but the bear people are known to be the most honorable of the mongrels, Alexius growled down their line.

Thali thought it strange that Alexius still behaved so, but she would ask him why later. She sighed. She'd never liked Cerisa much. After all, it had rejected her mother.

"I guess we're going to Cerisa."

CHAPTER THREE

THALI SPOKE PRIVATELY WITH Tariq and Bree before flying back to the rowboat with Alexius and Nasir. Thankfully, Tobias had disappeared for a walk. Thali was sure he had sensed their desire for privacy, as had Alexius and Nasir, the dragon having flown the guard to the rowboat.

Bree took her hands after hugging her. "Be safe. You are so brave, and sometimes I worry about how brave you like to be. Try to remember there are those who love you as much as you love others." She squeezed Thali's hands tightly. There wasn't a single sign of hurt or anger or blame in her eyes.

"Bree, you don't blame me?"

"For what?" Bree looked genuinely surprised.

Thali waved her arms in a wide arc.

"Surely, you're not confessing to being the mastermind behind all this? I know you well enough to know that you would never do something so reckless. You are not to blame."

Thali nodded, not sure if she could believe those words.

Bree gave Tariq a look and left the tent.

"Not enough time to ride to The Point?" Tariq grinned.

"I wish."

I did not think our duty to our kingdom would keep us here, Tariq said.

What do you mean?

I thought when this was all beginning that I would be able to join you, be at your side, fight alongside you. I never thought I'd have to stay back and play sentry. Tariq's face fell as he looked at her like a sad puppy dog.

Did you always think we'd be involved in something this big?

Yes? No? I don't know. I always dreamed of adventure and big things, but what's happening now is a little surreal.

Thali grinned wryly. *I just wanted to live at sea, on a ship, with an occasional fight here and there.*

Tariq chuckled. *On a ship filled with animals.*

Thali laughed as she imagined a sailing barn. Perhaps she wouldn't have ended up on an ocean for as long as she'd thought.

Be safe.

Did you do the thing I asked you to the last time we spoke?

Yes. Here. Tariq opened the neck of his tunic to fish out a ruby the size of a compass. It was edged in gold and attached to a gold chain. He pulled it over his head.

"You didn't," Thali said.

Tariq grinned. "You said to pick any gem and wear it after infusing some of my magic into it. I did that."

"You picked the most ostentatious gem you could find and gilded it in gold, on purpose," Thali said, fishing out the much smaller, more subtle emerald Tariq had given her years ago.

"Yeah, I'm going to have to replace that now," he said, pointing to the one in her hand.

"I think this is plenty, thanks," Thali said as she took the ruby and handed him the coin-sized emerald.

"It's your color." Tariq smiled, his teeth glaringly white.

Thali narrowed her eyes at Tariq as she draped the ruby's chain around her neck. She tucked it under her shirt, barely able to conceal it.

"A gem like that is not meant to be concealed. You should wear it over your clothes," Tariq pouted.

"And steal all the attention from you?" Thali asked.

Tariq shrugged and slipped the emerald around his neck where it joined the other chains of gems dangling on his sternum.

Thali felt the thread in her mind strengthen, like threads expanding and weaving together more tightly. "I think this will work," she said.

Tariq nodded, looking thoughtful.

A woosh of air waved the tent flaps, and a ping on her other thread told her Alexius was back and it was time to go. She threw her arms around Tariq. "Keep each other safe. If you need me, I'll be here," Thali said.

Tariq squeezed her tightly too. *I'll be watching you ...*

It sounded so intense that she laughed into his shoulder. When she pulled out of his arms, he was smiling too. She turned and stepped through the tent flaps, holding one open for Tariq. Then she strode over and climbed into Alexius's claw. Before the dragon took flight, she glanced back at Tariq. Her Bulstan brother waved.

Did it work? Alexius asked her.

I think so. I'll have to check when we get farther away. I wouldn't be surprised if the barrier prevents the gems from working though.

Perhaps.

Hey, where's that bowl I first climbed into when we first flew together? I think I prefer it.

That was to gain your trust. You had just found out I was a dragon, and I didn't want to scare you. Also, I didn't need tiger and dog claws gripping my scales.

Ah.

Thali was silent as they flew over Bulstan and back to the rowboat. They rowed it back through the barrier, but Thali looked over her shoulder. She hoped Bulstan would still look the same when she returned.

CHAPTER FOUR

T HE TWO SHIPS HAD stored the supplies before Thali and Alexius were able to bring the news to Elric and her parents.

"We have to go to Cerisa. Two gates are likely already open, and that should be the next one to open. It's our best chance to stop Rommy." Thali tried to hold her head high.

Elric nodded, and her parents looked at each other. She could tell they were deciding something. Crab had joined the meeting, and he watched her parents too. They all looked so intense that Thali could have sworn they too must be linked in their minds. Was that what she looked like when she spoke to Alexius or Tariq?

"It's probably better if we don't go," her father said. His expression was quite serious.

"We could go and hang back," her mother suggested. She put a hand over Thali's.

Thali knew her mother was trying to keep her safe.

Ranulf turned to his wife and continued before Thali could reply. "They'll know you're there, and as soon as they figure that out, they'll clam up and refuse to help. Thali at least has a chance," he said, resting a hand on his wife's shoulder.

Thali saw the pain on his face. She knew it was her father's greatest regret that he'd taken her mother's family away.

"I'll go," Crab said.

"They'll recognize you too," Ranulf said.

"They won't recognize me." Lobb stepped forward.

"Or me," Mouse said as he too stepped forward.

"We do have guards, if you're worried about our protection," Elric chimed in.

Ranulf finally turned to Elric. "Your Highness, we're not worried about your safety. You're going to need help in Cerisa, which means you'll need to speak with Amah. Thali has a chance at an audience with her as her granddaughter—one who is now a princess. But if Jinhua is so much as seen—or any of our known crew—Amah will turn Thali away, and that woman's people will follow suit for fear of angering her."

"Oh." Elric was left with his mouth hanging open.

Thali reminded herself to bring Elric up to speed with the family politics. She glanced at her mother. This was clearly difficult for her.

Her mother whispered with her father but hung her head low.

Thali swallowed. As much as she would like her family's strength and support, she was going to have to do this on her own. "Mom, I need you to do something for me," Thali said. If she could just make sure her family was safe, that would be enough for her.

Her mother turned to give her daughter her full attention.

"I need you to go home and protect Densria. Not only the animals there and the citizens, but also the silky white chickens. They're magical and might attract larger, more dangerous creatures. They also have the ability to heal. If we can protect them, they might heal the injured. We *need* to keep them safe," Thali said. She bit down on her tongue, hoping her mother couldn't tell that she wasn't telling the whole truth, that she was giving her own mother a mission.

Her mother's eyes narrowed a millimeter. She suspected.

Thali could only hope her mother believed enough of her words to follow along.

"All right," her mother finally said.

It was only a few days, thanks to the whales Thali recruited to help pull the ships, before their ships had to part ways. Thali and her crew would sail to Cerisa, and her parents would return with their crew to Densria.

Thali and her parents exchanged their customary letters after morning training, then had breakfast together as a family once more before Thali hopped back onto her own ship with Elric. She watched as her parents' ship sailed away. It slowly became a speck on the horizon, then it was just them—her and Elric—on their ship, in the middle of the ocean. Though she didn't feel alone, she did feel a little lonely. This had been what she'd wanted all these years, to sail off on her own, but now that it was finally happening, Thali was scared.

Chapter Five

"CAPTAIN," A VOICE SAID from behind Thali as she stood at the bow.

Thali smiled. She'd wanted to hear that word for so long, but it didn't seem to have the same effect now as she'd thought it would. It didn't feel as chest-inflating. She turned.

"Or do I call you Your Highness Captain? Your Captainness?" Daylor looked confused.

Thali grinned and threw her arms around him. She suddenly realized she didn't have to feel lonely. Her friends were here.

"Did you forget who your crew is?" Tilton piped up. Daylor pulled him into the hug.

Thali had been so preoccupied with what was going on that she *had* forgotten.

She patted Indi's head, and Ana leaned into her thigh as she turned her attention to her ship. Her ship. It was crazy to think that's where she was, finally on her own ship and sailing it on her own.

Tilton ran off to help with a sail as Isaia and Nasir coiled more rope. Lobb had the helm, and he nodded at her as she smiled. Then she saw another familiar face that made her smile as she swung on a rope from the top deck to the main deck. "Mouse." She hugged him.

He'd been showing Mia how to tie a knot, so he nodded at her and gave her the rope before patting Thali's arm. "Glad I'm not known enough to catch the kind of attention your parents would so I can come along," he said.

"Thank you."

"Chip and Dog are here too," Mouse said, and he jutted his chin toward the two sailors beside them, also tying rope and tidying the main deck.

Thali felt overwhelmed. She'd grown up with these men; they had been sailing long before she was even born. In fact, they had probably been there when she was born. "I'm so grateful to you all." Thali's eyes filled, and she swallowed down the emotion.

Chip looked at her and grinned. "Maybe we followed *you* here, or maybe we just followed the best cook." He raised an eyebrow at her.

Thali spun around and ran down to the galley. It was the tiniest galley there was, but there, humming to herself, was Carthy's large frame filling the tiny space. "Carthy?"

The large woman turned and smiled, waving a ladle at Thali. Carthy had been her family's cook since before she was born. Where her parents were, Carthy was, whether onboard or at home. Thali had never seen her anywhere else. "I can't save the world, but I can make sure you get a good meal while you do it." Carthy put the ladle back in the pot to stir some chopped vegetables.

Thali swallowed again. There just weren't words for how her family was supporting her.

CHAPTER SIX

THALI SAT DOWN AT the desk in her captain's quarters. She had asked Isaia to make sure she wasn't disturbed for the next hour—by anyone. Now that they were in the middle of the ocean, Lobb was teaching Elric how to man the helm. She appreciated that her crew was taking Elric on as one of their own. Now, she took a moment to luxuriate in being alone and put her booted feet up on the desk. For a moment, she could believe she had fulfilled her childhood dream: to captain her own ship. Thali ran her hands along the wooden desk, then looked out the back window to the wake cutting through the sea behind them.

She smiled. It felt like such a simple life now. She glanced at Indi and Ana on the bed nearby, Bardo curled on a corner of her desk, catching a sliver of sunlight. Ana raised her head as if asking if she wanted something, but Thali just smiled and looked back out the window. Minutes later, she finally opened the bottom drawer and drew out the orange silk pouch.

Three years ago, Ming had given her this thick cloth envelope. He'd said inside was a letter from her grandmother, the grandmother who had refused to see her family, who had disowned her mother when she had chosen her father. While Thali could understand the disappointment, for her mother had been promised to a Cerisan prince, Thali had seen nothing but hurt cross her mother's face whenever her family was mentioned.

Thali had been eight when she had asked her mother, "Why doesn't Grandmother want to see us?"

Her father had scooped her up, but her mother had placed a hand on his arm. So, he'd put her back down. Rommy had shot her a look and shaken his head.

Thali only remembered being confused.

"I love your daddy so much," her mother had said, "But when I decided to marry him, I left behind the life I was supposed to have. Your grandmother is angry with me for making that decision."

"So she's angry at all of us?"

"No, sweetheart, your grandmother is only angry with me, maybe your daddy. But she's not angry with you or Rommy."

"Then why doesn't she want to see us?"

"You know how you have Mommy's face but Daddy's eyes?" her mother had asked, and Thali had nodded. "Well, you remind Amah of my decision, so it upsets her, that's all." Her mother had wrapped Thali up in her arms and kissed her head a dozen times until Thali had forgotten all about her grandmother and broken into giggles.

Thali stared at the silk envelope on her desk now. She'd buried it in her trunk all these years because she'd truly never had any interest in what her grandmother had to say. Maybe she was being stubborn, but if her grandmother had treated her mother that way for so many years, then to Thali, she wasn't worth knowing.

But now, now she could really use her grandmother's help. Resources, information, relationships, anything could help her. And now it was about more than her family; this was about saving the world. Thali swallowed her pride.

Finally, she took her dagger and sliced open the thread that kept the pouch closed. Inside were pages of parchment and a cloth. As she opened the pages, the red cloth slipped out, and she recognized it as a family flag. She turned her attention back to the parchment.

Granddaughter,
I am sorry that we have never had the opportunity to
meet. Even though the way you came into this world
is a complete disgrace, I have realized that you did not
choose this.

If you choose to join our family, please fly this flag upon
entry to Cerisa, and we will show you Cerisan hospi-
tality at its finest, welcoming you into our family. I ask
only that you sever your contact with the one who is lost
to us.

This family is only for the honorable.
Amah

Thali laughed out loud as she remembered how this letter had landed in her hands: through the Cerisan prince of thieves at a meeting of global thief princes and princess. It was incredibly hypocritical to say "honorable" when a prince of thieves had delivered this letter. Thali looked at the cloth flag for a moment. It was a rich red with a large, black, rectangular box embroidered on it. Inside, unfamiliar strokes formed words Thali had never learned. She guessed it was her mother's family name or crest. The most impressive part was that both sides of the singular cloth had the same image. She'd have to ask Mia how it was done. The back of most embroidered images was a mess where Thali came from.

There were only two more pieces of paper. One had a drawing of a building on it. It was U-shaped, with a garden within and what looked like walls around that. In the corner of the paper, a tiny "X" with an "I" on each side within a square made Thali's heart skip. She recognized that symbol. It was Ming's, Cerisa's Prince of Thieves. Her hand went to the medallion she had tucked into her waistband, the one Garen had given her so many years ago. Had her grandmother given her a way to find Ming?

Thali pulled the third piece of paper out; it was a recipe. She recognized most of the ingredients, and interestingly, the recipe was not written in Cerisan. Why would her grandmother have sent her a recipe for some kind of bread?

The recipe didn't make any sense, and the letter was useless. There was no way Thali was about to hurt her mother and father just to be accepted by a family member who had never cared. The image of the building could be useful though. Thali dropped the flag in a drawer in her desk, ignoring the letter and the recipe.

Alexius knocked on the door. She knew it was him because he knocked on her thread too.

So much for Isaia keeping everyone out for an hour. "Come in," Thali said. She couldn't help but smile at how "captainy" that sounded.

"I felt distress and confusion," Alexius said, "And before you get mad at Isaia, know that it's been past an hour since you holed up."

Thali checked the time. It had indeed been an hour and a quarter. She wondered how she'd wasted so much time already. "What do you make of this?" Thali asked. She handed him the recipe she'd taken from the cloth pouch.

Alexius scanned it carefully, then turned back to her. "What am I supposed to glean?"

"I don't know. My grandmother sent it to me. I don't think it makes any sense." She handed him the other page.

"Ah," Alexius said, then read the letter. When he finished, he scrunched his brows. "Is your grandmother a seer?" he asked.

"I have no idea, Alexius. I've only ever seen her from a distance. I've certainly never had an actual conversation with her." Thali crossed her arms.

"Do you know where you got your magic from?" Alexius asked.

Thali shook her head. She didn't know anyone magical on her father's side.

"Historically, seers often give mysterious gifts, things that will only make sense when the time comes. Perhaps that's what this is?" he asked, lifting the page.

"A recipe though?" Thali asked. She wasn't as sure as Alexius about that.

Thali looked over the recipe again after Alexius handed the papers back. She searched through the letter again then, reading it carefully, trying to find another meaning. Were her grandmother's words as cruel as they had sounded the first time?

Alexius stood behind her and stared at each page too. When Thali looked over her shoulder at him, his forehead was scrunched in concentration. "I'm sorry about your grandmother," he said.

Thali shook her head. She'd done fine without her grandmother for so long, Thali didn't need her now. Especially after she'd hurt her mother so.

Eventually, she folded the papers and tucked them into her inner vest pocket. She sat back, and Alexius sat on a bench by the window. "That was anticlimactic," Thali said as she put her booted feet back up on the table. Alexius raised his eyebrow, but she didn't care what he thought. It felt like such a captain thing to do.

"What were you expecting?"

"Some kind of apology." Thali crossed her arms. She was angry, on behalf of her mother, herself, and her family.

"If she'd apologized and you'd made her wait three years for your reply, would it still count?" Alexius asked as he stared out the window at the ocean.

"My mother has waited over twenty years for an apology," Thali said.

"I don't think your mother is waiting for an apology," Alexius said.

"No ... no, I suppose not," Thali said. She watched a little row of marbles roll gently from one side of their tiny tray to the other. Bardo was wrapped around the tray, but the marbles didn't bother him at all. Her parents had always taught her to keep marbles in windowless rooms belowdecks so she could tell if she was actually dizzy or if it was just the ship listing from side to side. Now, even though Thali had a window, she found the rolling marbles comforting. "What do you think we'll find in Cerisa, Alexius?"

"I don't know. Hopefully a closed gate," he said.

"What do dragons think of Cerisa?"

"I can't speak for all dragons, but I can say that it's interesting that the people of Cerisa have ancient dragons in their drawings, but Adanek and the rest of the world depicts dragons as most of us are: young." Alexius crossed one knee over the other.

"What's an ancient dragon look like again?"

"You remember Xenon? He's an ancient dragon. My father is also an ancient dragon."

"What happened to your mother?"

"I don't really want to talk about it."

Thali nodded. The last thing she wanted to do was upset him. He may be one of her dearest friends, but he was also a powerful dragon.

Alexius sighed and looked out the window. "My mother was much like my sister, perhaps an older version. She was smiling, fun, strict. She had specific rules, and I didn't much mind them, but she always preferred loving and caring. She softened my father," Alexius said.

Thali was afraid to nod. She was afraid to move. It wasn't like Alexius to divulge what he didn't want to. It almost made her uncomfortable.

"As I understand human relationships, you ask hard questions to get to know me better, yes?" Alexius asked.

Thali nodded.

"You need not fear that I will injure you. After all this time, Thali, I won't hurt you."

"Well, you could. But it wouldn't make you happy in the long run," Thali retorted.

Alexius rolled his eyes.

Thali thought that was a very human thing to do. "You also don't have to answer any of my questions. I'm curious, but it doesn't mean you have to revisit something painful."

"Thank you for clarifying, but you should probably know a bit about my sister. Well, my other sister."

"Her name was Danx?"

"Yes." Alexius looked out the window. "Danxing, because she came out with her arms above her head like she was already dancing. And she did. She danced whenever she could and sang and smiled and made everyone laugh."

"What happened?" Thali asked softly, waiting for Alexius to answer in his own time.

Many heartbeats passed before he continued. "She died so the rest of us could live. There aren't many perfect creatures, but she was one. The crux of it is that it was supposed to be me. I was the weakest one. I was the sickly one. I figured—no, I knew—it was going to be me. It had to be. But Danxing wouldn't have that. She said I was meant for something bigger. And then she died so we could live."

"I'm so sorry," Thali said. Alexius's pain shot through her heart.

A knock suddenly sounded moments before the door flew open. Elric stood there, looking surprised at how quickly the door had flown open.

Thali startled, her feet falling to the floor.

"Hi," Elric said. He walked in and leaned over the desk to give Thali a kiss on the forehead.

"Hi," Thali said. "How was the steering lesson?"

"It was ... slow?" Elric said. He chuckled and it filled the room, easing the tension.

"It's not quite like riding a horse or driving a cart," Thali said.

"But it was interesting. It really takes a lot of teamwork to keep this thing moving smoothly," Elric said. He carefully slid the tiger and dog aside a little so he could sit on the bed. "What are you guys up to?" He asked then, looking from Thali to Alexius.

"Just trying to hash out what awaits us in Cerisa," Alexius said soberly as he crossed his arms and fixed a stony expression on his face.

"And?"

"Your guess is as good as ours," Thali replied, though she turned to Alexius as she spoke. As she examined his face, it suddenly dawned on her that whenever Elric was in the room with them, Alexius was grumpier, or at least seemed grumpier.

"If you're done, how about teaching me that game you promised? I want to win tonight." He paused and looked from Alexius to Thali again. "Unless you want to talk more about Cerisa?"

Thali shook her head, making Elric look hopeful.

Thali started to smile until Alexius spoke. "I'll get out of your way then." He stood and was out the door before she could even jump up.

"The cards are in that box next to Indi's head. I'll be right back," she told Elric over her shoulder as she hurried out and caught up to Alexius. She looked him in the eye but said in her mind, *What's with you and Elric?*

He does not trust you as much as he should.

What does that mean?

He doesn't seem to understand that there is no going back after this, no going back to the way things were, that fairytale life. Whatever's happening in the world, it's going to forever change.

How do you know he doesn't understand that?

He's a loud broadcaster. I can also sense his distrust of me because I'm a different species. He can't wait for all this to calm down so he can go back and live the life he was promised, rule a peaceful kingdom with nothing more to worry about than expanding trade routes.

Thali wasn't exactly surprised that Elric wanted life to go back to the way it was. Even she was in denial half the time. There had to be something more to this. *What's really bothering you?* Though she knew her guards were now staring at them, she stood firm, holding Alexius's elbow as he stood there as they stared at each other, unmoving.

He does not love you like he should.

And how is that?

He does not love you like that other one does.

Excuse me?

I am frustrated for you. You have a mate, a mate alive and well and able to love you, yet you are not together.

What does that matter? Thali swallowed. It had been a while since she'd thought of Garen, but she knew that's who he was talking about.

Yes, that one. He is your mate. And it frustrates me that your duty requires you to stay away from your mate.

Why does that matter to you?

As someone who only had months with their mate and has lived centuries without, I know better than most that your mate transforms you. And you ... here you are, separating your love from your duty. The two should work in tandem.

Well, that's all good and dandy for a cobbler or a captain, but I'm neither. I'm just some unlucky soul born to fulfill a prophecy. None of this is my choice.

I'm sorry. It's not helpful, I know. But we dragons believe that you only become who you are truly meant to be after you've met and lived life with your mate, hopefully for a long time.

Did Xerus change after he met Xenon?

Yes. He became who he is now. A leader. Before then, he had always been shy and reserved.

I still can't believe Xenon, my captor, is the same Xenon that's your brother-in-law.

You should return to your husband. He is waiting for you.

I'll return when I am good and ready to return. Will you be all right?

I will. It just ... it just irks me that he doesn't trust you as well as he should, that he doesn't love you as he should.

Fine, but maybe show it less and maybe he'll be less suspicious of you.

Fine.

At that, Thali turned on her heel and returned to her room. She pasted a smile on her face before she walked through the door and taught Elric the tricks to playing cards with sailors.

Chapter Seven

B ECAUSE IT HAD STORMED the previous night, they didn't pull into port until after the sun rose and the seas calmed. Thali still marveled that her ship ran almost as smoothly as her parents'. As they glided to the dock and Lobb and Mouse were preparing to disembark and find the harbor master, she heard a rather purposeful cough beside her ship.

She had hummed and hawed about what flag to fly as they had coasted in. There was no way she was flying her grandmother's flag, and with her parents' voices in her mind, she had decided not to fly her family's. This was not a merchanting trip anyway. In the end, she had decided to fly Adanek's flag. As much as she hated that they'd kicked her and Elric out of the kingdom, the official word was that she and Elric were on a sort of honeymoon. A tiny part of her was excited—she was representing her kingdom—but it also felt like she was representing herself for the first time.

The harbor master turned out to be the coughing culprit, saving Lobb and Mouse that task. Elric joined her at the rail, putting a hand on her shoulder. Together, they took in the harbor master. Thali recognized him. The same bald, portly man had greeted them every time Thali's family had ever docked here. He always combed the last few hairs he had across the top of his head as if to cover it up.

"Your Highnesses, we are honored to be receiving such special guests. When you are ready, if you would follow me, our humble town awaits you." He bowed a little awkwardly, and Thali turned around to look back at her ship.

"Well, there's a first for everything," Mouse said as she looked over her crew.

"They're going to want you to stay in town now that you're a princess," Lobb said.

Thali looked over her shoulder at the end of the dock, where a group of people had gathered. She swallowed. She had hoped to be well-received but hadn't expected a reception this size. "I should go change my clothes ..." Thali didn't bother to finish as she ran below and ducked into her room. Mia was already there, ready with a princess dress. Thali yanked it on, with help, then ran back abovedeck with Indi and Ana in tow, Bardo up her sleeve.

"Ready, my princess?" Elric had cleaned up too. He offered her his hand as he waited for her at the edge of the ship. He gave her his sunshine smile and she nodded. She could do this with him at her side.

She glanced behind her and saw that Mia, Tilton, and Daylor weren't hiding laughter as she'd thought they would be but stood proudly nodding at her. Isaia, Nasir, and Stefan followed her, along with Elric's guards.

Thali took a deep breath and placed her hand in Elric's. She called for Indi and Ana, and Bardo gave her arm a little squeeze inside her sleeve. If acting like a princess could get them the help they needed, she would be glad for it. They descended the gangway and strolled confidently down the dock, Elric letting her set the pace.

Thali pasted a smile on her face as they reached the edge of the group, and she instinctively glanced around, looking for weapons. But she needn't have worried. Most locals carried flowers or babies or nothing at all. Elric stepped in front of her to greet the townspeople, and Thali used the opportunity to flick the medallion she had tucked inside her belt outside so it was visible. If that would protect them even more, and possibly tell Ming she had arrived, she would use it.

Indi and Ana tucked in closer to her, one on each side, and she was glad that they inspired folks to give them a bit of a berth. People could not crowd her in their excitement. Many wanted to shake her hand or offer her flowers or gifts, but thanks to her animal friends, they could only approach from the front. So Thali smiled as she greeted everyone and accepted their gifts. Among them, she recognized many talismans her mother would often stock up on whenever their ships traded in Cerisa. Thali was grateful they were at least wishing her well.

"Princess, thank you for visiting!"

"Princess, you're so beautiful!"

"Princess, how did you get the prince to propose?"

Thali smiled through all the questions and well-wishes. But it was the children she was most excited to see, their faces so full of excitement and hope.

"Princess, can I pet your tiger?" one little girl asked. Thali turned to Indi and asked if she would tolerate the little girl petting her. Indi allowed it, so Thali nodded and guided the little hand to the tiger's shoulder.

Other children started reaching for Indi, so she ducked behind Thali. Ana eagerly took the tiger's place, diving in headfirst. Thali grinned at her animals. Then another little girl, maybe five or six, stopped in front of her, ignoring Ana. "May I pet your snake?" she asked.

Thali glanced down and saw Bardo now on full display across her chest. How he'd managed to squeeze up through her sleeve without her knowing she wasn't sure, but she asked him the same question, showing him what the little girl wanted to do. He slid down the outside of Thali's sleeve in response. Many people stepped back, to Indi's delight, but the little girl put her hand out determinedly.

Thali took the little girl's hand and gently slid it along Bardo. He stayed still as Thali held her arm steady. After petting Bardo three times, the girl stepped back, her smile filling her face. "Thank you," she said before melting back into the crowd.

Because the crowd had eased away from Bardo, Thali took advantage of it and made her way through the group quicker than she could have hoped.

A man and woman stood at the end, the woman nervously wiping her hands on her apron. They were familiar. Her parents' crew, including Thali and Rommy, often stayed at their inn while they were conducting business in town.

"Hello, it is good to see you again," Thali said, offering them a smile. She saw Elric speaking to someone who looked like the group's leader, but she focused on the innkeepers.

"Hello, Your Highness," the woman said as they bowed their heads. Thali stepped closer and they looked up. "We would be honored if you would stay at our humble inn."

Thali smiled. "We would be equally honored, thank you."

"The rooms have already been paid for," the innkeeper said.

Thali paused. "By whom?"

The man stepped closer to her. Indi and Ana tensed, but he stopped where he was and lowered his voice. "Your Uncle Renshu, Your Highness."

Thali nodded. Her heart leapt to think she would see her Uncle Renshu. She was hopeful she might finally get to meet other members of her family this time too.

Elric finally caught up to her then, and they walked together, following the innkeepers to their inn in the middle of town. Thali smiled as she remembered the courtyard, which now boasted different flowers but was otherwise much the same as when she had last been here as a teenager. She had sparred with Rommy under her Uncle Renshu's coaching. That brought a wave of pain to her soul as she remembered why she was there, how Rommy wanted to take over the world, and how much the world was depending on them. Thali let Elric guide her into the inn after their guards and followed silently as they were shown their rooms.

CHAPTER EIGHT

T HAT EVENING, AFTER THE group had all settled into their rooms, they crammed into Thali and Elric's room to eat dinner. Her uncle had paid for enough rooms so even Tilton, Daylor, and Mia could stay at the inn. Suddenly, a knock on the door had Isaia peeking his head out. He returned with an envelope that he handed to Thali.

"Who is that from?" Mia asked.

"Probably my uncle," Thali said, and she opened it without looking closely at it.

> *To the most honored guest, His Royal Highness Prince Elric of Adanek,*
> *My esteemed family would humbly request your presence for tea tomorrow afternoon.*
> *-Lady Qi*

Daylor peeked over at the note. "Is it strange that you're not mentioned?"

"That *is* your grandmother, yes?" Elric asked.

Thali nodded. She recognized the family crest stamped on the top left corner of the parchment. She shrugged. "Maybe it had to go to Elric specifically, for diplomatic reasons?"

There was a nagging in her heart, but she didn't pay it any attention. Her grandmother was their best hope for a clue to the gate, and even though she knew deep down that her grandmother held a grudge the size of the kingdom, she was hoping against hope that their meeting would be a success.

Thali swallowed. This was the moment she'd secretly dreamed of so many times. She stood in the lavish reception room, waiting to be presented to her grandmother. She'd only seen her grandmother in passing once or twice in town as a child, and she'd seen nothing but opulence and a ramrod-straight back.

She felt her meeting with her grandmother was a bit of a betrayal, for it was her grandmother who could not and would not forgive her mother for falling in love. But still, Thali had long wondered and dreamed of her grandmother embracing her, showing her the ways of Cerisa that she had never learned because she hadn't grown up here. She bit back a sob as she thought of her aunt, the aunt who had come to Adanek and then been burned to ash in front of her eyes. Did her other uncles look like her aunt? Her mother? Uncle Renshu? She'd only met Uncle Renshu because he always came to them. He would ride out in secret to meet them under the cover of darkness.

All Thali knew was that she had two other uncles and another aunt. Thali wondered if she had cousins. Guilt swelled in her heart again as she thought of her Aunt Qiao, who had given her life for Thali. Her aunt had been visiting with Cerisa's royal prince when Thali had encountered her first dragon; it was her aunt who had stepped up to protect her. It was Thali's fault her aunt had been killed. She probably wouldn't even have been there had it not been for Thali. If her Aunt Qiao had children, Thali would beg their forgiveness.

Elric put a hand on her shoulder, and she startled. "It'll be all right."

"Will it? How can you be so sure?"

"What's the worst that could happen?" Elric asked.

But Thali only raised her eyebrows. He did not know her family and clearly did not remember—or even hear—what she'd said about family politics. "The worst that could happen is that we have to fight our way out of here," she said. The guards that had accompanied them closed in tighter around them at that. Thali reached down to pet her animals, but her heart sank as she remembered she'd left them with Mia. She hadn't wanted to draw more attention to herself, and Cerisans didn't like pets.

"I doubt that your grandmother, if she's as politically savvy as you suggest, would attack the prince of another kingdom." Elric put two fingers under her chin.

Thali's shoulders drooped. "Then the worst is that my grandmother refuses to see us because she considers me an unwelcome stranger—which I am." A tear slid down her cheek.

Elric circled his arms around her then and squeezed, bringing their bodies together. She turned her head into his neck and breathed him in. He was a little saltier than usual, but he still smelled of sunshine and grass. "It'll be all right, really. No matter what happens, we still have each other. We'll figure this out." He squeezed her tight again.

She knew he was just trying to comfort her, but what options did they have? If her grandmother refused to help her, then the entire town would become an unwelcoming place. They'd have to steal away—or fight their way out.

The screen door slid open. The guards who had accompanied them—Stefan, Nasir, and Isaia—took up positions around Thali and Elric.

"Lady Qi welcomes the honored guest, Prince Elric, to her audience room." He bowed as he said it, and Thali wondered if this man was her uncle.

His gaze flit to her for a moment. He looked like her Uncle Renshu, but she still wasn't sure. Then she realized he had the same eyes as her mother.

Elric took Thali's hand and stepped toward the man.

"Lady Qi welcomes only the Prince of Adanek." The man bowed again.

"We are partners. If she welcomes the royals, she welcomes us both, or she welcomes neither of us." Elric squared his shoulders. The man held his gaze for a moment as Thali's fingers twitched. She tucked her elbow closer to her body, ready to eject the dagger tucked along her forearm.

The man nodded then and slid the door open wider.

Thali's eyes narrowed. He hadn't had to go back and ask. Had that been a test? A test to determine how loyal Elric was to her? Or to determine how much power Thali held? She wasn't sure. Her head started to ache. She had always hated politics.

They descended into a smaller room but then turned ninety degrees to step back up into another room, one that reminded her of her mother's garden. Potted plants rested on various levels, and in the middle of the room was a huge koi pond. A bridge spanned it and led to a space filled with the same cherrywood furniture in her own living room. Here though, a large, more ornate chair with two stiff, angled, couches and two chairs faced the elaborate dais.

Thali swallowed when she saw a woman who looked like her mother, but thirty years older, sitting with perfect posture in the largest seat, her hair braided down her back. Thali's glance moved to her Uncle Renshu and a man she hadn't yet met sitting to her grandmother's right, then to the empty couch on the left. Their escort took his place on the left couch, and an arrow pierced her heart when she saw the empty spot her aunt would have occupied, right next to another woman, the opposite of her mother—with sharp, pinched features. And next to her was a space she assumed her mother would have occupied.

Amah stood as they approached. Elric nodded his head, and Thali, following a half step behind him, also nodded as she bent her knees just a fraction.

"Welcome, Prince Elric. It is an honor to have you in my home," Amah said.

Thali hadn't expected her words to be so clear and her pitch to be so high.

"It is our honor. Thank you for receiving us," Elric said.

Amah gestured to the two seats before her and waited. Elric glanced at Thali, and they sat in unison. Thali watched as her grandmother's eyes never left Elric. She didn't even glance in Thali's direction. Uncle Renshu's lips were tight, but Thali saw a little wrinkle between his brows as he looked at her. If he was like her mother, then he was worried.

They waited as five women came in. They placed cups without handles on the chairs' arms, then poured tea. Two women attended to Amah, and one served Elric before serving Thali. Then one of the women placed a small plate of tiny, steamed buns next to the tea.

Amah smiled at Elric and gestured for him to go ahead.

Adanek protocol stated Elric had to wait for Stefan to take a bite and a sip, then wait another ten minutes before he was allowed to eat anything. The silence during that ten minutes was agonizing.

Thali went inside her mind to distract herself. She looked at the food through her own magical lens and saw no magic. *Alexius, is there a way to test for poison in tea or food?*

Yes. You can use magic to reveal the contents. I shine a light on it, but you could probably run a thread of magic through it, as if it were a spoon stirring the tea.

Thali pulled a thread of her magic out—no one was looking at her anyway—put a barrier between it and herself, then dipped the thread into the teacup. She swirled it around. Jasmine, water from the mountain streams, and minerals from the mountain came to her, but nothing deadly. She prodded the steamed buns. But that took too long, so she split her thread into dozens and raked through the buns with them. Pork, sugar, char from the fire, flour, rice flour, water, and yeast appeared to her, but she saw nothing out of the ordinary. Satisfied, she snaked the thread through Elric's tea and buns.

Her stomach grumbled, and she wondered if it would be an enormous breach of protocol to just start chowing down. How would her grandmother look at her then? At that thought, she decided she didn't care. She and her family had already been banished and dismissed, so why should she go hungry? Thali reached out and grabbed a bun, munching on it as she mused about the coming ramifications for her impulsiveness.

She must have been lost in thought for longer than she realized because she startled as Elric reached for the cup. Everyone else followed suit. Thali swallowed the last of her bun and took a gentle sip of her tea. The room remained silent. She had no idea how they could remain this quiet. She could hear her own heart beating in her chest, and it made her antsy.

Elric, however, remained calm as he continued to sip his tea, then tore off a small bite of the steamed bun and gently popped it in his mouth, all the while smiling and radiating sunshine. Never did he utter a word.

Thali considered dropping the plate on the floor. The quiet was starting to ring in her ears, and she wanted it to stop. She had already finished her steamed buns and her tea and was left with nothing else to do but watch as everyone else did so as slowly as they possibly could. Elric was the slowest of them all. She had no idea what was going on. It was like they were in a silent contest to see who would finish last.

That's exactly it, Alexius said.

Thali quietly moved to touch the gem hidden under her shirt. *Tariq, can you hear me?*

You bet, Lili, loud and clear. What's going on?

Thali was surprised at how clearly she could hear Tariq in her mind now. *Is there some political thing where you need to eat as slowly and silently as possible?*

Yup. Could be done with anything really. But in some cultures, whoever speaks first loses the upper hand. It's like a waiting game. Whoever breaks first loses. Could be done with food, silence, even sparring.

Oh great. I definitely finished eating first.

I assume Elric hasn't? Tariq asked.

How did you know?

He's a good politician. You're in Cerisa?

With my grandmother.

Ah. Good luck. Gotta go.

Thanks.

Thali saw a flash of the same meadow she'd left only days ago, except now leaves were starting to fall, the green landscape becoming a mix of yellow and orange and brown.

Then Thali blinked and she was back. She glanced around, moving her eyeballs only, and saw that she hadn't missed anything. Now only Uncle Renshu, Amah, and Elric had anything left on their plates. It was a true skill to continue eating so slowly without making it look as if they were done eating.

Thali knew exactly how little movement it would take to push her plate off the side of the chair. She could make it look like an accident. Just the brush of a forearm. Perhaps then her grandmother would be startled into looking at her.

At long last, her grandmother spoke. She smiled, a friendly smile, but the friendliness didn't move past her lips. "Your Highness, my family will talk of the honor you've bestowed upon us for many generations to come. However, I must ask the purpose of your visit. You are, of course, welcome to stay in our home and visit as long as it pleases you. We will be honored to see to your needs and wants for as long as you like." She nodded.

Thali felt very excluded.

Elric smiled the overly polite smile that he used to impart bad news. "Thank you. You are a gracious hostess. But tell me, will you not even look at your own blood? Your granddaughter, the Princess of Adanek, my wife, and the future queen of my kingdom, has come to visit her grandmother, and I dare say this is a colder greeting than we expected." Elric reached over to grip Thali's hand.

"I do not know of whom you speak. All of my children are here in this room. All but she who perished while protecting His Royal Highness Prince Feng as he visited *your* lands." Amah raised a single eyebrow into an arch.

"Power is held equally in Adanek. Should anything happen to me, my queen will rule."

Amah tipped her head in Thali's direction, without making eye contact. Thali thought that was talent. Amah's hand shook, and the teacup trembled as it landed back on the arm. Her two attendants were beside her in seconds, Uncle Renshu as well, and they helped her stand. "It has been a true pleasure, but I fear I must retire."

"Of course. It has been an honor to meet you. We look forward to our next conversation." Elric stood and bowed. Thali was seconds behind him as she stood and curtsied.

The attendants ushered her grandmother out of the room, and the same man as earlier, the one she was sure was her uncle, showed them out.

"We will be returning to our ship," Thali told him. She followed Elric out, but once in the reception room, she felt her silent uncle slip a note into the cuff at her elbow as she walked by him. She bent her arm to keep it there and looked up to see only Nasir and Isaia had noticed. Their gazes quickly slid away from the crook of her arm.

Thali held her hands under her chest so hiding the note was less conspicuous. As they walked along the busy streets, the guards closed in on them, and Thali was able to subtly grasp the folded note. She held it, hoping her sweaty palms weren't smudging the ink.

CHAPTER NINE

S O ENGROSSED IN HER thoughts was she that Thali didn't realize the pace at which they were walking until they suddenly reached the ship. She glanced at Elric. He was positively fuming. She slipped the note into her pocket and silently followed him onboard as he nodded tersely at the guards and crew, then continued to follow him all the way to their rooms.

"What's wrong, Elric?" Thali was worried. The note was burning a hole in her pocket.

Elric grabbed one of the many busts of himself in their office and smashed it on the floor.

Thali jumped back even as she felt Alexius wrap a magical barrier around her.

"I cannot believe that old woman! How *dare* she treat you that way. Ignoring you, not even addressing you. It's an insult to our kingdom! Kings have gone to war for less!" Elric paced in the tight space, reminding Thali of Indi, only the tiger tended to stay calmer.

Now that Thali realized the cause of his anger, she stepped closer to him, grasping his wrist to pause his pacing, then cupping his cheek. His hand trailed down her arm and settled on her waist, so she rested her closed hand on his chest. She could feel his heart racing, and his chest still heaving, but he stilled. "It's all right, Elric," Thali said soothingly.

His gaze finally focused on her, and she saw the hurt he felt on her behalf.

"I wasn't expecting a warm welcome. Truly. I'm a little hurt, but you have to remember Cerisan nobility has rules. My mother broke the rules. Therefore, my family pays the penalty—that includes me. But do you know what makes it all worth it?"

Elric calmed more and Thali smiled, focusing only on him. "My parents love each other very much. I grew up in a home filled with love. I met you. If my mother had kept her word and married Prince Feng, whatever iteration of me that union would have created would be stuck at the Cerisan palace, yes, living a luxurious life, but also being confined to the palace until I was married off in some trade agreement." Thali smiled.

Elric closed his eyes and leaned into the hand Thali cradled his cheek with. He took a few deep breaths, then she put her forehead against his. When his breathing slowed, Thali took her other hand and slid it behind his head.

"What do we do now? Traipse around the countryside until we find a gate?" Elric asked.

Thali swallowed. That had been on her mind since the moment she'd thought to come to Cerisa. She had always known what she would have to do, even though she'd hoped not to. She also had to hope it would work, because she wasn't sure about how he felt about her now. "I have an idea. But I need you to trust me, and I need you to stay out of it." Thali pulled back enough to search Elric's eyes.

His eyes narrowed, and she wished she could see what he was thinking. "I know someone here who could help us, but only I can go and ask," Thali said.

"Take Nasir and Isaia?" Elric raised an eyebrow. He was negotiating.

"He won't hurt me, at least I don't think so. I'll take Nasir, but I'm not sure Isaia would be a good choice."

"Stefan then," Elric said.

Thali's eyes widened, almost enjoying the bargaining. "Alexius."

Elric narrowed his eyes again. She could sense he wanted to ask, wanted to know who she was seeing and why he couldn't meet them. He nodded.

Thali suddenly remembered the note in her pocket and pulled it out to read it.

"Where did that come from? When?" Elric asked.

"My uncle handed it to me in secret as we left," Thali explained.

Elric looked dumbfounded but sat on a chair arm as she read the note.

"We should return to the inn," Thali said as she looked up.

"Is that what the note says?" Elric asked.

Thali handed him the note. "It only says the Double Pheonix Inn would be a lovely place to spend another night."

"What do you think it means?" Elric asked.

"I think it means one of my uncles will visit us at the inn," Thali said.

Elric nodded.

"This wasn't what you meant though, when you said you had to meet someone, was it?"

Thali thought for a moment. "Maybe I won't have to go, if this goes well," she said. Part of her wanted to meet her contact though, if she was truly being honest with herself.

Elric stood up. "Let's go back to the inn then."

Knowing she might have to meet her contact the next night, Thali had to prepare.

"Ready?" Elric turned and asked.

"You head up first. I've just got a few more things to bring," Thali said.

Elric strode over and planted a kiss on her temple, then left their rooms. Thali took the time to strap a couple more daggers on, then ran a thumb over the medallion in her belt. She didn't break promises, certainly not her promise to Garen to always keep it on her. So she always kept it on, just not always visibly—until now. She worried that Elric would notice and question her, but she would need this before they were done in Cerisa. Now that she knew they would not fall under her grandmother's protection, Thali hung the medallion more prominently outside her belt, visible to anyone who looked.

That done, she took a deep breath and went up on deck to meet Elric and head to the inn. Before disembarking, she turned to her guards and friends. "Amali, I need you to stay on board with Derk." At the guard's stiff nod, Thali turned to Mia. "Mia, would you prefer to stay on board or go ashore with us?" Then Thali hugged her best friend. "I need you to get Indi and Ana ready for a walk tomorrow after nightfall," she whispered into Mia's neck.

As they separated, Mia said, "I'll stay on board. I found some sails that need repairs." She nodded and disappeared belowdecks, ushering Ana and Indi down with her. Bardo stayed tucked up Thali's sleeve.

Tilton and Daylor looked at her questioningly just as Isaia and Alexius joined the group that would accompany her and Elric into town.

Thali leaned in close to Tilton and embraced him, whispering so low she barely moved her lips. "I need you both and Mia to meet me behind the inn tomorrow after nightfall."

Tilton only squeezed her in return, not showing any other acknowledgment of her words.

She disembarked then, and her little group walked through town back to the inn. Stefan and Nasir inspected the room before they all filed in. Then their guards spread out, two at the windows in the main living space, two more inside the door, and two outside.

Once upon a time, Thali had hoped that being shamed into leaving Adanek would have meant fewer guards, but that hadn't been the case. She would have to get creative now. "Nasir, Isaia, would you take the back window?" Thali asked. The guards shuffled around, looking confused. "Also, I think two in here is enough. It's not a very big space." Thali glanced at Elric's two guards, and they looked to Elric.

He nodded, then went to sit in front of the fire. Tea was brought to the door, and Thali brought the tray to the couches where Elric was waiting. Alexius disappeared into the bedroom. Thali felt a thread in the bedroom that was human and unfamiliar but felt like her mother's. She couldn't explain it, but as her strength had grown, even though she didn't have the same access to magic in this world as she did in Alexius's, her magical senses had heightened so she could sense individual human threads now.

Thali poured three cups of tea and handed one to Elric, who watched the door to their bedroom. Nasir and Isaia were also watching, hands on their weapons. Stefan was on duty in the hallway. He would not have been all right with what was going on, and even Elric looked a little uncomfortable.

The screen door slid open, and a tall man appeared, his empty hands in the air as he stepped into the room.

"Uncle Renshu," Thali said as she stood and ran over, wrapping her arms around his torso.

"My dearest niece," Renshu said as he closed his eyes and squeezed her back. "I am so sorry for Amah's behavior today. She is so stubborn in her old age, yet she still holds almost the entire town in her grip."

"It's all right," Thali said.

"She does approve of you though. I hope you know that. She said you looked healthy," Renshu said.

"Thank you for telling me," Thali said.

Elric scoffed from where he sat.

"Uncle Renshu, this is my husband, Prince Elric." Thali pulled away from him to introduce Elric.

"Your Highness," Renshu said as he bowed his head.

"You sat to her right earlier today."

"I am next in line, as the eldest, to take her position when she finally decides to give it up," Renshu said.

"Why not take it from her? Have you no sway?"

"I am here. That took all the sway I have," Renshu said. His jaw tightened.

"Uncle Renshu, thank you for coming. I know it's very difficult," Thali said. She stood to block Elric from view. He had become surprisingly grumpy.

"I could not miss seeing my favorite niece. You've grown up. Congratulations on your new title." Renshu beamed.

Thali saw he was proud of her, but she didn't feel deserving of it.

"How are your parents?" he asked.

"They are well, wishing badly that they could have come, but they needed to protect our home." Thali guided him to sit with them and handed him the third cup of tea.

"You'll have to catch me up on what's going on. I have felt a shift in the world, and we saw a giant shrimp-lizard beached on the shore the other day."

"Shore, like beside the ocean?" Alexius joined them from the bedroom.

Renshu looked at him, narrowing his eyes.

Thali didn't know how much to tell her uncle. She would need his help, but she wanted to keep him safe too.

"What is special about this one, niece?" Renshu looked at Alexius and put his foot between her and Alexius.

Alexius cracked a grin, laughing into his hand as he tried to hide his amusement.

"Uncle Renshu, what do you know of gates into other worlds?"

To his credit, Uncle Renshu looked only mildly surprised as Thali recounted her adventures so far. She said Alexius was a guardian of a gate and told him about the four gates, of how they were hunting for the fourth gate in Cerisa but they didn't know where to start.

"How did you get involved in all this, niece?" Renshu sat back and asked. Elric had moved to stand by the window and Renshu glanced quickly at him.

"It came to me. And now it's up to us to stop the worst from happening," Thali said. She didn't want to lay blame on Rommy or Xerus. And she wanted her uncle minimally involved.

Renshu narrowed his eyes skeptically. It was the same face her mother made when Thali lied to her, or told her half-truths. How was it that her whole family seemed to have a sixth sense about when someone was lying? Thali held her breath, hoping her uncle wouldn't try to seek out more answers than she could give him.

"Unfortunately, I cannot say I know much about any kind of gate. Our lives have centered around Amah and the school. If anyone would know anything, it's Amah. And I don't think she would tell anyone."

Thali sat back down. That's what she had thought, but it still hurt to have it confirmed. She wished at some point that something would come easily for them.

"What does all this have to do with your friend here?" Uncle Renshu glanced at Alexius.

"Well, Alexius is a dragon," Thali said.

"Is he?" Renshu asked as he looked Alexius up and down.

Thali wasn't sure if that signalled disbelief or acceptance.

Renshu nodded, looking deep in thought as he turned away to sip his tea. Then he looked at Alexius again. "My dear niece, is there somewhere we can converse in private?" Renshu glanced at the guards, but Thali had the feeling he meant everyone—including Elric.

Thali was curious, so she nodded but said, "Alexius will have to come." Elric looked curious too but nodded at that. "Let's go to the roof," she said, unable to think of another place that might be secure.

She crawled out the window after Alexius, easily using the trellis to climb to the roof. Once her Uncle Renshu had followed suit, they stood on the tiles that covered all the buildings in Cerisa. Not a soul was in sight.

Renshu glanced at Alexius, who in turn strode to the other side of the roof and looked away to give them the illusion of privacy. Thali was sure Alexius would still be able to hear them clearly from three rooftops over though.

Renshu sat then, crossing his legs, and Thali did the same. She wove a bubble around them, though she opened her mind's thread to Alexius to be sure he could hear the conversation too.

"Routhalia, is your brother involved in this?" Renshu asked gently.

Thali swallowed. She hadn't yet sorted out what she knew of her brother now and what it meant. Emotion choked her throat, and she could only nod.

Renshu seemed to understand. "Years ago, I was taking in the mid-autumn festival in town. It was a big year as our crops had done very well, and people had traveled far for the festivities. An old fortune teller did a reading for a friend, and when they were done, the fortune teller grabbed my wrist. He told me there would first be dishonor in my family but then balance. Siblings would be born to balance each other out, and the world would be their playground. I never knew if that meant you and your brother, but I suspected so given your mother's dishonor. Rommy has always been good at hiding his true feelings—and manipulating your parents."

Thali scrunched her brow. This was the first time she'd ever heard any-one say anything negative about her brother. He was always praised. She leaped to his defense automatically. "I think he's hurting, from rejection."

Renshu nodded as he looked at her with the same knowing look of her mother. "I'm sorry I cannot help you with the gates." He reached into his cloak, and Alexius was next to her in a moment. "Relax, dragon. It is only a gift for my niece, as is tradition." He smiled as he handed the long, thin box to Thali.

She wondered if it was another dagger. Her Uncle Renshu had gifted her all kinds of weapons in the past. She had a whole section for them in her armory.

Thali took the box and pulled at the bow. She opened the box and saw a dagger the length of her arm. But curiously, a bracelet rested next to it.

"Where did you get the bracelet?" Alexius asked.

"It is a family heirloom. I took it from our safe because I wanted you to have it." Renshu said. "When I am head of this family, your family will be welcomed back. You will be afforded all its privileges, and this is just the start." He nodded as if he had been practicing that speech and was happy to have it done.

"Thank you." Thali brought the box closer. The bracelet had an array of black and red gems hanging from it. She reached to touch it, but Alexius's hand shot out and stopped her.

Use your other sense first.

Thali furrowed her brow as she used her threads. She saw small bundles of threads in the gems themselves.

There's a lot of magic stored in these. It's old. And the magic is deceiv-ingly large.

What will happen when I put it on?

You might feel the magic, but it would need to be activated to be used. I'm checking now to see if there is anything evil in it.

A moment later, Alexius nodded.

Thali looked up to see her uncle watching her and Alexius. "There's magic in these gems. Gems that store magic are incredibly rare. I've only ever seen a few," Thali explained. She clamped her lips shut as she thought about the one she'd brought back from Alexius's world. She'd been about to say that she'd never seen any in their own world.

"Then I'm all the more grateful I chose it for you." Renshu glanced at it. "May I?"

Thali nodded. Her uncle leaned over, took the bracelet, and placed it around her wrist. She felt a huge weight on her wrist momentarily before it lightened like a normal bracelet.

"The gems in the bracelet match the dagger and sword," Renshu said.

Thali looked at the dagger. There was a rounded lump at the end of the pommel, but it didn't look very gem-like.

"The gem is inside. It's probably difficult to see in this darkness. Oh, and I left the sword in your bedroom. I hope those gems have magic in them too." Renshu said. "And I take that to mean you can use magic?"

Thali nodded, smiling awkwardly.

"I knew your gift with animals was so much more," Renshu smiled.

"You knew?"

"Jinhua confided in me once. I think she was wondering if anyone else in our family had similar gifts."

"Is there?" Thali asked, taking the opportunity.

Renshu shook his head. "You have a cousin who might have the gift of sight. He sees much farther than is normal for a human, but that is the extent of his abilities."

Thali wondered if the cousin had magic but needed to practice and learn more.

"I don't think it's magic though. I think he just has really good eyesight." Renshu grinned.

"Amah?" Thali asked, thinking about the recipe in her vest pocket.

Renshu's face crinkled. "Not that any of us know. She's beyond clever and has gained our family many advantageous deals, but I'd call it cleverness and luck."

Thali hefted the dagger again; it felt heavy and then light, and she wondered if the other daggers her uncle had gifted her had similar properties she'd never detected before. "Thank you," Thali said as Renshu moved away.

"I'm sorry I couldn't help more. While I'm not one to wish my own mother harm, I am saddened by her choices. None of us have ever stopped loving Jin and you and Rommy."

Thali nodded and Renshu disappeared as he slid down the back of the roof and into the shadows. She noticed her Uncle Renshu hadn't named her father.

Thali climbed back to her room, and Alexius followed suit. Elric looked up expectantly, and she filled him in on what her uncle had said and showed him the gifts. He just nodded and listened.

When she was done, they decided they should try to get some sleep. It was late. The guards set up their rotations as she and Elric went to their room, where Thali gasped as she found the sword her uncle had left. It wasn't really one sword but two. They were thin and could be held like a singular sword; her uncle had gifted her a beautiful set of butterfly swords with gems inlaid along the guard.

They crawled into bed, but as she lay there, sleep would not come. She stared at the ceiling as Elric pulled her close. *Alexius, how does one activate magic?*

You need to ensure it's good magic, without traps or conditions, then you connect to it like you do when you connect with animals. You might feel a barrier, but it should be easier than connecting with animals, especially now that you have practice connecting with magical, intelligent creatures.

Stones rolled around in Thali's stomach at the reminder of the horn-snoads.

You should sleep.

I can't.

Sleep, Alexius said, sending a wave down their connection. Thali yawned, then slept dreamlessly until she woke mid-morning, not remembering the last time she'd slept that well.

CHAPTER TEN

T HALI HID HER ANXIETY all day as she and Elric remained in their room, indulging in a light picnic lunch while playing cards. Elric still needed practice if he was to trounce the crew.

Mia sent a box just before dinner, and Thali could only guess that it was her outfit for her meeting tonight. She hoped it was the same one she'd worn to meet Garen's family a few years ago. That had given her the confidence she'd needed.

"You're really all right with no details?" Thali asked Elric.

"I am. I feel useless, but I can understand that especially here, your family might have other contacts, contacts that may not wish to be known," Elric said, glancing up from the book he'd chosen after dinner. "Can I help in any way though?"

She shook her head.

"All right, then I'll be right here, reading until you get back," Elric said. True to his word, he put his feet up on the table and eased back in his chair. "And I'm not moving until you *do* come back."

Thali narrowed her eyes. She wasn't sure she could be as trusting of others as Elric seemed to be of her, no matter what Alexius said. She placed a light kiss on his forehead, then slipped into the bedroom with the box Mia had sent. The outfit inside made her gasp. It was much like the one she'd wanted to wear. Trust Mia to be so intuitive. This time, the dress had been cut of the deepest black silk with swirls of red embroidered on it—Adanek's colors—and boasted a high neckline that shouted sophistication and superiority. Once she was dressed and about to leave, a gleam from the box caught her eye. Leaning closer, she discovered a necklace half-tucked under a cloth.

It was a gold necklace adorned with some of the biggest sapphires she had ever seen. But she knew why it was there. Together, her dress and necklace represented her: the blue and gold of her family with the black and red of the kingdom. Thali smiled and invited Bardo to encircle her neck as she checked her image in the mirror once more. It would do. She climbed out the window and down the trellis behind the inn. Indi and Ana greeted her as Nasir and Alexius stepped out of the shadows with Tilton, Daylor, and Mia.

"Thank you," Thali told Mia.

"Wait," Mia said, pulling a kohl pencil and some berry stain out of a leather pouch.

Thali groaned but held still.

A few quick moments later, Mia said, "There." She stepped back, then took a small mirror from the bag to show Thali her makeup job.

Thali was awed. She looked ... well, fierce, and not quite herself. The whites of her eyes stood out with the heavy kohl lines, and the gray of her eyes looked almost black. Her lips were as red as the swirls on her dress—and blood. "What would I do without you, Mia?" Thali looked at her friend.

"You would wear terrible clothes and be forever a sailor," Mia said.

"I love you and appreciate you more than I could ever express, Mia," Thali said, embracing her. Indi and Ana pushed their way into the group hug, and she hugged her animals too. Bardo popped out to greet Indi and Ana from the back of Thali's neck.

"Can you two keep an eye on the guards outside the room?" Thali turned to Tilton and Daylor. They nodded and turned the corner towards the front door of the inn.

"Stand still," Mia said. Thali did as instructed while Mia walked around her once, then backed up a step. "Good," she said with a nod before turning and disappearing around the corner too. From the shadows, Thali heard her say, "Why, yes, Isaia, what a coincidence. Thank you for walking me back to the ship."

So Isaia had been trying to follow them. Thali should have thought of that. It was fortuitous that Mia had left when she did because any surprises that night would be bad. Isaia's bright blond hair was too noticeable. Thali needed guards who could disappear. Taking a deep breath then, she took the medallion that always hung at her waist and put it around her neck. Now it sat just below the jeweled necklace.

It was the cherry on top of the most symbolic outfit she'd ever worn.

Now came her biggest hurdle. She wasn't exactly sure how to find him. All she knew was that the dark of night would be the best time, and her attire and the medallion would be the message. Her only thought was to find the seediest place in town and hope one of his crew would pass along the message she was sending. That said, she was no idiot. Hidden beneath her extravagant outfit were all her weapons—even the newest dagger.

Alexius and Nasir had dressed more plainly in shades of black and gray. Thali hadn't bothered dulling her appearance with a cloak because she was already incredibly conspicuous with Indi and Ana beside her. She glanced at them and decided it was now or never. Taking a deep, steeling breath, she asked them to stick close to her. And off they went.

The moment she stepped out of the alley and onto the street, a woman in bright-pink silk, toddling on what looked like wooden bricks, walked toward them. She had been standing half a block down, and now she smiled, making eye contact and approaching slowly. Her hands were outstretched, her right hand on her left, palms up. Thali knew she'd done that on purpose.

The woman had raven-black hair like Thali's own mother, and her skin was white with powder. Thali waited for the woman to approach, and when she neared, she bent ever so slowly at the waist, bending until she knelt on the ground and touched her head to it before rising slowly and gracefully. "Your Highness, we are honored by your presence. If it pleases you, I will guide you to my master," she said.

Thali blinked. There wasn't a soul on the street other than this woman. Suddenly, Thali knew without asking that he'd known she was here the whole time. She'd needed no plan.

She followed the woman down the street, though they didn't wander as far as she had expected to. They'd only turned a couple corners before they entered a tea shop Thali had passed numerous times before. As they walked up to the door, a young man with a braid down to his ankles and dressed in traditional warrior silks opened the door and bowed his head, not making eye contact with anyone in her group as they walked through.

They strode to the back of the tea shop, the woman balancing delicately on the wooden blocks as she ascended the rear stairs. Bundles of tea littered the stairs, yet she navigated them as if they were nothing, impressing Thali. Indi managed the stairs too, but Ana somehow kicked a tea bundle every few steps. Luckily, Alexius caught each one and placed them back in their spot.

Thali too had learned to walk on the wooden blocks that were supposed to be shoes, and the first time, she'd fallen over, nearly twisting an ankle within moments. Naturally, her mother had made her wear them while training until she could walk and run and fight in them, so Thali had much respect for how this woman moved so gracefully in them.

At the top was a small landing. A young man and woman in traditional clothes sat waiting. Rich silks in yellows and reds brightened a room constructed all of agar wood. The couple rose and bowed, then opened a set of double doors to a screened room with intricate wooden panels along the walls. Thali wished she could get a closer look at them and hoped she would have a chance to examine them. Indi and Ana tucked in next to her as they all walked into the room: her tall, curly-haired dog and tiger prowling, heads high; her snake upright and draped around her shoulders; and her two guards, stiff and intimidating, two steps behind them.

Filling the middle of the room was the most ornate cherrywood table she'd ever seen. The carvings on its legs were so delicate and detailed, Thali was worried they would fall apart. She wasn't sure how they were holding the weight of their burden because the table's surface was plated with pure gold, protected with a layer of glass. An entire scene of a dragon and phoenix dancing around each other was even carved into the gold. A white stone tea set sat on top.

Ming stood the moment she entered. He was dressed in black warrior silks, looking exactly the same as when she'd last seen him three years ago. He smiled brightly as she approached with her entourage. Thali was surprised to see no one else. She used her magic and found only one other thread of interest in the room.

"My beautiful, fellow princess, thank you for visiting," Ming said as he bowed his head.

Thali smiled widely and took his hands in hers. "Thank you for the warm welcome, brother." She smiled ever so sweetly. "I see there are only three of us here today." She glanced at the pillar where she'd detected the extra thread.

Joren stepped out from behind the pillar. He wore a bright pink-and-yellow silk robe with sleeves as big as the skirt. Surprisingly, a "V" of his chest showed, though it and his face were painted white, just like the woman who'd escorted her here. Painted atop the white powder were bright red cheeks, and his eyes too were lined in kohl, though far more heavily than hers.

"I see your skills have improved," Joren said as he glided over. He took Thali's hand, bowed low over it, and kissed it. "Your Highness."

Somehow, Thali realized Joren meant that more as an acknowledgment of her marriage to Elric than her position in this court.

Indi rubbed her head against Joren, so he patted her and scratched behind her ears before moving away.

"Let us sit for tea," Ming said.

After greeting Joren, Thali didn't take her eyes off Ming again, though Joren lounged in his own chair. She'd sensed his thread the moment she'd entered the room but found herself surprised that her magic only reached the room's perimeter.

There's a magical barrier in the wooden panels, Alexius said.

Thali didn't twitch a single muscle. She smiled politely as Ming stood, pouring powder into a bowl. She watched quietly as he ceremoniously made their tea. His every step was meticulous, and Thali was surprised when Ming served her first. Though Joren looked as if he wasn't paying attention, she could feel his gaze linger on her, watching, assessing.

Thali waited until Ming had served everyone at the table, surprising her yet again when he took Alexius a cup. Thali hid a smile behind her hand, wondering what Ming knew of Alexius's true form. She wouldn't offer that information up easily—if at all.

Thali took deep breaths as she waited, trying to resist bouncing her leg. To combat the urge, she tucked her ankle behind her other foot. The corners of Joren's lips turned upward. Princess lessons had at least taught her something.

"So, Ming, how has business been lately?" Joren asked. He seemed especially preoccupied with one of the many jewels on his fingers.

Ming took a deep breath in and then out. "The fishermen have reported some strange beasts in the distant waters, large pink-and-purple fish. One fisherman even returned to port and no longer recognized his family," he said.

Well, that settles it, Thali thought. *The North's gate is definitely open.* That made her wonder what kind of creatures had entered and if she should learn more about that world.

I suspect the North's gate is connected to Aeceal. The world of Aeceal is water based. However, the waters here are less oxygenated than they're used to, so they'll move slower here, Alexus explained.

Thali decided she was out of patience with the politics, so she smiled at Ming. When he turned to her, she asked, "Ming, what do you know of a magical gate to another world?"

To his credit, he didn't startle. In fact, he turned his attention to pouring them another cup of tea. After that task was done, he sat and turned to Thali. "How did your grandmother receive you?" Ming asked.

"She didn't. Well, she received me but did not acknowledge me," Thali said. her grandmother's rejection still twisted something inside her that she shoved away. His question surprised her though. Joren turned to her, scanning her face earnestly.

"I am sorry," Ming said. He truly looked saddened by the news, though he didn't offer words of comfort. "But until you shared that knowledge, I did not know of such gates. Nor did I know there was a gate in these lands." Ming was nothing if not methodical and thoughtful, and Thali wondered what small percentage of his thoughts he was sharing. "Will you leave this with me for a week?" he asked, turning again to her. "I will find the gate and inform you of its location. I assume your goal is to protect it?"

Thali nodded, surprised once again by his confidence in her. She had expected more posturing, or at the very least, a convoluted, mysterious conversation.

"In the meantime, will you follow me? There is something I would like to share with you." At her nod, Ming rose and headed to the other side of the room.

After telling her animals to stay with Alexius, she and Joren followed him through a door next to the bank of windows. He opened it, and they descended a narrow set of steps into a lush garden bisected with stone paths and lined with a beautiful array of strange plants. Once they'd descended, Thali likened it to a fortress with its lofty walls. Three walls were of sliding paper doors, however, and the fourth was instead a set of heavy wooden doors as tall as the walls. It was exactly as her grandmother's drawing depicted.

Opposite the gate, a waterfall poured out of the wall. But it wasn't a rushing waterfall. Instead, it was a gentle one that fed into a koi pond.

"Is it not too cold for them?" Thali asked before she could help herself.

"The walls keep them warm, and we do not get winters like Adanek does," Ming said.

Thali turned again to look around. It looked like three houses boxed in a courtyard. She supposed she'd never really seen the inside of Cerisan homes. "What is this place?"

"It is known to outsiders as the manor of a powerful, secret lord from faraway lands. In truth, it is my home." Ming bowed his head.

"It's beautiful," Thali said.

"I'm glad you think so because I would like to invite you and your husband to stay here while you are in Cerisa. You will have your own building and can use it as a home base during your time here." Ming led her to the left wing. He slid the doors open, and Thali walked inside. She couldn't see the length of it from outside, but it was impressively large inside.

"There are five bedrooms upstairs and staff quarters on the lower floors. I do hope you'll stay here as it's much easier for me to secure."

Thali wondered what Ming needed to secure them against.

"I will also make myself scarce as I understand your husband is not aware of your dual status." Ming stated as he crossed a large, expansive room. Mats dotted the floor and cushions were stacked against a wall. As Thali explored a doorway, she found a sitting room furnished as she was accustomed to with long, wide couches and white silk screens so thin they looked like windows and let light into the room. An enormous rectangular dining table occupying the opposite corner told Thali the space could easily accommodate thirty people.

"I'm across the way, but I'll make myself scarce as well," Joren said.

Is it me, or does he seem more serious than usual? Thali nodded. "This would be wonderful, thank you."

"To maintain my guise, I will send a note to your inn today, inviting you to stay with the lord of the manor," Ming said.

"Thank you." Thali wondered how much she trusted Ming. He'd offered so much more than she'd expected, yet she couldn't detect—or think of—any reason for him to deceive her.

"If you have need of me, simply ask the gardener," Ming said as he nodded at an old man with long white hair raking an empty garden bed.

Ming walked her back upstairs, and after heartfelt farewells, she saw herself back out to the street, her animals flanking her and her guards trailing. That had seemed too easy. *Shouldn't it have been more difficult?* she wondered.

As Thali walked back to the inn, few people were still out. But of those, only a couple turned to stare at her entourage. It was the majority that did not look who bothered her more. Those were the people loyal to her grandmother, who would not serve them or even talk to them while they were in town. She'd never forget the time Rommy had had a fever so high he'd fainted, and her parents, desperate for a healer, had rushed from storefront to storefront, looking in vain for someone who would help him. After that, her parents always traveled with a well-stocked healer.

"Are you all right?" Elric asked. He hopped over the low fence surrounding the inn and came to take Thali's hand.

"I am, thank you." Thali looked up into Elric's eyes. She saw a line of worry there, but also the sunshine that blasted away all her problems. "I thought you were going to stay in that chair until I got back."

"Technically I did. You're back." He winked. "But we got a strange invitation while you were gone," Elric said. He pulled a card out of his sleeve as they entered the inn and climbed the stairs to their room.

Thali was dumbfounded at Ming's hastiness. The card was indeed an invitation, as Ming had promised, to accept Lord Wong's hospitality even though he had to leave on a business matter and would not be available to meet them.

"What do you think?" Thali asked. She pressed her lips together to prevent herself from saying too much.

"I think it's gotta be better than this inn." Elric waved his hand around the room. "Given this card has gold leaf on it." He brought the card up to the light and tilted it, making the gold leaf shine.

Thali looked at the card. "I think we should take everyone."

"What about the ship?"

"Mouse and Lobb and the rest of the crew might choose to stay on board, but I'd really like at least Mia, Tilton, and Daylor to come with us," Thali said.

Elric nodded, so Thali wrote a note and sent it back to the ship with Stefan.

Chapter Eleven

MING HAD SENT A small army of people to help them move their things into his compound, so many in fact, each easily carried only one item on the short walk from the inn to Ming's home. As they entered their allotted space, Elric spun around, clearly impressed by the opulence. The space was filled with much more gold than it had been the previous evening. Though Thali was happy to be here, she was saddened that the innkeepers had been happy to see them go. She wondered if her grandmother had leaned on those trying to help them.

The next week was spent in luxury. Even Elric relaxed as they savored extravagant meals, bathed in a hot spring, enjoyed the music of talented musicians, or lounged in the library. Thali spent the days eating, resting, and trying to distract herself with her friends, reminding her of her time at school. The world outside Ming's compound had been harsh, so Thali took the coward's way and remained within the fortress walls.

She still trained in the morning though, and if she was early enough, Ming would show up in the shared training room, dressed plainly to practice with her.

"Your skills have grown," Ming said one day. "Do you use magic?"

"No, though after having done so before, it feels as if I can move faster now," Thali said.

Ming nodded as they circled each other, brandishing their staffs. Though Ming was a good deal older than her, he was calm and reserved, making him extra dangerous.

Thali glanced around to see if there were any plants nearby before she finally asked, "Why is Joren here?"

She had been trying figure out if Joren wanted to insert himself into her life again or if he just wanted to be part of the magical events. Not that she really minded either way. If he wasn't Garen's brother, she would have been glad to have him. Even though he was as slippery as a fish, he would save his people. And his magical abilities with plants always came in handy, especially with the ease with which he used it. She didn't think she would ever be that good.

Ming didn't reply right away, but Thali was learning that was just who he was. He liked to think things through. Any words that left his mouth were concise and important.

He grabbed her wrist and locked her staff with his own, using it to roll his body close to hers. Then he paused. "He cares about this world as much as you or I. He knows you're at the center of this next big change and has kept very close tabs on you."

Thali wondered if that was a warning or information. She wondered too if it was because of Garen. A dagger sliced her heart as she thought about how they'd nearly chosen each other. It would have been selfish, but they would have been enough for each other.

"We'll need all the help we can get," Thali said. If she was going to play a role in whatever was about to happen, then she would at least make sure the cards were stacked in their favor.

Ming nodded, tilting his head as if he wanted to add something. But then he turned and pulled his hood up before disappearing behind the door to his building. A moment later, Elric slid the doors of their building open and sleepily approached with two cups of tea.

"Good morning," Thali said.

"Good morning. I think I'm enjoying being away from the palace too much." Elric grinned. His hair was tousled, but even with sleep still clouding his eyes, he glowed like the sun. "Would you come and sit with me, or do you still have drills to finish?" Elric asked.

"I'm done," Thali said. She took the tea he offered and followed him to the courtyard. He sat in a large basket seat, and Thali pulled the blanket draped over the back over them as she climbed into the chair with him. Elric lay his head on her shoulder and they watched the sun rise as they sipped their tea.

As the building woke and they emptied their teacups, a sleepy tiger and dog joined them, Bardo hitching a ride on Indi and sliding up Thali's arm and around her neck.

When Elric finished his tea, he put the cup on the small table and repositioned them. He slid his arm around her and pulled her closer. She put her head on his shoulder and he rested his cheek on her forehead. "Thali, how do you feel being here?"

"What do you mean?"

"I mean, back in Cerisa. I know you didn't spend lots of time here, but you've spent some. It's where your family is."

"Being in the same room as Amah was as close as I've ever been to her. Sometimes though, when we were here, a small package would show up at the inn my family would stay at. It was never marked. There wasn't even a note or signature on it. But my mother always thought it was from her mother. Usually, it had small things for me and Rommy." A lump rose in her throat at the thought of Rommy. She'd been pushing it away because she didn't know what to make of her brother's decisions. Her mind was constantly trying to think of excuses or explanations. Perhaps she'd heard wrong, maybe she hadn't asked him the right questions and she'd misunderstood what he said. But the image of the colors on the map all becoming the same, of the pawns and figures moving and building and multiplying, haunted her dreams.

Would she be able to face her brother? Could she stop him in time? What would she do when they found the gate in Cerisa? What if they managed to get through Bulstan's gate? What would happen to Uncle Mupto?

"Thali?" Elric interrupted her thoughts.

"Hmm?" she replied as she blinked her way back to the present. She closed the lid on the many questions bubbling up.

"Are you seeing what I'm seeing?" Elric asked. He removed his cheek from her head and the top of her head chilled.

Thali turned to see what Elric was looking at. Sure enough, servants were carrying a huge pink fish with a blue-gray tail bigger than Indi through the courtyard's front gate.

"I don't think I've ever seen a fish that big," Elric said.

"Me neither," Thali said.

Alexius stepped out of the sliding door of their quarters. *That is a finnifenba.*

What are they like?

They are peaceful, intelligent creatures, beautiful to watch in the water. People would make pilgrimages to their lake to watch them dance as a way to celebrate an occasion like a marriage or a new baby.

Thali wanted to ask if they were poisonous but thought it was insensitive.

They're attracted to large magic reserves. You should eat as much as you can tonight.

Really? Thali was surprised.

Because they've caught one, they will not be able to catch another. The finnifenba are too smart to get caught again. But eating it has been known to help retain larger reserves of magic within oneself. My parents often took the finnifenba's sacrifices seriously. The population in Etciel sacrificed one of their own to my family on occasion in support of their reign.

What did they get in return?

Their lands, or rather waters, were well protected, and dragons tended to their homes.

Is that a big deal?

I forget how little you know of dragonlore. We are royalty. All dragons are noble. To have dragons tend to your habitat is to make it sacred.

Oh. Thali blinked to focus on Elric, who had been watching her.

"Is it safe to eat?" Elric asked as the servants carrying the fish disappeared into the kitchens.

Thali smiled and nodded.

"I wonder if they'll make some for breakfast," he said as they rose and he guided her back to their quarters.

Thali stopped, so Elric turned back to her. "Thank you, for being so calm about all this, and accepting." she said.

Elric smiled and her insides melted. He was definitely her sunshine prince. "We'll be back in Adanek in no time, I'm sure of it. But I'm excited to finally be on one of your adventures with you." He grinned and Thali didn't have the heart to tell him how arduous their journey was probably going to be.

Chapter Twelve

T HE GARDENER PRESENTED THALI with a note on a tray one morning when she was practicing her drills with Nasir and Isaia. They may have been in waiting mode, but she would keep up her skills as much as possible. She grabbed the card and glanced at it.

Follow the gardener after breakfast. I have answers.

Thali halted her drills and hurried to breakfast. She couldn't inhale it fast enough. What Alexius had failed to mention about the finnifenba was that it was also delicious. It was melt-in-her-mouth tasty and so flavorful she thought her tastebuds might cry every time she ate it.

"I think you're eating even faster than me," Daylor said.

Tilton looked a little taken aback too as Thali shoveled rice and fish in her mouth with her two stick utensils. Mia knew how to use them, but Tilton and Daylor had been learning from Elric, who scooped food into his mouth more than picked it up. Alexius just sat calmly eating his own breakfast, a knowing look on his face.

"Sorry, I think we're going to be ready to head out soon," Thali said.

Ana had gotten used to sitting between Daylor's legs as he was the messiest eater, and she rushed over to clean some grains of rice from Thali's frantic eating.

"To the gate? You know where it is?" Tilton asked.

Thali nodded. "Maybe."

"So we should be packing up?" Mia perked up.

"You don't have to come. You'll be safe here if this is where you'd rather stay. Actually, I think I'd rather most of you stay behind. It'll probably be dangerous," Thali said. She thought of all the creatures that had already attacked villages and people.

"We're coming with you, Thali," Tilton said.

"Or, you could stay here, enjoy yourselves, recuperate from your busy schedules at the palace." Thali started patting a few of her daggers to make sure they were there. Her animals stirred and came over as if they too did not want to be left behind. Even Bardo slid up Mia's chair, across the table, and into Thali's lap.

Mia narrowed her eyes. "I know we're not as skilled as them..." Mia waved a hand at Nasir, Alexius, and Isaia, "...but we can help."

"It's not that I don't think you'll be able to help. It's that I ... I don't want to be ..." Thali looked down and away from them. "I don't think I could handle it if you got hurt."

Daylor put a hand on her arm. "You didn't force us to come here. We've come to help you, and we've made that choice on our own."

"I don't think you've fully thought out the possible consequences," Thali said.

A cough behind them made Thali turn to find the gardener. She nodded at her friends, and they nodded back. They would pick up this conversation when she returned. She wondered when they would start asking questions about the mysterious lord or who she was meeting.

Thali walked along the edge of the stone path as she followed the gardener, her animals and Alexius trailing her, until the servant slipped into what she'd thought was a wall. There was a small gap though, so she stepped through it and up some narrow stairs that ended on the roof. She found she could walk across it without being seen, however, as it was hidden by a false wall. Strangely, they dipped back down a few more stairs and across the rest of the building until she saw a small table and tea set and Ming meditating on the roof's edge. Thieves and roofs were something she would never understand.

The gardener bowed as he left, and Thali sat on the cushions by the low table waiting for Ming to return from his meditation. Indi wrapped around her back, and Ana sat on her side, head on her shoulder. They didn't love Ming like they did Joren, but they didn't dislike him either.

Thali glanced into the other part of her mind and saw Joren was nowhere to be found.

"There are three possible places in Cerisa your gate might be," Ming said, his eyes still closed. "To the north is an isolated population. They survive off what they catch and are not friendly to guests. Many report seeing dancing lights emanating from there, so they may have magic."

Thali silently waited for him to continue.

"To the northwest of us is a forest. Within it is a desert, and an oasis within that desert. There is a group there also rumored to have magic as they protect the oasis. They are very hard to find. It is said they offer help to travelers who make it near, but no one who has met them has ever returned."

Ming still had moved nothing more than his mouth. "To the south, on a small island hard to find because of the ocean's drift, is yet another village. It is whispered that they are much more than the small fishing village they seem to be. Again, no one that has entered has ever left. However, they appear at the market, though rarely, and their wares are much finer than one would expect for a mere fishing village."

"So where do you think the gate is?" Thali asked. She hated the cold, so she was hoping he would choose the jungle oasis or the fishing village, though being at sea with more magical creatures was also a risk.

"Are you asking my personal opinion or which I think you should go to first?"

Thali looked to Alexius. "What do you think?"

"If we consider that the locations usually fit the worlds the creatures are accustomed to, then I would say either the isolated town to the north or the island. Etciel has more desert than other worlds, and that gate is already open," Alexius reasoned.

Ming interjected. "My gut tells me the ice village to the north is simply unfriendly. I was going to encourage you to go to the desert oasis or the fishing village." He opened his eyes and put his hands on his knees.

"Good." Thali nodded. "Fishing village it is."

Ming nodded. "I will send you with whatever supplies you need."

"Thank you. And ... would you look after my friends while I go?"

"They aren't coming with you?" Ming asked.

"I would prefer they stay here, safe," Thali said.

Ming paused, looking as if he might say something, but then he nodded deeply.

Thali looked around for a plant. She found a vine that was drying up along the edge of the roof and touched it, suffusing it with magic to bring it back to life. Then she tapped on it consistently until a leaf started to unfurl.

Coming, princess.

Ming watched her silently, then came and settled on a cushion. The minutes passed in silence until Joren appeared, rising on a vine over the side of the building and stepping onto the rooftop. Indi shifted to rub a head into Joren's waiting hand, but Ana continued pressing into Thali's side.

"You called," Joren said.

"I need a favor," Thali said. She had thought long and hard about it. Owing Joren a favor was a dangerous thing and she worried about it, but what she needed was more valuable than anything he could ask for.

CHAPTER THIRTEEN

T HALI RETURNED TO THEIR quarters and shared the news. "We'll leave tomorrow morning." They would have one last night in luxury.

"Where are we going?" Daylor asked.

"I'm still figuring out a route there, but that should be sorted by tomorrow." Thali grinned. A knock sounded on their screen door just before it slid open to a feast as dish upon dish was brought out.

Thali jumped into the celebrations. She and her friends ate their fill and drank sweet wine. It was late when they all retired. Thali stayed up until it was just her and Elric.

"You're leaving tonight, aren't you?" Elric asked.

"I said tomorrow morning," Thali said. She smiled too sweetly at him.

"Was it in the food too?" Elric asked.

He was reclining on a cushion. Thali had not seen Elric eat much, but she'd seen him drink, or so she had thought.

"I've been avoiding poisons my whole life, Thali. I recognized the gritty powder in the drink and perhaps the scent in the food," Elric said. He looked suspiciously at her.

Thali's shoulders fell. She had wanted to keep Elric safest of all. "Your anger was going to be a small price to pay if it meant you were safe," Thali said.

"Oh, I ate and drank anyway," Elric said.

"You did?" Thali froze, then turned to him.

"I'm not a total fool, Routhalia. I know you have some powerful connections here. And if I haven't been introduced, I assume they're associated with things I'm not supposed to know about. But you're underestimating your friends. You're underestimating me. I know you want to keep us all safe, but tomorrow morning, when everyone finally wakes up, they're not going to give up and stay here. They're going to pack up and come find you. And I *will* be part of that. I will ensure you and they make it as safely as possible."

"I'm sorry," Thali said.

"Will you lay with me for a little while?" Elric asked. He patted a spot on the cushion next to him. She nodded. He tucked her into his arms and rested his head on her shoulder. She tried to memorize the moment: his smell—he even smelled like sunshine—the warmth of his skin, his hands holding her, the slow breaths that deepened as he slept, the gold in his hair.

As she waited until the whole place was quiet, she thought back to earlier that day.

"Joren, I need a favor," Thali said.

He cocked an eyebrow.

"I need a sleeping potion. Something that will make it difficult for everyone to wake up. But it can't work until they're asleep."

Joren looked at her for a full minute before he nodded. He pulled a vial from inside his cloak. When he uncorked it, a seed slid out onto his palm. He grasped a cup of tea, and Thali watched as the tea disappeared back into the leaves. Then the leaves sailed out of the cup and onto a nearby plate. From a pitcher, he poured some water into the teacup, then placed the seed into the cup of water. There it grew into a plant, sucking up all the water. Suddenly, the flower blossomed, the largest flower she'd ever seen. Its petals were as large as her hand. She had no idea what kind of plant it was. Then, just as fast as it had grown and blossomed, the flower dried and fell into Joren's open palm. He closed his fist, crushing the dried plant and dropping it back into the teacup. "For the record, I think you're making a mistake," Joren said.

"I want to keep them safe."

"Do you have the same concern for me?" Joren asked.

"You have extraordinary skills to protect yourself with."

"And him?" Joren nodded at Alexius.

"He's a dragon," Thali said.

"Your guards won't eat or drink. You should know that. And they don't have magic."

"They can handle themselves."

"So do you want to keep your friends safe, or do you not trust their abilities?" Joren asked.

Thali didn't respond.

He placed the cup in her hands, but Ming took it from her instead, nodding. "Eat little at supper," he said.

"Thank you, Ming." Thali left, but Joren's words stuck in her mind.

Thali strapped on the last of her daggers, including the one her Uncle Renshu had given her, and slid out the door. Alexius, Nasir, and Isaia accompanied her through the compound's gate, and they made for the small ship and crew she'd bought through correspondence. She wasn't about to endanger her own crew. She'd also asked Indi, Ana, and Bardo to stay with Mia, to keep her safe wherever they might be.

She and her guards climbed aboard the much smaller ship in the dark of night, where she asked some of the fish nearby to help them along as the ship started to sail off. She waited until they were some distance from the harbor before she asked some larger porpoises to assist. When they agreed, she tossed ropes over the bow and asked them to grasp them, to tow them to the fishing village.

Onward they sailed, faster than was usual, making the crew look worried. They didn't have far to travel though, so it was still night when they stopped. The island was still a couple of hours away, but she thanked the porpoises and waited. She wanted to approach in the light of day, not at night when the island's inhabitants might think they were being attacked.

She hadn't even looked her guards in the eye when she'd started packing. They'd only followed her silently. She'd felt Isaia's disapproval but hadn't addressed it. Now he approached her as she stood on the bow and waited.

"You're angry we left everyone behind?" Thali asked.

"I'm disappointed you think so little of your friends."

"I'm just trying to keep them safe."

"They chose to come with you. They deserve to choose for themselves again."

"Do you really think they'll come after us?"

"Perhaps. I would." Isaia said.

"And what do you think, Nasir?"

Nasir emerged from the shadows. "I think it would have been safer for them to travel with you than without you."

Thali nodded. She hoped they would stay put. She hadn't given them any clues as to where she was headed, but that didn't mean there weren't ways to find out. If they asked the right people, they would figure it out. Then she realized they would know to check the docks, to ask which ship had left, and to ask the harbor master, or perhaps even an observant member of her own crew if they had seen her—or a small group leaving in the middle of the night. Maybe she should have disabled a rudder in her own ship before leaving. She should have thought of that. Ah well, it was too late now.

Chapter Fourteen

Thali exhaled. Ming had given her a map, but in truth, it wasn't much of a map. All she knew was that the village was supposed to be southwest of their current position. At least more creatures would be awake since she'd waited till morning.

Ready whenever you are, Alexius said. They'd talked over the plan last night. Thali would search the animals in the area for information about the surrounding islands. She would investigate each island through the animals, mostly the birds and fish, and once they found their island, they would sail in that direction.

Alexius would be on the watch for magical creatures. Using magic in the water would likely call the villagers to their location, and drifting around the ocean without direction was a waste of their resources and energy. But it was a risk they would have to take.

He put a hand on her shoulder now, reminding Thali to focus on her breathing. She put her hand in her pocket and held the blue gem she'd taken from Etciel, feeling the abundance of magic it contained. Doing what she needed to would require a large source in her world. Part of her wished the gates opening between the other worlds and hers meant that she could feel the same powerful flow of magic here, but that wasn't the case.

Thali took another deep breath. As she exhaled, she spun hundreds of spools of thread outward. She reached whales, fish, and even some birds above them and used them to make a mental map of the ocean beyond them. Then she started to sort through memories, sights, sounds, and smells. It was a lot to take in, but she cataloged it all, placing it in her mental map as she continued filling in the details. She analyzed all the information she received, narrowing down the candidates as she discovered islands that did not fit their criteria.

We're not alone, Alexius said.

Thali was down to five possible places, so she sent a message to the porpoises to head southwest. Four of the five locations were in that direction, and sitting around waiting for whatever Alexius said was coming was the worst idea.

She focused on the whales then. They would know the ocean best. She sorted through their memories and narrowed the choices down to two because the whales didn't like them. They didn't feel right. Thali pulled in her magic spools and sent four threads out: two in each of the directions she had narrowed down to. Suddenly, one hit a wall and she pulled the thread back immediately. She directed the porpoises in that direction and asked them to go faster. "Hang on!" she yelled.

Everyone sat and gripped the sides of their small ship. Three more porpoises joined them, and they all swam where Thali had directed them. She hoped she was making the right choice. She could sense a large magical creature heading toward them now, chasing them. It was still far away, but it moved quickly. *Do you know what it is?* she asked Alexius.

I do not. I don't know all the creatures that exist in all the worlds. I can only tell you it has fur and is moving swiftly through the water.

It has fur?

Yes. It's also long with six paws and a long tail.

What if it's friendly?

Do you really want to find out?

Just then, Thali sensed the place where her thread had hit a barrier, so she sent threads out toward it. If her thread had hit a barrier, then she didn't want their ship to go *splat* against it. When the new threads hit the barrier, she whittled one down as small as it could go until it pierced the barrier. Then she expanded the thread in the opening until she could open a space big enough for their ship to pass through. The porpoises followed her guiding thread, and the moment they were through, she patched the hole she'd made. The barrier snapped back into place, so she removed her threads. There was a loud *thunk* behind them, and they spun around.

Teeth. All she saw was sharp teeth, rows and rows of them. The teeth gnashed at the barrier, and Thali wondered if it would hold. She looked beyond the teeth and saw a huge furry purple body with six paws scrambling at them. It tried to scurry up the barrier, and Thali saw the thick tail before the giant creature slid down and stared at them. Two large eyeballs in a round, flat face stared at them through the barrier.

"It's kind of cute," Nasir said out loud. Everyone turned to look at him. It was true in a way. It did look like a giant sea otter with an extra set of paws in its middle. But there were those teeth. Those were shark teeth, ready to gnash them to a pulp without a thought.

Thali glanced down at the gemstone in her hand. Its surface was now dull, and she knew she had used up all the magic in it. In Etciel, it would have taken days to charge it, so she wondered how long it would take in her own world for the magic to build.

Her shoulders drooped. She felt the drain on her own magic too.

Alexius coughed and Thali looked up. They were surrounded. Sharp, pointy narwhal horns covered in metal, like armor, were pointed at them. Thali swallowed as she looked around and counted thirty surrounding their little ship. They must have come from under the water's surface; otherwise, she surely would have seen them approach.

"Who are you?"

Thali spun her head in the direction of the voice, wondering if a narwhal had spoken in its native tongue. Beyond the glint of the horns though, Thali saw a woman with tanned skin and thick braids atop her head holding a horn to her shoulder. She looked angry, and Thali swallowed. She didn't know which title would offend or please these people, so she dropped the gem into her pocket and put her hands up as her friends were doing. "My name is Routhalia," Thali said, lowering her eyes to the woman's knees. The woman was riding the narwhal like one would ride a horse. Thali scrambled to think of all her parents had taught her about encountering a new culture. The most important thing was to appear less threatening. With so many points ready to pierce her body, looking less threatening was definitely a good idea.

"You will let us bring you to shore," the woman said.

Thali nodded slowly, but as she watched the narwhals herd both the porpoises and their ship, she knew she had to protect the creatures that had brought them all this way. "I don't know where those creatures came from or what they're doing." Thali jutted her chin out at the porpoises now ramming the narwhal guard surrounding them.

The woman only narrowed her eyes. Thali looked around and decided to extend her threads out to the narwhals as she waited to reach the shore. Her threads were met with walls, but she could tell they would be easier to break through than the hornsnoads'.

Don't. Leave them be, Alexius said.

Thali left the narwhals alone, a little surprised at herself for wanting to push into their minds. At the same time, she wondered if the plate armor they all wore was part of the magic she was feeling.

As they approached land, smooth stone structures with rounded tops appeared, dotting the island. She thought the island must be warm given all the open-air buildings and outdoor furniture. As they neared the shore, people came to stare at their little ship. All the locals textiles and clothes were brightly colored and boldly patterned. Thali took a last opportunity to dive into the porpoises' minds, and she gasped out loud before covering it with a cough. Alexius shot her a look.

Did you see underwater?

Alexius raised an eyebrow. Thali knew that her gift with animals was unique and that it took considerably more effort for him to do something even remotely close to it, but she couldn't help but wonder if he had some other way of seeing. The only reaction she got from Alexius was him pursing his lips.

She would have liked someone else to have seen what she had. At first, she'd thought she was looking at a reflection in the water, but as she'd looked closer, she'd realized she was seeing a series of white-domed buildings that dove further into the depths of the ocean than she could see. The island didn't look very big, but it was truly much bigger than it appeared.

The narwhals parted as their ship neared a dock. There, more people in metal armor and carrying various tusks and horns coated in metal stood at attention in a tight square. They eyed the group on the ship without flinching. When it rubbed along the side of the dock, they fanned out so no one could either escape or see beyond them.

"You may step out now," the woman instructed.

Nasir stepped onto the narrow dock first, followed by Isaia, Thali, and finally Alexius.

The group closed in on them then, and they were forced to walk single file as they were ushered down the dock. Thali was surprised no one had confiscated their weapons. Not that they could move with the guards a hairsbreadth away from them. They were so close she could feel their body heat on her arms. Worse yet, she was so short that she saw nothing but chest and back plates around her. Isaia and Alexius were the tallest of her crew, but the guards in metal armor were still taller. *Can you see anything?* she asked Alexius.

We're approaching buildings.

Do you see many people?

Some stopped to look. Their shore is very much like any shore, though. I haven't seen anything odd yet. They seem to survive on fish, but I haven't yet determined what their building materials are.

Do you think they're friendly?

Silence was her only reply. The hairs on the back of her neck prickled. Thali looked up then, only to see a soaring golden tower in the middle of the island. It reminded her so much of the tower she'd seen on Star Island, a shiver went down her spine. She hoped she was wrong. Maybe that tower had nothing to do with the gates, but then, what else would it be for?

CHAPTER FIFTEEN

T HEY WERE USHERED INTO a low building with a rounded roof. Thali ran into Isaia's back when he stopped suddenly. She blinked a few times as her eyes adjusted to the darkness inside. When they did, she noticed the ground was hard with a sandy texture to it.

The woman said, "Please remove your shoes."

The guards around them didn't move, and Thali struggled to kick her boots off since she didn't have much space to bend over and use her hands.

Use your magic, Alexius reminded her.

Thali thought that was a silly use of her magic, then realized there was more to his suggestion. She raised her foot, making the boot slide off, then did the same with the other foot. Almost daringly, she made her boots float between her friends' feet to an empty spot along the wall. Next, she did the same with Nasir's and Isaia's boots.

Alexius used his own magic to shed his boots. Their hosts could clearly see their magic in use but didn't react. Interesting. Thali didn't even feel the effort drain her as badly as usual. She wondered if this place had magic.

The guards didn't take their boots off, nor did they enter the building any farther. They simply prodded Thali's group forward, so Nasir took a step. Barefoot now, Thali followed Nasir farther into the space, where a new set of guards—also barefoot—surrounded them. The new guards wore similar armor, but it looked like it was made of coral or maybe shells.

Thali noticed the difference in the floor's texture here right away. She looked down and used her magic to test it, discovering the ground was made of woven kelp. It wasn't dried kelp either. It was still malleable, giving their steps some shock absorbency. She marveled at it and tried to figure out if the kelp was still alive or if it was in the process of drying. Though she didn't know why she was fixating on the kelp, part of her wondered what Mia would think of it. Would she make a kelp dress? Something twisted in her heart at the thought of Mia.

She'd left her friends behind. Much of her wished she hadn't. Not only would they hate her for it, but she really could have used them right now. Then the metal point of a horn swam into her sight, and that thought burst abruptly. *No. It is good my friends are safe.*

Thali looked up and saw Nasir and Isaia standing next to each other before her. They were clearly protecting her, though their weapons remained strapped to their bodies. For that, she was glad. They were smart not to increase the tension. Thali looked around and noticed that the walls were of white plaster, or maybe white sand. Though she had to peek through Isaia and Nasir, she saw three steps, three people in long robes standing on the bottom one.

"It has been a long time since we have had guests." An authoritative voice filled the room.

"Will you not move aside so we may greet you all?" a musical, breezy voice said.

"They have been brought here at horn point. Of course they are defensive," a huskier, melodic voice said.

Thali didn't want to look juvenile and rise on her tiptoes between Nasir and Isaia, but she did need to speak for them and hopefully take the focus off them. So she put her hands on their arms. They looked at her questioningly before stepping aside at her nod.

Alexius followed behind her. Thali gulped when she saw three stunning women—all with black hair to their waists—standing before her. They had the same ivory Cerisan skin tone, but they were tall, as tall even as Nasir and Isaia.

"Ah, that's better." The smallest, thinnest one smiled at her. She squeezed her hands together as if she was keeping herself from rushing to greet Thali.

"What are you doing here?" the woman on the right said. She looked like a warrior. She was broad in shoulder and hip but had a small waist. It was impossible not to be jealous. Only her voice indicated she was suspicious and angry.

"Sister, stop. Please. Let us at least enjoy some refreshments. It's been so long since we've seen new faces," the little one said.

The woman on the left, a mix of the other two, stood and watched carefully. She didn't seem as suspicious or eager or as ready to fight. If anything, she reminded Thali of Xerus.

"You would serve tea to those who would just as soon kill you in your sleep?" the warrior asked.

"We do not wish to harm anyone," Thali piped in. She knew she had to start advocating for them before these leaders made up their minds about her group.

"Not wishing and not doing are two different things, young one," the warrior said.

Thali swallowed her anger. It had been a long time since someone had dismissed her because of her age. "If you do not harm us, we will not harm you," Thali said.

The warrior studied her then.

The tallest one, the wise one, spoke, "Then perhaps tonight we shall dine and discuss in further detail why you've come to us? I'm sure you'd like some time to rest and clean up?"

Thali recognized the peace offering and bowed her head in thanks.

The number of guards that escorted them out was halved. Alexius kept his hand on her shoulder as they turned and walked through an archway to the side. They headed down a hallway. Isaia balked when they faced an open box.

"It is much faster and easier than taking the stairs." The woman who had escorted them to shore had returned, without shoes. She stepped into the box. It had two sides missing. The first was the one they were to walk into, and the second had a simple railing. Thali swallowed.

You have magic. We'll be fine, Alexius said.

Thali nodded and stepped in. Isaia and Nasir followed; then Alexius did the same. Thali stood at the railing as the room started to descend. She became so curious, she leaned over the railing. At first, she didn't see anything but the same white-sand walls moving past.

Thali jumped back suddenly. A cavernous space with rows and rows of shells and wooden railings appeared. It began to look like a curious mishmash of branches and shells as their box started to descend faster and faster. Swirls of seashells and open spaces flashed before her as the box descended too quickly for her to see anything clearly. Thali's stomach flip-flopped for a moment, but she reminded herself she'd flown down her own cliffs faster than this, more recklessly too.

She leaned over the railing again, then moved away as a tiny pod of three narwhals with thick green ropes tied around their horns swam right at them, darting up. Thali dared to lean over the railing again, checking below before looking up. The box was attached to ropes, and those ropes were tied to the narwhals' horns. As the narwhals swam up, the box moved down. "Huh," she said.

Their box slowed, then stopped. Nasir pushed Isaia out of the box and Thali followed as they stepped out onto a completely different floor. Thali looked around and saw that this hallway too had white-sand walls. Their guide tried but failed to hide a grin as she stepped out of the box. As they strode down the hall, Thali walked next to Alexius, who steered her with a hand on her shoulder as she tried to take in their surroundings. At the end of the hall, they turned and saw the ocean just beyond.

How are we breathing air when I can see fish swimming in the ocean on the other side of the walls?

Alexius squeezed her shoulder, and Thali stopped. The woman stood in front of some double doors. She pushed them open and said, "You may rest in here. There will be guards posted outside, so no exploring. We'll come and retrieve you for supper."

Despite their lack of freedom, Thali thought they were being treated well. She walked into the room and saw that all the furniture was made of a strange combination of white sand and wooden branches, making for some unique furniture. A smaller room with a bed in the center adjoined the main room, which was full of couches—hard, sandy ones—and a table with chairs. She explored further and came upon two more bedrooms and a bathing room. When she returned to the main room, Isaia, Nasir, and Alexius had their heads together.

Nasir finally nodded at Thali, then headed for one of the farther bedrooms. Thali went to explore the first one, the one she assumed was hers. She stepped through an intricate archway and discovered the bed was a sand block. Pressing her hand into the fluffy covers, she was surprised to feel the bed was soft and squishy. Curious, she sat on it and sank farther than she had expected to. She heard a swish of water and put her ear to the bed. It was filled with water. She wondered if she would ever wake up on the hard sand, completely soaked.

Now that Thali didn't feel as wary, she strolled around the room, examining everything. Most of the furniture was made of sand or was at least covered in sand. Instead of dressers the room had built-in shelves containing simple clothes. She went to explore another archway and found she had her own bathing chambers. But there was no faucet to fill the tub with water, nor any buckets nearby. She saw only what looked to be a drain at the bottom, and she wondered how it worked.

"Miss, may I show you?" a small voice squeaked. Thali jumped. This woman hadn't been there a moment ago. Thali nodded, and the woman approached the tub and turned a few levers on their sides. The tub started to fill from the bottom.

Thali stuck her hand in the water and found it was warm, hot even. "That's wonderful."

"It is very convenient, yes. It's better than hauling water up the stairs and back down." The other woman nodded.

Thali wanted to know more. If this woman knew about hauling water, then had she originally come from another place?

A cough brought Thali's attention back to the bedchamber. Isaia lingered in the entryway, peeking into the bedroom to get her attention. When she made eye contact, he disappeared. Thali turned back to the woman. "If you could continue, I'd love to bathe in a few minutes."

The woman nodded.

Thali went to the sitting room and sat as Isaia paced in front of what she assumed was a hearth. Instead of fire though was a mess of glowing orbs dangling in a net. "Spit it out, Isaia," Thali said. She wrapped them all in a thread bubble so no one would overhear their conversation. Isaia came closer and sat on the other end of the couch. She'd not seen Isaia this nervous before and it made her anxious, so she placed her hands on her knees.

Isaia took a deep breath. "My sister was a big fan of fairy tales. She devoured books about them. And she read them to us all the time. There was this one fairy tale about three sisters who ruled an underwater world. They looked kind and gentle, but they lured humans to their arenas to kill them—and eat them. Shiny horns appeared in the water as a warning for all fishermen to stay away."

Thali could see the resemblance to their situation, though they hadn't been violently treated and no arena had been introduced. It was strange they had been allowed to keep all their weapons though. "You think that's where we are?" she asked.

"I do," Isaia said. "I think we need to be careful. This has been too easy."

Thali thought about how much magic she had used to get through their magical barrier. That hadn't been easy. She nodded though. Isaia was as dependable as any of her guards and friends, so she trusted his instincts. "What happened in the story?" Thali asked.

"A fisherman heard the women were beautiful and decided one of them was the only bride for him. He was prideful, so he trained as a warrior to overtake them and then sailed to find them. The tale goes that three women locked him up, and the next day, tossed him into an arena. They promised him his pick of bride if he could defeat their champions. Each woman had a champion, and after those came a fourth. All were monsters. The man defeated all four, yet when it came time to pick his wife, they chained him to the middle of the arena and devoured him piece by piece until there was nothing left." Isaia gulped.

"Well, that sounds terrible," Alexius said.

Thali swallowed. They hadn't seen enough of this place to know the story wasn't true. And with how many creatures from stories she'd seen with her own eyes of late, she couldn't deny that it was possible. "We'll stay vigilant. Thank you for sharing your knowledge with us."

Isaia nodded. "I'll stand guard by the door, but I think you should be careful what you say to our hosts." He rose and went to take his position.

Thali wondered if Isaia ever got bored. He could have been a merchant, experiencing his own adventures and markets. Instead, he stood staring unblinkingly at a blank wall, one hand always on a weapon.

Maybe she should have tried to leave *them* with Ming too.

I would have followed regardless, and those two didn't eat, drink, or sleep because they knew you would try something, Alexius said.

This isn't what they should be doing.

But maybe it's what they want to do now.

Thali sighed. She tossed her threads out into the hall. She felt nothing but the guards posted outside, so she pulled her threads back into herself and noticed her reserve of magic hadn't dipped very far. *Is there magic here?*

It does seem to refill faster than in the rest of the world. Maybe they have their own source, or there's a leak, or the gate is already open. Given the finnifenba though, I'd say it's open. We should try to get to the gate as quickly as possible. Alexius replied.

Thali nodded. The woman waved to her from the archway to her bedchamber, and Thali nodded. "But first, a bath." She dashed away from Alexius before he could argue. Whatever they had to face, she would love to get the grime off her first.

Thali sunk into the hot water, but despite wanting to completely relax, she kept a magical tether on her clothes and her weapons. She'd also sent the woman away so no one would learn of all the weapons she carried as she undressed.

Alexius stood guard at the door to her bedchambers, using a blanket as a curtain.

Thali took her time and wondered whether Elric was enjoying some quiet time or if he'd followed through on his threat to pursue her. She hoped he would stay put. At the thought of their time at Ming's compound, she realized she was glad that he'd seen their time away from the palace as a vacation instead of as punishment. At the same time, she hoped they would make it back to Adanek in time to save it. She could just imagine what a bunch of dragons would do to the palace and kingdom.

Her relaxing moment ruined, Thali climbed out, dried herself thoroughly, then dressed. She switched her shirt with a similar one she found on a shelf. Then she found some trousers that fit too. At least they would be fresh.

When she emerged from the blanket-door, Alexius and Nasir were talking quietly. Isaia was still at his post. Thali found a book on a shelf.

Surprised she could read it, she curled up in a chair adjacent to two others and began to read. It wasn't long before she fell asleep.

Wake up. Alexius brushed Thali's mind, and she opened her eyes. Still curled up in her surprisingly comfortable stone chair, she looked around and saw Isaia and Nasir were still awake, and Alexius sat across from her. He looked at the door, so Thali turned her attention there too. Then a knock sounded, and the door opened.

The same woman who had escorted them to their lodgings nodded her head in greeting.

"What is your name, by the way?" Thali asked her.

"I am called Sumac." The woman nodded her head. She didn't seem either friendly or unfriendly.

Thali bowed her head. "It's nice to meet you, Sumac."

Sumac narrowed her eyes, then turned and walked away. Thali followed, Alexius next to her as Nasir and Isaia brought up the rear. They all wore clean clothes and looked at least a little more rested.

They were led to a room with exactly seven cushions around a table. They sat down and waited. The three women appeared through a doorway, this time draped in pale pink as they glided over and sat down. They were definitely more graceful than Thali was.

"We welcome you as guests to our home. Please, go ahead and eat," the small one said as she smiled.

Thali looked down at the table. Suddenly, piles of food appeared: buns and dumplings of all kinds and vegetables. She'd seen them all in Cerisa but couldn't identify them all. Thali swallowed apprehensively and used her magic to pick apart the ingredients. But because she didn't know them all, she didn't know if there was poison in the food.

"Please, let us show you there is nothing worry about," the small woman said. She took one of each item and divided each between her sisters, who all ate without hesitation. A small part of Thali wondered if there was something in the food the women would be immune to that might harm her and her friends.

I think it's safe, Alexius said.

Thali smiled then and chose a few items, transferring them to her plate with her sticks. At least those were familiar. Nasir and Isaia followed suit, as did Alexius.

The food was delicious, though Thali noticed there wasn't any meat. There was fish and other seafood—shrimp, maybe oyster and lobster—but no meat. She also noticed the vegetables were mostly variations of sea vegetation.

They slipped into silence as they ate, and while Thali wasn't unused to it—her family often ate in silence—she did notice that it was a comfortable one. She'd expected it to be filled with tension. That made her wonder if there was a magical reason for it, if one of the women had an ability to influence the emotional state or energy within a room.

When the remaining food was cleared out the normal way, tea was served. Thali wondered what they wanted to know and how much she should tell them. She decided to dive in. "We are sorry for any inconvenience our appearance has brought you, but we've come for an important reason," Thali started. She took a deep breath and explained, "Beyond your island, magical gates have been opened and magical creatures are attacking the world."

The sisters exchanged a look, and Thali wondered if that was how she looked when she spoke with Alexius in her mind.

The wise one turned to her. "What is it you hoped to achieve in coming here?"

Thali swallowed. It was time to lay out all her cards. "I had hoped to secure your gate."

The warrior laughed. "You and what army? There are only four of you."

"Sister," the wise one admonished. "Do not insult a dragon, for their wrath lasts long."

The warrior slammed her lips together and glanced downward. *They didn't deny having a gate. Did they know about the other gates already? About the creatures loosed into our world?* Thali wondered exactly what they knew.

"My sister is quick with her words. Please accept our apologies. We are sure you are more than strong enough to protect whatever it is you wish to." The wise one bowed her head at Alexius. She bowed so low in fact, that the back of her neck became visible.

Alexius's eyes narrowed.

"We know very little of the world outside but have felt a disturbance in it for some time now. What do you know of that?" the little one asked.

Thali still couldn't quite believe her brother was behind it all, so she gave them little detail. "There are four gates between our world and other, more magical worlds. We think two have opened—a third is protected. We have not found the fourth."

"You seem to be quite knowledgeable about this," the wise one said.

"I've been thrown into the center of it."

"If there was a gate here, what makes you think we cannot protect it ourselves?" the warrior asked Thali, though her gaze shifted to Alexius.

"It's not that I think you can't. I just want to offer assistance. We don't know what kind of world connects to them. Our world is in danger because of these gates. "

They still watched her with narrowed eyes. They didn't trust her.

"What can I do to earn your trust?"

The sisters looked at each other. Thali needed to speed this up. She worried creatures were pouring through the gate, preparing to attack.

"Well. There is one thing that would earn our respect," the warrior finally said.

Thali swallowed, wanting to glance at Isaia, because if he was right, then she'd be fighting for her life. She took a deep breath and nodded. "I will do what I must to earn your trust."

"You will be tested tomorrow then," the wise one said.

The door behind them opened, and the three women stilled their movements. Thali knew a dismissal when she saw one, so she stood, turned, and left.

"A moment, Sifu Lung, if it pleases you," the wise one said to their turned backs.

Thali looked over her shoulder to see Alexius pause and turn back to face them. *Wait for me on the other side of the door,* he said.

She nodded and continued with Isaia and Nasir out of the room. When the doors closed, instead of having a staring contest with the guards at the doors, Thali went to a nearby railing and peered out. They were in a massive column-shaped building. It reminded her of the tower on Star Island, but bigger. The center was open, all the way up to the clear ceiling that let light into the entire building.

Thali leaned over and gazed down at the rows and rows of balconies. There were so many of them. And they were all similar—made of the same white sand—but also different. One had undulating edges like waves leaving a beach, another had the sharp peaks and crests of an ocean, and another had intricate, almost lace-like latticework. She wondered whether the designs were significant or just random. Then she realized that the floors higher up were all level, but as they neared the bottom, they became irregular. Some balconies jutted out while others were sunken.

The doors behind them opened again, and Alexius stepped through. His expression was unreadable. She was surprised. She had expected him to give something away. She would have to ask him later. They silently followed their escort back to their rooms.

"Your evening meal will be brought to you," Sumac said. She paused, as if she was going to say something else. But then she inclined her head, turned, and left them alone.

"Too bad Daylor's not here. Another meal tonight?" Isaia said.

"So, what happened?" Thali asked out loud so Isaia and Nasir could hear as well.

Alexius's cheeks turned pink then, and Thali raised an eyebrow.

"They...they paid their respects to my...heritage," Alexius said.

Thali suddenly got a flash of the three women, torsos exposed, standing in front of her. It quickly disappeared, and she wondered if Alexius had let it slip. Or maybe her magic was stronger than Alexius had expected. *What kind of offering did they make?*

Not one I accepted.

Thali pressed her lips together to hold in a laugh. Heat climbed to her own cheeks as Nasir raised an eyebrow and Isaia calmly looked around.

"Do you think they'll let us join you during the challenge?" Isaia asked.

Thali sobered as she realized that tomorrow she might fight for her life. "I hope not."

"We're your guards. It's our duty to fight for you," Isaia said.

"I do not want your injuries or deaths on my conscience." Thali strode over to the pitcher and sniffed it before pouring herself a cup of water. "Besides, they need to trust me." She dipped her magic in the cup and finding nothing besides water, downed it in a gulp.

Thali's vision swam. She knew she couldn't do this all alone, but she didn't want her friends hurt. She heard someone approach her and headed for the balcony at the other end of the room. There, she marveled at the shell that was so thin, she could see through it to the ocean beyond. The air wasn't quite as fresh as the air outside, but it was better than being cooped up in that room. Two stone stools beautifully carved and shaped like barrels sat on the balcony, so Thali chose one, putting her elbows up on the railing as she stared into the blue of the ocean. A fish swam by every once in a while, but she mostly saw empty ocean.

Eventually, Thali heard more footsteps, softer ones this time, but they didn't come into view and she didn't feel the warmth of another body. Instead, she heard the doors of the balcony close and the scrape of the other stool moving closer. Only stillness followed, allowing her to close her eyes, settle her mind, and be calm.

When she had become a princess, she had struggled with the idea that she would never have to fight again. And now, now she found herself struggling with the idea that she would have to fight for her life. There was so much that depended upon her surviving and winning tomorrow. It felt like the start of her journey, yet the warrior in her, the one who had listened to Isaia's story, knew that this could also be the end.

"You know, when I was a child in the orphanage in Bulstan, I had a friend. He was the same age as me, and we were both around the same build." Nasir spoke quietly.

Thali put her head between her arms and focused first on her breathing, then on Nasir's voice. She wondered what lesson he was going to impart now.

"His name is Amir. And yes, I know, Amir and Nasir, it was like we were meant to be brothers. We both wanted to join the palace guard, but when it came time to, he didn't pass the physical test. He did not have the lungs to run for long periods. We were sad to be parted, but he found a position in the royal stables. We still met to dine together or walk together. Anyway, you know that Prince Tariq is impulsive. Back then, he would often dash off on a horse from the stables whether they were saddled or not, especially if a certain dear friend was coming to town."

Nasir paused there and Thali could practically hear his smile.

"Often, Amir would send a messenger to me directly to tell me that the prince had left in this or that direction. The prince has his own guards of course, but once I joined them, I realized it was useful to have friends in certain places because the prince often tried to do things secretly. Well, one day, I got a message saying, 'PT upset. To Point?'

There was a storm that day, and I rode out anyway because that was my duty. Amir had offered to ride out with me, but I didn't want to risk his health. I rode after Tariq, and the storm got worse and worse. It got so bad that I couldn't see where I was going and used my horse as a shield after I hopped off and walked. And I walked right off a cliff."

Thali gasped and looked up.

"I still had the reins in my hands, so that caught me for a second before the horse reared from being jerked so hard. I had the wits to grab onto something and managed to grasp some slick rocks. My toes found a very thin ledge. I looked down. I was sure I would die falling that far. I cursed myself for having gone alone. The horse had run away, and my fingers were getting too cold to feel anything. I thought how stupid I was not to have accepted my friend's offer to come with me. But then I saw a rope dangle into my vision. Amir had come anyway."

Thali knew her challenge would be easier with her friends. She knew they wanted to be there. But her fear of them being hurt, or worse, prevented her from accepting their help. Bree had only sliced her arm, and Thali still couldn't look at her without feeling guilt. "How do I live with the guilt?" Thali asked.

"Whether your friends die because they were helping you or from some other cause, it will bring you sadness. But think of how they would feel knowing they could have helped and did not? We would all rather help the ones we love than stand by and watch them fail." Nasir was very still.

"What happened to Amir?"

"He still works at the stables. It's more difficult now, but we still exchange letters when we can," he replied.

Thali wondered if she'd ever meet Amir. She would like to next time she was in Bulstan. "You're saying I should let my friends in? That if I can choose tomorrow, I should let you all stand at my side as we fight for our lives?" Thali asked.

"Yes. That's what I'm saying. We've chosen to be here."

"You also think I should have brought everyone when we left?"

"I can see why you did what you did, but I think it's likely they're coming anyway. As I said, it would have been safer for them to travel with us than without us." Nasir rubbed the back of his head.

Thali cringed at that. She hoped more than anything they wouldn't come after her. Thoughts of the nasty biting otter creature popped into her head. While they at least wouldn't get through the barrier, they'd still be left to contend with monsters. "I hope they stayed put."

"Do you really think Elric, who loves you dearly, will sit back and relax when you're out here, in who knows what kind of danger?"

Thali thought back to her last conversation with Elric and how he'd known about the potion and had taken it anyway. He had taken so much in stride, but if her princess lessons had taught her anything, it was that putting them both at risk was worse than putting one of them at risk. Adanek still needed a ruler and a future. "I can only hope Elric stays behind."

Nasir scoffed. "I doubt it."

"But wouldn't he for Adanek?" Thali asked.

"His parents kicked him out of his own kingdom. If anything, it's given him permission to be reckless and take risks," Nasir said.

Thali swallowed hard. She didn't know if she could live with herself if something happened to him, to her friends. Her plan could very well backfire.

CHAPTER SIXTEEN

T HE NEXT MORNING WHEN Thali woke, her feeling of impending doom came flooding back. She didn't feel as rested as she would have liked, but she got up, did her stretches, then went to the main room to find Alexius, Nasir, and Isaia eating at the table.

"Did you sleep well?" Thali asked, even though just by looking at them, she could see they had not.

Isaia looked the most miserable.

"Isaia, what's the matter?"

He looked up, dark circles under his eyes. "Will you let us follow you into the arena?"

"How do we know it's an arena?"

"That's not an answer," Isaia said.

Thali looked at Nasir, who only raised his eyebrows at her, then at Isaia. "Am I the reason you look so miserable? You're worried I won't let you follow me into the arena?"

He nodded.

Thali couldn't believe how miserable she'd made him.

"So, you will let us go with you?"

She nodded.

Isaia threw his arms in the air. "Oh, thank all the creatures in all the worlds."

"Did it really matter that much to you?" Thali sat down and took a bit of porridge.

"Alexius is blood-oathed to you, Nasir was personally assigned to you by your best friend, but I have no proof of my dedication to you."

Thali thought about that. "Do you need one?"

"I didn't think my life debt would sway you." His eyes pleaded with her.

"I'm sorry to have caused you so much trouble, Isaia." Thali said. She hadn't realized her keeping them safe would put such a burden on them. She finished her porridge, took a piece of bread, or something that looked like bread, and took a bite.

When she bit down, she heard a *whooshing* in her ears. She blinked and found herself facing a giant white-sand wall. Were those blood stains?

She turned around and saw Alexius, Isaia, and Nasir standing with her. But behind them was a sand floor with tall sand walls. Thali looked up to see stands of people sitting so silently and still, she wondered if they were frozen. Suddenly, she realized they were in an arena.

The small woman from the day before stood on a platform at the top of the sand wall. Thali could barely see her sisters sitting behind her. "Welcome. This is Princess Routhalia of Adanek. She wishes to earn our respect by entering the arena to test her skills," the woman said, and the whole crowd cheered. It rocked Thali, and she heard it echo off the walls as if they were in a deep underground pit.

"Magic," Nasir whispered as he took up his position on Thali's left. Isaia was to Thali's right, and Alexius protected her rear.

"You will face our champions, and if you survive, you will earn our respect. There are four tests," she said. Then she clapped her hands together. The crowd quieted and three cracks appeared in one sand wall. They widened ever so slowly, making Thali wonder what she and her friends could possibly be facing.

Water started to fill the arena. Thali hadn't seen that coming. The water would soon reach their feet, and she wondered how quickly the massive space was filling. Suddenly, she realized she wasn't wet. Not even her feet were wet. She glanced down and realized the square cutout beneath them was dry. As the arena filled with water, the square they stood on began to float. She grabbed her friends, and they all moved to the center of the floating square.

Thali watched the arena fill. The walls were tall, so the water could get several feet deep. Yet it felt like mere moments before the entire arena was water, leaving her and her friends just one level below the crowd that had gathered to watch. They sat solemnly, as if bearing witness. Thali suddenly wondered if she'd made the wrong decision. Maybe she shouldn't have challenged the women to trust her. And maybe she should have done this on her own, not let her friends take part.

She looked into the water. Surely there would be something swimming around in there, something that would try to eat them. She wondered if she'd be able to communicate with it, to access it. *How much magic do you have access to?* she asked Alexius.

Not enough. This arena blocks a lot of it. We can communicate, so there's some. And I can draw a little from the land above, but you'll only have what you hold in yourself.

Before them, a splash drew their attention, and Thali's eyes widened as a large, wide, flat snout protruded from the water. It reminded Thali of a crocodile but bigger. It leapt out of the water, showing off a long, slender body covered in the impenetrable, rough skin of an crocodile. She felt Isaia step back, and they all shifted to rebalance. Thinking back to the leviathan that had taken a chunk out of Isaia's leg in their first year, she swallowed. The creature seemed to float above the water for a moment, then somersaulted, almost brushing the edge of the audience. Then it dove back into the water, drenching the crowd.

"Any experience with that creature?" Nasir asked.

"I've never seen or heard of it. I don't think it's magical," Alexius squeaked.

"Croco-whale seems an appropriate name," Thali said. She felt Isaia tremble next to her, and her heart hurt for him. Looking at that creature must bring all that fear and pain back.

Small splashes turned their attention to the water around them. Snout tips started to pop out of the water—by the dozens. They were smaller than the one they'd just seen, but by her rough count, there were over fifty. The creatures all started snapping their jaws, rocking her floating island. Thali closed her eyes for a moment, then forced them open. Never with her eyes closed. She went into her mind and saw the faint strands of her magic, like a field of wheat. She pushed them out and connected with the croco-whales. The creatures' threads weren't sparkly like mythical creatures, and they were faint; her magic was also faint. But if she didn't do something, they were all going to become breakfast. She pushed her threads to connect with the croco-whales, to calm them.

"It's working." Alexius said.

Nasir and Isaia said nothing as the snouts closed and sunk below the surface.

"So don't fall into the water. Is that the challenge?" Nasir finally asked.

Thali felt a trembling at her feet, and she looked down. The four grabbed hold of each other as the piece under their feet started to separate. That was going to make this an even greater challenge. Thali wobbled as she looked at the others. Her balance was probably better than most, and she was grateful that Alexius, Isaia, and Nasir had equally good balance. They glanced at each other quickly. Thali was glad that Daylor was not here. She had only recently taught him to swim, and he had always had terrible balance.

Then she heard a door start to open, and she turned to look. Her heart sank as a raft floated out. On it was Daylor, Tilton, and Mia. They sat huddled together in the middle. Thali was at least glad their raft was thicker than her piece of floor and that it had a bit of a ledge. She hoped it wouldn't break apart like her square had.

"Don't move," Alexius said.

She held her body still though she wanted to wave to the three on the raft, to shout to them, to see if it was really them. How had they gotten here? How had they found this place, and how had the three sisters known they were with Thali?

"I told you it was a bad idea to leave them behind," Alexius muttered under his breath.

Mia shouted, "We're coming!" and she shuffled slowly to the edge so as not to rock the raft.

She was about to stick her hand into the water when Thali shouted back, "Don't use your hands!" Though she hadn't so much as moved her head as she'd spoken to Mia, she still rocked a little. Thali stayed afloat on the tiny piece she was on, but her ankles were getting sore from the balancing, and she knew the others would be starting to feel tired too.

Thali moved only her gaze to Mia, who was kneeling on one edge of the little raft. Tilton was on the other side, and Daylor sat in the middle to keep the weight even. Mia had removed her shoe—as had Tilton—and they slowly paddled their way over.

The croco-whales stayed put, their snouts just below the water's surface, while Mia tried to paddle around them, careful not to hit any of them.

The raft drifted over until it bumped into Nasir's square. Tilton grasped Nasir's ankle, tethering the raft.

"Isaia, go first. You'll rock us least," Thali said.

Isaia hesitated for a moment before carefully shifting and stepping off his piece and onto the raft. Then he reached out and grabbed his piece of floating sand and placed it in the raft. The four on the raft shifted to make room and keep their balance.

Thali nodded. "Alexius, you're next."

"Not until you go."

"That's not how this is going to work. Now go," Thali said. Her magic was starting to flicker, and she knew she couldn't hold it much longer; she was running out.

Alexius moved Thali's hand from his shoulder to Nasir's, then jumped off his platform onto the raft, landing surprisingly lightly.

"Nasir, you next," Thali said.

"Together," he said.

"No. You go first," Thali argued. She looked up for a moment, and Nasir's eyes narrowed. He knew what she was about to do.

He held still, as if deciding whether he would let her. The croco-whales started to pop out of the water as her hold on them began to slip, and one popped right up at Tilton's arm. He pulled back while still holding onto Nasir's ankle, pulling him into the raft.

Tilton had made the choice for him.

Before anyone could say anything, she placed both hands on the wall they had drifted into and used her foot to push the raft away. With her friends all safe on the raft and moving away, Thali dove into the water. She would have a better time connecting with the croco-whales if she was amongst them. It should take less magic.

"Thali!" Mia shouted.

The magic that held the creatures snapped, but it filled her own reserve in part again, so Thali spun a thread to pull her through the water as the croco-whales followed. She swam deeper and faster, around and around. She wanted to tire them out. At least using a single thread to propel herself was much less taxing than holding fifty of them. All the creatures fell into line behind the leader, exactly as Thali had hoped. One croco-whale led the hunt; she was the prey.

She guided her thread out of the water and then back down, inhaling a gulp of air as she breached. The croco-whales breached with her. As she took them for a fourth lap around the arena, they suddenly backed off. She felt them stop, then swim away. Before her, an underwater gate began to open.

Thali felt the creature before she saw it. It was angry. She tried to connect with it, but it dashed out, ignoring her. It was almost as wide as the arena itself. It would only have to open its mouth and swim forward to catch her and all the croco-whales in its mouth. She swam up; above the water was her only chance. She dug into her magical reserves and tried again to connect, but she didn't have enough magic left.

The creature turned its enormous, rounded head toward her and opened its mouth. It was aiming right for her. She kicked her feet with all her might as the creature neared, its maw gaping. Thali could see the surface, but she wasn't going to make it. She was out of magic. She swam as fast as she could, but she felt the change in the water as its mouth started to surround her body. Its bottom teeth were level with her chin, and she tried not to look at the bits of fabric caught on them.

She felt herself being lifted out of the water. Two strong hands had grabbed her by the arms and hauled her out of the water and onto the raft.

Thali panted and saw Mia holding in both hands the piece of sand that Isaia had brought onto the raft. Mia smacked it on the tip of the creature's giant maw—hard. She was leaning too far over the raft to be safe, but Tilton held her while Daylor held Tilton.

The creature snapped its jaws shut, catching the piece and snapping it into an explosion of sand before sinking into the water in a blink. As it did, it displaced the water and sent their raft careening on a wave, right toward the group of croco-whales. Thali and her friends all grabbed onto each other as the raft landed in the middle of the croco-whales.

The huge creature was gone for now, but the croco-whales turned their attention to the friends. Thali had long since run out of magic, so now she didn't know what to do.

"Squid turds, Thali, don't you ever do that again!" Mia shouted.

Thali sat stunned as she looked at her friend. Then she looked at all her friends. Nasir, Isaia, Daylor, even Tilton looked angry. "What?"

"We're in this together, you dolt! When will you get that through your thick head?" Mia said. Hurt replaced the anger in her voice. "We know we're not as strong as you, not as magical as you, but we're here to help you. Stop fighting us," she said before catching her breath.

Thali again looked around at her friends. She swallowed. Wasn't this exactly what Elric had warned her against? "Wait. If you're here, where's Elric?" she suddenly asked.

"He's here somewhere. We came together, but they separated us when we arrived," Daylor said.

"I hate to break up this emotional moment, but we need to do something soon ..." Alexius interrupted.

Thali glanced behind her friends and saw that rows upon rows of croco-whales were closing in tighter and tighter around them. Snouts in the air, they started snapping. She watched as they swam closer and closer. Panic rose in her chest as she realized the creatures were surrounding their little raft, swimming so tightly together their snapping became smaller and smaller as the space became limited. The croco-whales soon pressed up against the raft, no longer snapping but leaving their snouts open a few inches.

"Thali, look!" Mia said and she pointed to the far end of the arena. There, past the croco-whales, a platform had appeared. They had to get there. As if confirming that thought, their raft started to creak, and Thali didn't waste any time.

"They're so close together that they can't open their mouths more than a couple of inches. I think I know how we can get out of here, but we're all going to have to move at the same time—and move quickly," Thali said. "It sounds crazy, I know, but I think we can use the crocs as stepping stones to get to the platform." She looked at her friends. Isaia and Nasir looked grim but nodded. Alexius nodded, and Mia looked terrified but determined as she nodded.

They all turned to Daylor.

"What? I think I can do it," Daylor said. He had the worst balance. He still couldn't stand on one foot at a time for more than a few seconds, let alone hop from one croco-whale snout to the other.

"Daylor should stay between us," Alexius said as he looked at Thali.

Tilton nodded. "I'll go behind."

They lined up in two rows along the edge of the raft and each of them took a deep breath.

"Ready?" Thali looked at her friends. Mia, Alexius, Daylor, and Thali made up the first row, though she'd have preferred to go in the second row, but Daylor needed help and they were running low on time. Who knew when the other creature might make another appearance?

Daylor, Alexius, and Mia nodded. They held hands and stepped onto their first croco-whale.

It sank an inch and tried to shake them off but couldn't. Thali was glad she'd worn boots with flat, hard soles. She and her friends all wobbled, then found their footing.

"Step," Alexius said, and they all took the next step.

"Step," Thali said, and they did. They had two rows of croco-whales left.

As Thali watched, the croco-whales started to shift.

"Step!" Mia shouted. Her croco-whales were starting to disperse, so she had to leap to the next one and ended up blocking Alexius.

"Go!" he said, and she made two more leaps onto the new platform. Daylor was wobbling, and Alexius held his upper arm to steady Daylor as much as he could. "Step!"

Daylor, Alexius, and Thali all stepped together to the last row, then jumped to the platform. But then Thali's magical sense tingled.

Nasir, Tilton, and Isaia were behind them. She spun and threw her hands out. "Stop!" They froze, wobbling on their croco-whale snouts. Thali pulled her arms back as the giant creature breached the water and snapped but disappeared back into the depths. "Jump!" Thali shouted. The croco-whales had been pushed backward by the wave, but the three remaining friends leapt forward over it and landed in the water near the platform.

Thali, Alexius, and Daylor reached into the water, ready to pull their friends in. Thali hoped the other creature was not coming back. The three in the water swam furiously. Everyone on the platform but Mia grabbed someone and hauled them up, everyone landing on top of each other on the new platform.

Isaia scrambled off Thali, and Nasir pulled Alexius to his feet. Tilton and Daylor held each other, covering each other's head and face in kisses.

Thali looked away, realizing that the platform was starting to lower and the walls were beginning to rise. They must be done. They had survived their first challenge. The water was draining, and she looked out to see the croco-whales swimming toward an opening in the wall. She hoped the other creature was gone too.

Thali was panting hard. She had to put a hand on her knee just to hold herself up. As she glanced around, she saw everyone else was also crouched over or sitting. But they were all alive. It took a concerted effort to control her breathing. As she closed her eyes so she could focus on slowing her air intake, she felt the platform hit the ground. The water was gone.

A door slid open, and a building rolled into the arena, a tent-like structure. After that came a lumbering giant tortoise carrying crates and water jugs. Thali was so thirsty, she wanted to grab a jug from the large tortoise, but she waited. The tortoise stopped just outside the tent and turned to pull on a rope, loosening all the items from its harness as it stepped away. The load slid off its carapace to the ground. Then the creature lumbered out, and Thali said a quick, "Thank you," for the tortoise's gentleness.

Once the doors of the arena had closed again, she looked up to the three women.

"You will have tonight to rest. The next challenge begins tomorrow," the small one said. At that, the auditorium darkened. Only the soft glow of a few orbs filled the space. It was quiet too. They had been left alone, or at least that's what they were supposed to believe.

"Let's find out what's for dinner, shall we?" Daylor asked as he slung an arm around Thali, Tilton tucked under his other arm.

Chapter Seventeen

THE NIGHT HAD BEEN surprisingly peaceful. Thali hadn't really recognized their food but had eaten it anyway. Then they'd walked into the tent to discover a cot for each of them. Tilton and Daylor had pushed their cots together, and Alexius had taken the cot next to hers. Mia had taken her other side, while Isaia had chosen the first watch. Thali had barely made it to her bed before she'd closed her eyes and fallen asleep.

She woke blinking at the bright light that filled their tent. She thought for a moment she was on a beach but then remembered, simultaneously, how this place controlled the light.

Everyone else began rousing then too, so they left the tent to find a table of fruits and meats. Thali looked around the arena. People were starting to trickle into the seats, but it wasn't full yet, so she figured they still had time. They ate inside the tent so as not to be on display. When they finished and the buzz of the crowd had built, they all stepped out, ready to face their day.

"Your next challenge is …" the wise woman began. Strange mounds appeared in front of her: eight mounds in two rows, four across. They were translucent but colored: some green, some red, others purple or yellow. They reminded Thali very much of gelatin desserts but dragon-sized. They would tower over her by several feet. But what exactly were they?

"… to move the zelatono through the door," the wise one said, motioning with her arm toward them. Behind them, the wall slid open to reveal a space only big enough to hold maybe two mounds at a time.

Thali wondered what would happen to them once she had wrangled them into the space.

She jumped at a noise from the zelatono. She whipped back around and saw that the great jelly-like mounds were bouncing up and down, or rather scrunching and unscrunching vertically. If gelatin could scrunch. The sounds they emitted were akin to small trumpets as they continued to bounce up and down in a colorful rainbow of sorts.

"Are they creatures?" Mia asked as she came to stand next to Thali.

"I ... I think so?" Thali wasn't sure.

"They are. I've never seen one in real life. I've only heard of them," Alexius said. "They're notoriously slow. And be careful. You can be absorbed into them."

"Then what? Do they dissolve your bones and flesh?" Daylor asked. He didn't even sound scared. He sounded resigned.

"No," Alexius said. "I don't think so. However, I've also never heard of them killing anyone, and they aren't considered dangerous, generally speaking."

"That's reassuring," Daylor said.

"Are you all right, Daylor?" Thali turned to him.

He nodded. "Just looking forward to the next threat that wants to eat us." He smiled.

She nodded and slung an arm around him.

"If they're creatures, can you ... um, do your thing?" Mia asked.

Thali nodded and went into her mind. The night's rest had refilled her magical reserve a little. Glittering light-red threads caught her attention, but when she slid toward them, she felt as if her mind was being slowed. Each thought took longer, as if she were falling asleep or incredibly tired. She pulled back. "Their thread slows me down."

"You didn't blink for a solid minute there," Daylor said.

Alexius nodded.

"What if we push them along?" Daylor asked.

No one had a better idea, so they each chose a spot between the two rows. Thali looked over her shoulder at those behind her, and they nodded at each other. Daylor and Tilton faced one mound, Alexius and Nasir had one, she had another, and Isaia and Mia took the last one in the first row. "Maybe let me go first," Daylor said.

But either Mia and Isaia hadn't heard him or thought differently because all three put their hands on the translucent wall in front of them and pushed—and got sucked into them.

Because the creatures were translucent, Thali laughed when she saw Daylor slowly pinwheel his arms, swimming through it to the edge and popping back out. Mia and Isaia also emerged from the wall of squishy translucence. All three were covered in goop.

"Are you all right?" she managed between breaths as she calmed her laughter. Nasir, Tilton, and Alexius covered their mouths with their hands, trying to control their own laughter.

Daylor spat out the goop he'd accidentally gotten in his mouth when he'd tried to speak. Then he said, "I'm glad you taught me how to swim."

Thali laughed harder at that. Mia and Isaia nodded their agreement.

"It's much wetter inside than it looks on the outside," offered Isaia as he tried to scoop the goop off his face and out of his eyes.

"So we can't push them," Tilton said.

Thali shook her head.

Daylor shook his head so violently that goop went flying and hit Tilton on the arm. He made a face, backed away, and brushed it off. "Hug?" Daylor grinned and Tilton ran to hide behind Alexius.

"What if we pull them?" Nasir asked.

"The leaves of our tent are wide, as wide as half their base. It's possible that with their greater surface area, the leaves won't get absorbed." Nasir looked at the ground, and they followed his gaze. The zelatono were resting on the ground, not melting through it. So it was possible. They ran over to their humble abode, and Thali scrambled up it, Nasir following. They analyzed the roof's construction, then started gently removing the large leaves. Two leaves overlapped would be as large as the zelatono's base. The two tossed eight leaves to the ground, then slid off the roof and down the tent. Isaia had found some rope and made a quick fishing net to support the leaves.

Thali hoped it would work. They had all day, but she felt they could save time on this challenge. It was about their intelligence more than their physical strength.

They made one net and decided to try it out before they made another. All six friends wrapped it around one zelatono carefully. They dragged the lead rope to the front. Then four of them went around the back to both hold the net wide and hold the two massive leaves in place, leaving Alexius and Nasir in the front.

"All right, we're ready. Pull now!" Thali shouted. They started slowly tightening the slack until the leaves rested on the zelatono's side.

"Pull more on the bottom," Thali said.

They did, and she watched as the leaves hugged the zelatono. She held her breath as she watched to see whether they would be absorbed or if they would hold.

They held at first, but because they couldn't cover the entire creature, as they pulled harder, the leaves and the net started to slide into the zelatono. They would chop it in half if they kept going. She wondered if that would kill it. At the same time, people had swum right through them, and they had seemed unharmed. Could they move the top and bottom separately?

Thali ran back around to the front to see what it looked like there. But as she did, she saw that the bottom of the mound where the leaf ended had the same problem. They could move a part of the creature but not the entire mound.

"Stop!" Mia shouted as she ran over with Thali.

"We're just chopping it in half," Tilton said as he caught up.

"Only the part touching the leaf might move. But either it'll be absorbed as we get further, or we'll cut it in half by accident as we move it." Isaia said.

Alexius and Nasir dropped the ropes.

Mia balled her fists and let out a frustrated, high-pitched squeal. It startled Thali, but the zelatono moved—horizontally, toward Mia—shocking them all.

"Wait, do that again," Thali said.

"Gladly," Mia said. This time, she did it longer. The zelatono slid closer by a foot.

"They're attracted to high-pitched sounds?" Thali asked as she turned to Alexius, who shrugged. "Mia, go stand where Alexius is. Try it there," she said. Surely this was too good to be true.

Mia screamed again and the blob moved toward her.

Thali watched the ground as the zelatono slid a foot closer to Mia again. She looked at the other mounds. They had all slid closer to Mia. "Try talking to them in a high-pitched voice." Thali moved to stand between the blobs. They were large enough that it was difficult to see them moving, but if she watched the ground, it was easier.

Mia ran further ahead. "Come on, globby things! Come to Mama!" she shrieked in a happy, high-pitched voice. It was the same one she used to get Ana to run to her.

The zelatono slid, slower this time. And only the one right in front of Mia moved.

Thali crossed her arms. "Come closer again, Mia. Try that same voice once more."

Mia did and the same zelatono slid closer to her.

Alexius ran over to a zelatono on the far end of the same row. He opened his mouth, but nothing came out—or nothing Thali could hear. His zelatono slid closer to him a little quicker than the one in front of Mia had.

Thali looked at the others. In that moment, she was saddened by the number of males with her instead of higher-pitched females or dragons who could talk in such a high pitch no one could hear it.

Tilton moved in front of one and Thali in front of another then. She opened her mouth, and in the highest pitch she could manage, said, "Come on, Zela, you can do it. Come over here!" It slid toward her. She was surprised when she heard Tilton do the same while Mia continued. Her zelatono was the furthest along, and she started guiding it toward the opening as it outpaced the others. They were moving slowly, maybe one foot at a time. But at least it was progress. Perhaps this was a test in patience rather than intelligence.

Thali could speak in a high pitch longer than she could scream, so she stuck with that. Alexius was right behind Mia as they got closer and closer to the opening.

"Wait!" Thali shouted as she looked at Mia. She was about to step into the enclosure.

The zelatono slid and hit her feet. She jumped back.

Thali abandoned her zelatono and ran over to Mia's. Alexius came over too.

"What do you think happens when we go in there or when they go in there? There's only space for two of them, so they must go somewhere," Thali said.

Mia edged closer then tapped the floor past the threshold with her foot. "It's a grate. You can't see it, but I can feel it through my boot."

Thali looked in carefully.

Nasir ran over with a rope then. "Here. Tie this to Miss Mia and then we can find her if we need to."

Thali knotted the rope around Mia's middle. Then Mia stepped into the space. Thali, Alexius, and Nasir moved aside, the men holding the rope and feeding it as Mia walked further back. Mia shrieked as loudly as she could, and Thali slapped her hands over her ears. The zelatono suddenly slid into the enclosure. Once it was fully inside, it started to melt. Thali looked at the floor. It looked like the blob was melting through it.

"The floor is warm now. I can feel it through my boot. It's not hot though," Mia said as she walked out.

Thali nodded. "Good to know. Glad you didn't fall through or get gooped again."

Mia nodded. "Me too." She ran off to the furthest zelatono, and Thali returned to hers.

"One large, lengthy bit to go," Alexius said.

Thali went back to encouraging her zelatono and quickly came to realize that it moved farther with positive comments than negative ones. She narrowed her eyes and only gave it encouragement. It slid further. She did it again, keeping her voice the same pitch. "Come on sweet Zela. Let's go this way!" she said excitedly, and it slid farther than before. *Interesting,* Thali thought. "You can do it! Just a little farther now! You're almost there! I'm so proud of you! Look at you go! What a wonderful little zelatono!" It moved ten feet with that string of praise before Thali had to stop to take a breath. She was now overtaking

Tilton's zelatono. She watched out of the corner of her eye as Alexius's zelatono slid into the enclosure and melted through the floor. She was starting to hope the creatures were all right after melting.

Thali looked behind her. Her zelatono was at the edge of the enclosure, so she stepped inside. She tried to look through the grate, but she couldn't see through it. She had to hurry. Tilton was coming. She could only hope these people didn't kill the blobs. "Come on home, Zela! That's it! Come on in! You can *doooo* it!" Thali went as high pitched as she could, and the zelatono slid right in and stayed there. She felt the bottom of her boots heat, and the zelatono started sinking lower and lower until it disappeared through the grate. She stepped out, her heart plummeting a little as she wondered if her little red zelatono was all right.

"You all right, Thali?" Tilton came up to her and put a hand on her shoulder. She nodded and smiled. "You get a little attached to them, eh?" He smiled as he looked at his own zelatono on the edge of the dark floor.

Thali nodded. She hugged Tilton because she needed it, and he squeezed her back. They'd been through so much together, and he'd read her mind. She left then but could hear Tilton talking in a higher pitch than she'd ever heard him use.

"Come on, Zela, Zela, Zela!" he said, and his yellow zelatono slid into the enclosure. The others were not far behind. All the zelatono were edging closer, and with four already returned, there were only four left. She went to join Nasir, and when he took a breath, she yelled some praise in her own high pitch. It slid faster. Nasir nodded and they alternated. As one breathed, the other yelled, and back and forth they went, moving consistently now as the zelatono slid toward the entrance. They were the last ones in.

"I hope they're just going home," Daylor said.

"They don't seem to be distressed," Alexius said.

Thali went into her mind to check. Indeed, the translucent glittery red threads were under their feet and calm. She would have guessed they were snoozing. But she didn't connect with them. She didn't want to take more time than she needed to in this challenge.

Chapter Eighteen

That night was much like the previous one, though they slept under a partially open roof after eating. They all had aching heads from all the high-pitched yelling and were asleep before long. The next morning, they found fruits on tables outside again and gathered there to eat.

"Was that last test perseverance?" Mia asked.

"I don't know, but I'm hoping there's only one more." Tilton said.

"Nope. Remember, there's four," Isaia said as he held up four fingers.

Tilton groaned as his shoulders sank.

"It's gotta be a physical one," Daylor said.

"How do you know?" Thali asked as she turned to him.

"Because the rest has all been brainy stuff. So, there's got to be one brawny one now."

"Is that your specialty?" Tilton teased.

"It's about balance," Daylor said, sticking his tongue out at them.

A hissing sound filled the air. They all drew their weapons as fog filled the arena. Thali swallowed, thinking of the first time she'd been in a peculiar fog. It had been during their first-year final exam—or so they'd thought. They had been facing the last challenge when a mysterious fog with hallucinogenic properties had settled around them. It had made her and her friends look like fish. Thankfully, Thali had recognized the enemies they'd had to battle as their own classmates in time to prevent anyone from injury. But the fog now made her uncomfortable.

"Remember what I told you about what happened at the top of the tower in our first year!" Thali told them all. They all nodded, then they disappeared. The fog thickened so much she could see nothing around her. Thali felt like she was inside a cloud. She waved her hand up and down and felt only cool softness before it dissipated around her fingers.

The fog wrapped around them again, then started to move away. Or was she moving backward through it?

Thali flexed her toes to confirm that she was still standing. And she was. She could feel the solid ground beneath her feet.

The fog kept flowing, and in her periphery, she could see her friends' outlines. They also stood still. At her nod, they came closer as the fog swirled and condensed. The fog descended, then started to reform as people, people with heavy armor. Thali swallowed, guessing they had to fight this army of soldiers. Warriors made of smoke and fog could not be hurt. Worse still, invincible warriors were reckless and dangerous. But at least she could see now.

"Have you ever fought smoke warriors, Alexius?" Isaia asked.

"I can't say I have," Alexius said. He sounded grim. That made Thali more nervous.

Before their eyes, the smoke coalesced into twelve warriors. The only thing that made Thali feel better was that the warriors all looked similar. They all had the same weapons and stood in the same stance, telling Thali maybe they thought and responded the same. The fog finished solidifying, becoming dark-blue-and-black plate armor. Small tiles overlapped over the warriors' thighs in a skirt of armor, and their helmets reminded Thali of the rooftops in Cerisa. The helmets even curled out like hair that was just beyond shoulder length. She narrowed her eyes and saw nothing but dark-gray shadows where faces should have been.

The warriors shifted into different positions. Thali gulped. That was what she had been afraid of. If they adopted independent positions, then they moved independently. She wondered if they were controlled by warriors outside the arena, if they were many people's magical creations, or more frighteningly, a single person's. The latter would require a lot of magic.

"Best guesses for how to take down a smoke warrior?" Mia squeaked from behind Thali.

Thali had long ago made sure Mia could hold her own, but everyone else in their group had years of experience in battle, including Tilton and Daylor. "Mia, if I asked you to stay within our circle, would you? If you see an opportunity, take it, but otherwise, stay behind us?"

"Even though it looks like there's supposed to be two of them for each of us, gladly. I know when I'm outmatched, and this is one of those times," Mia replied, putting a hand on Thali's shoulder.

Thali nodded. Her friends closed in tighter, surrounding Mia, then started forward. They stepped in half steps, weapons drawn. Thali had her daggers strapped on and her twin butterfly cutlasses out in front of her. Her staff was strapped to her back, and her blood was starting to thrum in her ears as the anticipation built.

Her skin prickled as her body hummed, excited to get into a fight. Part of her had missed this. She twirled the butterfly swords in anticipation. "Alexius, Isaia, with me. When we tire, we fall back, and Tilton, Daylor, and Nasir will take our place," Thali said. They approached the warriors, and Mia squeezed her shoulder a couple times before she sunk back behind Nasir. Alexius was to Thali's left, Isaia to her right. She knew these two warriors best as they'd both been her sparring partners. Her heart started to beat faster, and she was a little surprised at how much she anticipating what was about to happen.

As the three friends approached, six warriors peeled away from the group, stepping forward and spreading out to line up. Two warriors then faced Thali, Alexius, and Isaia each.

"Let's do some experimenting, shall we?" Thali asked before charging forward.

The two warriors in front of her each held two short swords longer than her cutlasses. It was four swords against two. The last warrior held two long, skinny daggers. Just before reaching her warrior and making contact, Thali kicked the staff on her back up, and it sailed upward. It came down at an angle, and she caught one end with her foot, using her forearms to knock her staff down and between the warrior's legs. He tripped, and as he fell off balance, Thali came up with one sword and then down with the other, swinging it sideways so the warrior with the short daggers had to block.

The warrior with the swords fell in half when her blade sliced him, then he puffed into smoke. Unfortunately, it hung in the air a moment before floating to the back with the others.

She kicked the staff with her feet so it rolled toward the other warrior. He was clever enough to leap up. But it gave her the opportunity to slice upward, and he landed back down on her blades. His arms fell off but then grew back.

"Interesting," Thali said. A mortal wound would kill the smoke figure, or at least reset it, but limbs would regenerate.

With a flick of her thumb, she fit her cutlasses together, creating a massive, double-edged sword. Then she kicked her staff up and caught it. Now she had a deadly weapon in each hand.

The remaining warrior bent at the knees. Thali knew he was getting ready to jump in. She waited for him. The blood sang in her ears, yet she was incredibly calm. Time slowed as she headed into the lethal warrior zone her mother had taught her to fight in.

"When you are prepared and your body knows what to do, you must let your body do the work. Calm your mind and let your muscles react to what your body sees and hears and feels. It will not steer you wrong. Do not let your mind think. Observations are always key, but they are not important right now. Store them for a later date." Her mother's voice floated into her mind, and Thali nodded as if she stood right next to her mother.

The warrior with the two long daggers switched his grip. Now Thali was convinced these warriors were mirroring real fighters, ones that could see her actions but did not fear being sliced, kicked, or stabbed—or dying.

She saw his move before he made it. He tilted one dagger, showing her his next move. Thali braced herself, ready for him. He took a wide step, and she ducked right into him, jerking her staff and releasing her last secret: a blade at the end of the staff. She stabbed it in between the armored plates on his shoulder, then under his helmet. Knowing she wasn't taking a real life let her be more aggressive too.

The warrior puffed into smoke. It too rose and then zoomed backward like a cloud on a mission. She looked around and watched as Alexius played with his warrior, drawing him into a trap as he learned more and more about him.

Thali turned to Isaia as she caught her breath and watched as he went for the kill. His blade sliced out, separating the head from the body in one smooth move. Quinto swords were wickedly sharp—among the sharpest in the world—and she wondered if the warrior had known that.

Isaia came over to her, and Alexius, seeing them done, finished off his own warrior and then closed the circle with her.

Those behind Thali came closer, and the last six warriors slowly started to approach. They stopped though. It seemed they would not fight those who had already fought. Thali nodded, and Nasir stepped up beside her.

"Fatal blows will make them go *poof*," Thali said. "Anything else will regrow."

"Go for the heart or the neck, decapitate them, or deliver a fatal blow to the gut. Nothing else will make them disappear. Or you could slice them in half," Alexius said. Isaia nodded his agreement.

Nasir nodded in return, as did Daylor and Tilton. The six warriors remained where they were until Daylor, Tilton, and Nasir stepped forward. Then the six started their march forward. Thali, Isaia, and Alexius sank back and watched. Thali's hands twitched. She wanted to get back into the fight. Her body hummed again as it recovered, and she jumped at any movement in her direction. Alexius and Isaia each put a hand on her shoulders. Their hands were heavy, and they weighed her body down, calming her twitchy muscles.

The second shift performed admirably. Daylor received a cut on his upper arm, and Tilton had a slice across his chest, making Thali glad he'd worn armor.

They were all huffing and puffing—except Nasir—when they completed their task and turned to Thali. Nasir's eyes had darkened, and his movements were calm, almost unnaturally so. She wondered if she looked like that as she recognized the warrior calm Nasir had sunk into.

They all turned to watch then. The smoke that had zoomed away hovered near the end of the arena. Thali hoped it would dissipate into the sky, but as they watched, part of her wanted more, and part of her wanted the fight to be over. The part that was worried for her friends wanted the smoke to go away, but the warrior in her hoped the smoke would reform into fighters.

The cloud descended to the ground, then started to condense again. Thali swallowed her excitement. It wouldn't suit to show it. This time, there weren't twelve warriors; there were six, one for each of them.

"Ready?" Alexius asked.

Isaia and Thali both nodded, and Thali stepped forward, her double-edged sword in one hand and her staff in the other, blade out. It had a blade on the other end too that she had yet to release, but she would only use it if she needed to.

These new warriors were bigger, bulkier. Their armor appeared smoother too, with fewer gaps between the plates. Thali wondered if that had changed because of what had happened in the last round.

Are they connected to real warriors?

Yes, I believe so, Alexius said. *I think there are real people controlling them somewhere nearby.*

Thali nodded. She wanted to confirm her suspicions. She started running then, and Isaia and Alexius did the same. The three warriors ran toward them in return.

She leveled her staff first, blade out, to make the warrior dodge to the other side—to her waiting cutlasses. He threw his sword up in time to block her blade from slicing his torso, but the power with which she came in forced him to use his other hand to brace himself against it with his blade. She slid her hand up her staff and jammed the blade in the gap in his armpit. This time, she twisted the staff into the smoke creature and extended the blade. It felt like it had sunk into real flesh.

The smoke creature grunted, but instead of *poofing* away as she expected, he simply backed away from the blade. Smoke filled the hole her blade had left. The warrior shook itself and charged at her again.

Thali didn't let it faze her. She parried and blocked with her staff, then sliced upward and then down again with her dual-edged sword.

"You have fancy weapons," the smoke figure said as he sliced downward.

It could speak! Thali saw her opening. She brought her swords up, tangled with the warrior's second sword, then blocked from below with her staff. The sword came clattering out of the smoke-warrior's hand.

She swung her staff around and knocked the warrior's hand away as she took her opportunity. Slicing her cutlasses sideways into his middle, she dropped her staff and held her double-edged cutlass in one hand. She continued to slice through the warrior, then twisted her wrist and doubled back, slicing the other way. The cutlass finally severed the warrior's spine. Its lower half *poofed*, but his torso floated for a moment more. She couldn't see his expression but felt his shock as his top half finally *poofed* away. Thali blinked. She half expected to be covered in blood and gore. But she wasn't. She only felt the cool mist of fog on her skin as she blinked and looked around her. Isaia was still fighting his warrior: a very talented woman. Thali wondered if it was Sumac.

Alexius had dispatched his own warrior and was watching her. He came closer. "I don't think the goal is to test our abilities."

Isaia dispatched his warrior then, so they took a step back as Tilton, Daylor, and Nasir stepped forward. Thali was still catching her breath, so she put her arm around Isaia's shoulders as he bent over, breathing heavily as well. Alexius was calm and cool and breathing normally, which annoyed her a little bit.

Thali watched the others fighting their smoke warriors and she started to see what Alexius meant. None of the warriors were outmatched. In fact, they matched the fighter in front of them almost exactly, like a perfect sparring partner.

"If the goal is not to beat us, then what is it?" Thali asked.

"To tire us," Isaia said.

Thali took a deep breath. Of course it was.

"Yet, if we pull back, I think they'll still injure us," Isaia said. He glanced at his shoulder, which had the tiniest of cuts. "My family won't let me live that down." He grinned, and Thali grinned back. She knew exactly what that was like.

Thali had barely caught her breath when Tilton, Daylor, and Nasir backed away, huffing and puffing themselves. She stepped forward. Now there were two warriors for each of them again, and Thali found herself trying to kill them as quickly as possible.

She was more out of breath after that battle, and this time, she'd caught a shallow cut on her thigh. Thali backed away with Isaia and Alexius again and noticed Daylor and Tilton looked sluggish as they stepped forward.

"When do you think it'll end?" Daylor moaned, gripping his sword and holding it up as he passed them.

Thali turned to Alexius.

"I'm not sure," he said.

Mia dabbed everyone's brows with a piece of her skirt and brought them water. She was sweating almost as much as they were. "So you think this is just to tire everyone? But why?"

"What if the next challenge follows immediately after this one?" Thali asked.

Isaia nodded. "That would be my guess. Or maybe they just want to see our true colors."

Thali nodded in return. She was getting tired. The battle lust was coming back slower and slower with each encounter.

There was nothing like pushing someone past their limits to see what they were truly made of, after patience evaporated. Thali watched the others fighting and saw that Tilton and Daylor were struggling. They sliced their swords slowly and were barely blocking. They were on the defensive more than the offensive.

"How do you think we end this?" Thali asked Alexius.

"I've been trying to figure that out, but I don't have an answer for you yet. I don't know if it's going to take one of us to collapse or all of us to collapse. I am curious to see what happens when only a few of us are left standing," Alexius replied.

Thali swallowed. It had been a while since she'd truly been exhausted. Alexius would outlast them all easily. *It must be magic dragon energy,* she supposed.

Nasir supported Tilton, who in turn supported Daylor as they stumbled back. Thali was surprised that they came back without additional scratches—and that they'd managed to dispatch their warrior. Tilton and Daylor flopped to the ground, and Nasir placed his hands on his knees. He was breathing hard, and it wasn't often Thali saw a Bulstani warrior breathing hard.

Thali swallowed. She too was still breathing heavily as she, Isaia, and Alexius stepped forward. Alexius and Isaia stayed closer to her this time. They formed a small semicircle, and the warriors responded in kind. There were only six of them now, and Thali waited for them to make the first move. She wondered if they would if she did not.

Surprisingly, one warrior hung back, while the other came forward, swinging his sword at her. She separated her butterfly cutlasses to block, then twisted, bringing one down to slice behind her as she spun into his chest and used the other to keep his sword locked outward.

The warrior *poofed* away, and she found herself facing the other one. This was the one with two short daggers, the more skilled of the two.

"What do you want from us?" Thali asked quietly. She truly wondered if he would respond. He didn't. Instead, he tried the same move she had tried on their first round—except Thali saw it coming. She countered and stepped back, using her staff to flip inside his guard, then swirling her swords deep into the smoke-warrior's gut. Though the armor was hard, her swords were sharper. They did not dull with use as others did. The move surprised the warrior, and he *poofed* off too. Thali was panting again and just wanted to lay down. It would be wonderful to have a nap right now. She turned to look around and saw Isaia finishing. Daylor and Tilton were still prostrate on the ground. They didn't even push up to their elbows to watch them. She could go again, maybe. Alexius could go again. She turned to see Isaia breathing hard too, but there was still some vigor in his eyes.

Thali stayed where she was, but Nasir put a hand on her shoulder. Isaia stood firm too, as did Alexius.

"Isaia can go again, and allow me to go again. You can come back refreshed then. You are the most valuable of the three of us," Nasir said quietly to her. "Please."

Thali nodded and finally backed away. She wouldn't mind the breather.

As the new warriors matched their new opponents, Thali walked over to Tilton and Daylor. She stood by their heads and looked down. "Are you two all right?" she asked.

They both nodded. "Tired. So, so tired. Is it our turn already? That was fast."

"It's all right. You two sit this one out. Alexius and Isaia are going in your stead."

"How do they train for this?" Tilton asked quietly. He looked completely and utterly drained, as if he couldn't even bear to lift a finger.

A cry tore Thali's gaze away. Isaia was bent over, and before Thali knew what she had done, she was right there. She threw up her swords, blocked, and pushed the warrior off Isaia as he bent over his thigh. A curtain of blood was pouring from it. It was the same leg the leviathan had slashed four years ago.

Adrenaline rushed through her as she tapped into her magic, spinning and diving and fighting with ferocity. She left the others to tend to Isaia.

Her anger that this creature had injured a friend re-invigorated her, and her adrenaline renewed. She pushed the smoke warrior further and further back. Nasir and Alexius pushed their warriors back too until all three warriors were pinned against the rear wall. She watched her teammates out of the corner of her eye, and they all went for the killing blow at the same time. Suddenly, all the smoke—including the cloud that had gathered at the end of the arena—*poofed* and dissipated.

"Finally," Daylor said a little louder than he may have meant to.

Thali ran to Isaia. He had a thick gash on his thigh that would need stitching. Mia had tied a tourniquet with a piece of her skirt. If she kept this up, she'd have no skirt left.

"Thank you, Mia," Isaia said through gritted teeth.

"Stop." The commanding voice made them all freeze.

Thali wondered if they had done something wrong.

A jellyfish floated down from above, and Thali looked up to where it had come from. The wise woman stood at the edge of the arena looking down upon them. The crowd had backed up to give her space. The jellyfish floated down to Isaia's leg and plastered itself there, spreading out to cover the entire wound. Thali watched as the creature sucked up some of Isaia's blood, then flew off his leg, which was now covered in slime. Then in front of her eyes, his leg started to knit itself back together until it was only a scar. Knowing where the scar from the leviathan was, Thali almost laughed. Isaia's leg would look more like a tree with its crisscrossing scars now.

"Our intention was never for you to be mortally injured," the wise woman said. Then she sat and disappeared. Thali's adrenaline ebbed, and she reached out. Alexius was under her arm immediately, holding her up as she sagged against him.

CHAPTER NINETEEN

A TINY COUGH BROUGHT their attention back to the rim of the arena.

"The last challenge is one of finesse and stamina," the small woman said.

Thali gulped. Her hands shook from the adrenaline. She turned to see that Isaia's and Nasir's hands were shaking too. Finesse would be difficult.

The entire back wall of the arena slid up, and a huge tray with what she thought were boulders slid out. As it neared them, she saw the boulders were actually four mounds of kelp—attached to each other. The far right bundle had a loose end that sat on the middle of the tray. On the edge of the tray were two sticks as long as masts and about the same thickness as Thali's arms. It would take strength to move each strand of kelp, and she would struggle considering her exertions so far.

"You will knit your way to the end of the arena," the small woman said. "No magic is allowed."

"Does anyone know how to knit?" Thali asked. She turned to Mia.

"Don't look at me. I sew, not knit." Mia had her hands on her hips.

Isaia coughed.

Thali was again very glad she had her friends.

"I've never knit on this scale," Isaia said, "but my mother forced us all to learn. She said it would help us develop our fine motor skills and appreciate the fine winter garments our grandmother made us."

"I also know how to knit, but it's been a long time and I don't know how to start," Alexius said.

That surprised Thali, though she supposed when you were hundreds of years old, you knew how to do a little bit of everything. "Well, Isaia, you take the lead," Thali said. She looked at them. Now she was wishing she'd paid more attention to Crab sitting on his chair with yarn in his lap. But he didn't knit, he crocheted. That used one stick; knitting used two.

"All right, the first thing we need to do is make a slip knot on the end." Isaia moved toward the kelp.

Thali really hoped it wasn't slimy, though that was the least of their worries. The chatter increased as the crowd lost interest. Thali wondered if something would be unleashed on them to make it more exciting for those watching.

Isaia made a slip knot, and Nasir ran to grab a stick. She watched as their muscles bulged. This was going to take a lot of energy, energy they did not have.

Can we use magic to infuse everyone with energy? Strengthen them?

We'd have to take from somewhere or something. It's no different from eating.

Thali thought it was very different from eating. Then she wondered if she could siphon a drop of energy from the crowd around them.

"No magic, remember," Nasir grunted as he and Isaia took the strand of kelp, made a loop, and twisted it around the stick.

"How did you know I was thinking about magic?" Thali asked. She ran over to help Nasir hold the stick up so Isaia could continue making loops.

"You get a furrow between your eyebrows when you think of or use magic," Nasir said. He stepped back to take a break from holding the stick.

Thali looked around as she held it on her own for a moment. There had to be an easier way to do this. The platform caught her attention. It was about two feet off the ground. That would work. "Hold on."

Nasir took the stick again, and Thali moved up the end of it. Then she dragged it with Nasir's help so a third of the end hung over the edge. Alexius helped her as she went to roll the ball of giant kelp yarn closer. He focused on feeding the yarn as Thali went back to help Isaia and Nasir. Nasir still held the stick steady while Isaia made loops, so Thali joined Isaia. With the slack on the kelp yarn, Thali made loops, then handed them to Isaia. He twisted them and put them on the stick. Nasir pushed each group back along the stick. This was going to take them a long time.

Soon, they had to readjust. Now that they had their initial stitches, Thali and Nasir, Alexius and Isaia moved the stick in place. They used the platform to angle the pointy end up, keeping the other stick nearby as if the platform was a giant lap.

"All right, so knitting is basically making loops with the yarn and putting them onto the sticks." Isaia lifted the kelp yarn and twisted it to make a loop, then Alexius took the loop off the first stick and placed it around the loop Isaia had made. Then Isaia moved the loop to the other stick.

"This is tedious," Nasir said.

Thali swallowed. Daylor and Tilton were still recovering, and Mia wasn't strong enough to help make loops, so she sat on the stick to stabilize it. The four settled silently into their task. Sometimes their arms shook so hard they couldn't put one giant loop through the other. When that happened, someone put a hand on their shoulder and took their place, allowing the other to lie down and rest.

They had no idea how long it was taking them, but eventually, they got into a rhythm: two people knitting, a third pushing loops down the new stick, and a fourth making sure there was plenty of kelp yarn to keep them going without tension. They switched as they tired because the two making loops had to expend the most energy.

The platform took up half the arena, so Thali figured they only had to knit enough for half an arena. She felt like time was moving slowly. They took short nap rests here and there as they moved from one task to another, and her arms were so sore, they shook. But as long as they didn't shake too much when making the loops, she continued. She had lost track of how long they had been going when she bumped into the sand wall behind them.

They had finally finished the last row. They stepped back, nearly falling. Only about half a ball from the initial four was left. She had never felt such exhaustion. Her arms felt like lead, her feet dragged, and even her vision swam. She tripped on the kelp as they walked away from the wall to the platform. Thali didn't even care. She plopped down on the platform, and Nasir followed. Isaia wanted to stay standing, but Alexius pushed him to sit as he stood behind everyone. Thali wondered if dragons had extra strength reserves or if he was as tired as she felt. She wanted to sleep for a week after this.

"Very well done," the women said in unison.

Thali just wanted to lay down and close her eyes. And she didn't care if it was in that order. Her eyelids were so heavy.

"Unfortunately," the wise woman said—Thali was awake and standing in an instant—"there has been a complication. We promised that if you won, you'd have our respect and could wander where you like in our kingdom unsupervised. But I'll now give you a second option."

Thali's eyebrows furrowed. A second choice. She wanted to shout that she preferred the first choice; that's what they had come here for. She didn't care about anything else.

Alexius put a hand on her shoulder though. She should wait to hear the other option. Perhaps it was better. However, the stone rolling around in her stomach told her otherwise.

Another door, several feet above the ground, slid open. Another platform slid out. Thali's throat went dry when she saw who was on the platform.

"We do not take kindly to strangers here. It has been centuries since we have seen outsiders. Yet this week, we have had so many!"

Elric's shock of golden-blond hair was unmistakable. He looked around, and his eyes found hers almost immediately.

"I guess I know where Elric is," Thali whispered.

As if the women had heard her, the small one said, "Our defenses normally keep out all outsiders, but your friends are clever. Our defenses do not protect against animals."

Indi stuck her head out from behind Elric. Even from here, Thali could see Ana's tail wagging as the dog scented her. Her heart sank. Those she wanted to keep safe, keep protected, had come here. Now, instead of finding the gate, she had to make a new choice.

"Your friends can suffer through similar trials, or I, with my mercy, will let them be your prize. Should you choose them, you will not have access to our lands. But they will be safe and unharmed," the small woman said.

The entire crowd held their breath, but Thali knew there was no question. "I choose my friends and their freedom." The crowd booed at that. They really didn't like outsiders.

Thali saw the whole group's shoulders sink. She would not put more of her friends through the challenges.

The small woman nodded. For being such a small woman, Thali thought she had more cruelty in her than her larger companions.

Chapter Twenty

T HIS TIME, A PREVIOUSLY unseen door near Thali opened, and the challengers walked out of the arena. Sumac was waiting for them. She sat in a box with two benches inside, and Thali climbed in without even thinking of asking if it was for them. And away they went, gliding along the ground without a word. Thali was glad they wouldn't have to walk because she would have much preferred to lay down right where she was and sleep. Then she thought of Elric and Ana, Indi and Bardo. At least she would be reunited with them. And after today's trials, she now saw the advantage of doing things with other people, sharing the burden. She wouldn't have survived any of those challenges by herself. There certainly would have been no way for her to have knit that entire kelp carpet alone.

She sighed and put her head on Alexius's shoulder. He scooted closer to her. It wasn't long before she was falling asleep as the box traveled.

"Sleep," Alexius said out loud, and Thali knew it was for the others. Isaia at the very least would probably not have slept until he'd known for sure they were safe.

She watched them slump over before she drifted into darkness and a dreamless sleep.

Thali lay still, vaguely remembering waking up, having some broth brought to her lips, and swallowing it. She remembered green eyes and little bits of conversation.

How long were the trials?

It was cruel to make it three days.

Her eyelids fluttered open then, and the room was dark. She felt the warmth of a familiar furry body beside her and one draped over her legs—and the solid chest of someone on her other side.

Thali remembered the trials, she remembered her friends, and then she remembered that she was not in the palace, at home in Densria, or on a ship. She was in a foreign land where the locals rode narwhals.

She sat up suddenly. It was dark, though she could see Elric's golden curls next to her. The boy could sleep, that was for sure. He was still asleep now, though his arms encircled her waist. He mumbled something as he tried to pull her body against his.

Thali carefully extracted herself instead. She had to see that her friends were safe. She contorted her way out of bed, replacing her hand with a tiger's tail, then made her way as softly as she could to the blanket that had been hung for her privacy. She had to leap to the side when she almost stepped on Bardo. She moved him to a tabletop, then caught a soft glow on the other side of the blanket and wondered who was still awake. When she pulled the curtain aside, she saw Tilton reading a book by the fireplace and Mia sewing. "What time is it?" Thali asked.

Their gazes flew up to her. Mia squeaked before pressing her lips together. She ran over and threw her arms around her friend, and Tilton rose to join them. Thali hugged them both tightly. "I'm so glad you guys are all right. You are all right, aren't you?" She pushed away to examine them herself.

"We are completely and totally fine," Mia said. Then she slapped Thali across the face.

Thali reared back in horror.

"That's for drugging us and leaving us." Then Mia hugged her tightly again. Thali went rigid, wondering if she was about to feel more pain, but Mia added, "And this is for saving us. And for your attempt to keep us safe. But we can make our own decisions—and we can help."

"I know. I'm sorry," Thali said. They moved back over to the hearth and away from the bedroom. "How did you get through the barrier anyway?" Thali asked as she sat.

"Well, Indi and Ana knew where you were. They stood at the bow of your ship and leaned in your direction. They passed through the barrier with the bow. Then the ship stopped. We couldn't see them. So we turned the ship, and they reappeared. Then I held onto them, and we tried again. I passed through the barrier. So we hopped into the rowboat, hung onto the animals, and rowed over. Your ship is on the other side, by the way."

"Huh," Thali said. "Did you see the people riding narwhals?"

"Yes. I'm surprised, honestly, that you're not getting along with them better. This whole place reminds me of you," Tilton said.

Thali thought about the animals here and their relationship with the people, the narwhals with their riders, towing porpoises, crabs moving things around, fish swimming by in open tubes.

The floor creaked, and Thali turned to see Daylor, wrapped in a blanket, shuffling over to them. He looked as sleepy as she had felt, but he smiled at her before sitting down next to her. He kissed the top of her head. "I'm glad you're all right, but please, do not do that to us ever again." He opened one side of his blanket and Tilton climbed in.

"I'm sorry." She looked at them, really looked at them in this strange place. "Those trials were the hardest thing I've ever done, but if it's taught me anything, it's that I shouldn't have tried to keep you safe, though it would kill me if any of you got hurt. I know I couldn't have completed those challenges without friends. And it would have gone a lot faster if I'd had *all* my friends." Thali said. She stared at her hands.

Daylor took one and Mia took another. "Thank you," Mia said.

"Will you tell me about your journey here?" Thali asked.

They exchanged looks and laughed. Then they told her what had happened when they'd woken up from being drugged. Soon enough, the tension in the room began to lighten, and Thali heard the soft pads of tiger paws on the floor.

She went to pull the curtain aside, and Mia bustled over. "I'll take them." The tiger and dog followed Mia, so Thali took a deep breath.

She walked into the bedroom. Elric was stirring, patting the bed and looking for her. "I'm here," Thali said, sitting on it. She sat with her legs crossed feeling incredibly guilty as Elric slowly blinked awake.

He smiled and pulled her back into bed with him. He circled his arms and legs around her, wrapping Thali in his limbs. "I told you we'd come after you." Elric whispered into her hair. He kissed her head, her neck, her shoulder.

"I hoped you wouldn't. Didn't you say you needed a vacation?"

"I think I got bored before you even left." Elric grinned into the top of her head.

Thali snuggled closer to him, breathing him in. She'd missed him. How was it that even now, at the bottom of the ocean with light barely reaching them—and she wasn't even sure it was real sunlight and not some kind of mirror trick—Elric still smelled of sunshine?

"I'm sorry," Thali said. "I'm sorry I didn't let you choose your own path. I shouldn't have taken the choice away from you. Though I'm sure if anything happens to you, your parents will chop off my head and post it on the front gate."

Elric's laugh rumbled in his chest. "We're more of a display-the-whole-body type ..." But he couldn't keep a straight face. He showered her with kisses instead.

Thali giggled. "You're not mad?" She pulled back.

"It was probably childish of me to take the draught, but I understand where you were coming from. You want to protect the ones you love. I get that." Elric's emerald-green eyes bore into hers, and she basked in them for a bit.

"So, if I'd asked you to sit it out—" Thali began.

"Not a chance," Elric said. He grinned again.

Thali sighed. "Fine. But you start training with me."

"Deal," Elric said. He pulled her back to him, and she listened to his heart as he tucked her head under his chin. His heartbeat was steady and strong.

This was nice. She didn't want to think about the gate or her brother and what he may or may not be doing. She didn't want to think about whether more dangerous creatures of who knew what sort were about to be released into the world.

A loud cough came from the other side of the curtain—then again.

"Yes?" Thali called out.

"You should dress. We'll soon have company," Alexius said.

If he'd spoken out loud, it meant he'd said it as much for Elric as for her. Thali groaned. She slid to the end of the bed, forgetting the furniture was made of sand and scratching her legs. "Squid turds," Thali grumbled as she went to change into clean clothes.

Elric did the same, then took Thali's hand and they emerged from the blanket hung across the archway. "I wanted to ask you about this," he said as he turned and pointed at the blanket.

Thali raised an eyebrow. "They apparently don't believe in privacy."

"But a blanket? Don't you two have magic?" Elric asked, glancing between her and Alexius.

"Apologies, Your Highness," Alexius said. The blanket melted away, then became solid, ornate, double wooden doors.

"Nice," Elric said.

Thali bit her tongue. Did it really matter that they had used a blanket? Instead of using his magic for saving lives, Alexius had just used his magic to make a door. Thali's jaw tightened. It was a waste of precious magic.

Elric didn't seem to notice, and a knock captured their attention. They turned to the main doors, the ones that could lead them out to the rest of these lands.

Sumac opened the door and entered. Everyone stood mutely, waiting for her to speak first, which she did. "I take it you are all well rested?" Sumac asked. Her hand twitched, making Thali wonder what was going on beyond their rooms. At Thali's nod, Sumac continued. "We were wondering if Sifu Lung would come. We have a matter of importance we'd like his esteemed opinion on."

"Only if her—Their Highnesses—can come too," Alexius said.

Sumac looked tired. Her forehead wrinkled and she looked at their entourage.

"Don't worry, I'll stay," Mia said.

"Us too," Tilton said, nodding at Daylor.

Sumac sighed. "All of you might as well come."

Mia clapped her hands together excitedly. Thali noticed her friend had strapped the dagger she'd gifted her before they'd left for school on a belt around her waist. In the same breath, Thali noted that Mia should probably have a proper sheath for it.

They filed out of the room, Alexius leading and Elric taking the rear. The local guards followed, though Thali noticed they had fewer of them now. Only four followed and one led them rather than a whole crew forming a tight square around them. Their group outnumbered their guards. Perhaps they *had* earned some trust.

Chapter Twenty-One

S UMAC DID NOT TAKE them to the same room as previously. Instead, she brought them up, closer to the surface, but not quite above water level. She led them down a side hall to a room with two guards posted outside. They nodded at her and opened the doors. Thali gulped at the ornateness of the room. Golden shells, seahorses, narwhals, and even dolphins decorated the white, sandy surfaces. The most impressive was a wide column of water in the middle of the room. It was twenty feet across, and the ceiling soared three stories high. She scanned it and saw a flash of something dark, like a shadow.

Use your other sight. But be careful, Alexius said.

As they spread out around the column, Thali saw a smaller channel that fed into the column with a series of gates. They'd trapped something in there.

Thali switched to the threads in her mind, putting barriers up naturally as she reached out toward the column of water. She sensed it before it sensed her. She kept her thread out of its mind, though she felt the water and the shape of the creature within.

It was like a seal but with much larger pectoral flippers. And it was female, with a tail made of many strands of what resembled kelp, but could not be. The creature had incredible dexterity in each strand, and Thali could tell the creature controlled the strands of her tail with incredible agility and accuracy. Not once did the strands touch each other.

As the group walked around the column, they saw the three women dressed in long cream dresses that reminded Thali of more sand.

"I thought we were only inviting the dragon?" the warrior said.

"He would not come without the others," Sumac replied, which Thali thought was interesting because that wasn't completely true.

The wise one nodded. "This creature swam through our barrier and killed five of our people last night. We corralled it into this space, but another died in the process.

"How does it kill?" Elric asked.

"We're not sure," the wise one answered.

Alexius, do you know what this is?

I do not. But I can tell that it is not as docile as it wants you to think.

Do you think it's safe enough for me to connect with it?

You risk killing it.

Thali thought back to the hornsnoads she'd infiltrated in Etciel. She hadn't known they would all die afterward. She shuddered to think of it, and Elric put an arm around her shoulders and glanced at her, silently asking if she was all right. Thali nodded. No, she would not infiltrate another's mind without consent—unless her friends were at risk. Even then she wasn't sure she would.

"From what we saw of the bodies, they were ... burnt," the warrior said. She swallowed.

Thali wondered if the warrior had known someone that had been killed.

"Burnt? In the water?" Elric asked.

The women nodded.

Alexius stepped forward. "I know this is incredibly difficult, but could we examine one of the bodies?"

The sisters looked at each other, then back to Alexius. They scanned the rest of them before answering. "Yes," the wise one said, "but first, there is something you need to know."

Chapter Twenty-Two

S UMAC AND A GUARD led them down a hallway to more opulence. They walked into what Thali thought must be some kind of reception or ballroom, except this one had a wall of murals. They were sculpted of sand, with a few colors added to the white to highlight different parts. If these people read left to right, the group was standing at the end of the story, but maybe they read right to left like Cerisans.

The small one continued walking to the couches in the middle of the room and sat down. The warrior stayed on their right and the wise one on their left as they faced the first mural.

The small one said, "It is said that our people originated from a love story. A man and woman fell in love but could not marry on the mainland, so they ran away. They stole a boat and sailed to a place where they could live in peace."

Thali looked up at the mural of two people in a rather small boat. They wouldn't have gotten far.

"They landed here and started to build a life as they explored the island." The next panel showed the two people building a home together.

"The man got very sick one day, and the woman did not know what to do. She took him to a mysterious place they had found earlier, where three monoliths had been erected. She placed him in the middle. Having found it earlier, they had taken care of it, cutting down overgrown vegetation and keeping the area clean and tidy. The woman lay down with her husband, and they held each other through the night. The woman was sure she would wake alone. But when she woke—"

Here they moved to the next panel. It was incredible. It had the most detail and was of a woman next to a man who, instead of legs, had tentacles like an octopus. The image was so detailed Thali could see there were no little suction cups on the tentacles. They were smooth and scaled like a snake. And, he had six, not eight tentacles.

"The woman was so shocked, she ran away. But in time, her husband convinced her it was truly him, and they continued to live their lives on the island. When the woman was very old—though the man had not aged since the day his wife had brought him to the monoliths—the man took the woman and lay her on the stone in the middle of the monoliths." The small one paused.

They moved to the next panel, and Thali saw for herself that the woman had also become an octopus person. Or was it a snake person? Or a squid snake? She wasn't sure what they would be called.

"The monoliths not only restored the woman's life and youth but also healed whatever had prevented them from having children. And so they populated this land." The wise one finished the tale.

Thali had questions. When had the monoliths and gate appeared? And were they under the ocean? Because there was no way they'd missed it aboveground on their trek here to the tower. Or maybe it was inside a building? And who or what had created them?

A cough behind them made them all turn around. The small one—still on the couch—undid the tie to her skirt. It fell open and revealed six tentacles, just like the woman in the panels.

Elric swallowed audibly.

It was truly strange to see a half person, half hepto-snake. But Thali didn't want to forget her manners, so she stepped toward the small woman. "Thank you for trusting us enough to reveal your true form," Thali said.

The other two women also untied their skirts, revealing their own six tentacles. They were colorful, not skin-colored, making Thali wonder if there was a specific meaning to each color.

The wise one nodded. "If you'll follow me, we'll take you to the bodies of our dead." Thali watched as the woman's legs undulated—like a snake—but then rose and fell in a three-beat cycle as she moved.

Thali forced her gaze away as she and her friends followed the woman through another room to a somber chamber with seating areas.

Mia grasped Thali's elbow. "I think I'll stay out here, if it's all the same to you." She glanced at the heavy curtain separating the couches and where Thali assumed the dead were.

Thali nodded. Tilton also stayed behind to keep Mia company. Daylor joined them though. Ana and Indi too stayed behind to comfort Mia. Even Bardo slid to Indi and then to Mia. Thali would have to check in on her; this was a lot for her to take in, and she looked pale.

The women stayed outside, but the warrior held the curtain open for Thali's group. They filed in silently. Five bodies lay on separate edged tables. The tables were wide, likely to accommodate their tentacles.

Thali didn't want to touch them out of respect, but she strolled around each table. She swallowed down the bile and pushed away the eerie thoughts. The echoing emptiness of the room made it difficult.

Elric followed Thali closely, but Alexius observed from the far side of the room. A swathe of fabric covered faces and other parts, but Thali didn't think she needed to move them. She looked carefully at their torsos though, for there, the skin was puckered like it had been burnt, like the creature's tail strands had burned them. *But how could the kelp have wrapped all the way around the victims?* Thali wondered. *When you touch a hot stove, your instinct is to move your hand away. So surely, they would not have let themselves be wrapped up in burning kelp.*

Another body was not only burnt all the way around but was also sunken, like he'd been squeezed then burned. But why? Why had that creature harmed all these people—and not eaten them? This was the first time anyone had seen this creature, so protectiveness was unlikely. It could not have been here long enough to build a home or have babies. Besides, the creature in the tank had not been agitated.

When there was nothing left for Thali to see, she left the room and sat with Tilton and Mia. Indi and Ana came over, and she noticed for the first time that their hosts were not at all bothered by her tiger, dog, and snake. Their hosts hadn't even said anything about how her animal friends followed her or how they roamed freely. Bardo stayed with Mia, curled around one arm as she petted him absentmindedly.

Alexius came out last, Elric and Daylor emerging just before, both pale and wan. Elric sat on the arm of the chair Thali had parked herself in.

Do you think this creature is from the water world? That she came through the open gate? Or is she from theirs? Thali asked Alexius.

I'm not sure. There is a world where elements combine unnaturally, like fire and water. But there are also creatures of all kinds from the world of water. The only thing I do know is this creature is not from this world.

The women guided the group solemnly to another room with more seating.

"Sifu Lung, we have never encountered a creature like this one. What can you tell us of it?" the wise woman asked. The three women sat across from the friends on one couch. They perched on the edges, looking delicate, though Thali now wondered if that was the most comfortable position for them considering their many tentacles. Then she wondered whether anatomically, they preferred to sit on a stool with their legs fanned out around them.

"It is also the first time I have seen such a creature. I'm sure you've seen that it burns its victims. It looks as if its tail is camouflaged as kelp, but each strand has independent control. I would also propose that the creature has full control of its abilities."

That was pretty much what Thali had seen too. They weren't telling these women anything they didn't already know. It was frustrating. Suddenly, words came unbidden. "Why are you so comfortable with my tiger and dog roaming around?"

Even Eric jumped as her question had come out of the blue.

"Animals here are more than companions as they are in the other lands. They are essential to our daily lives, and here they are treated with the utmost respect and care. They roam as they wish and are cared for before we care for ourselves." The wise woman turned to Thali as if she knew Thali had more questions.

"And what is to be done with us now?" Thali asked. They were all thinking it, and she was tired of the guessing and the waiting.

"What do you wish to do?" the wise one asked.

"You are obviously capable, intelligent, and brave. You can deal with this new creature. So I would like to see the gate with my own eyes, see that it's intact, if it's not breached. Then we will leave."

"Do we offend you so much?" the warrior asked.

"It is not that you offend, but that you don't seem to like strangers. So, I would as soon leave you alone and be on our way."

"Where would you go?"

That made Thali hesitate. She wasn't sure where they were going next. They hadn't received word from Elric's parents to return. She could impose upon Ming for a while longer or return to Bulstan. She could probably even go home to Densria if she wanted so they could plan their next steps. Her parents and the town would hide them and keep their secrets.

"Perhaps let us work on getting you to this gate before you consider your next move," the wise one suggested.

Thali looked around and saw that all her friends were all watching her. They nodded at her, so she turned back to the women. "Thank you. We would greatly appreciate your assistance."

"It is quite a journey to the gate, so it would be best if we depart tomorrow morning. We will be gone for three days," the wise one said. The warrior looked grumpy, as if she would have preferred to fight instead of taking them to the gate.

They all filed out of the room, Thali and Elric last.

"Are you all right?" Elric asked. He placed a hand on her elbow.

She stopped to face him. "This all just feels so out of our control. Is this how you always feel?" Thali asked. She realized that at least she had a handle on magical animals and magic, but Elric was constantly facing new things out of the realm of his imagination.

He smiled and she warmed at that bright, brilliant smile. "You get used to it," he said. "Or perhaps, it's more like you survive the first few and realize it's possible to get through it. So we'll get through this too. We'll be home soon enough."

Thali didn't even want to think of the state Adanek would be in once they did return. "You're a remarkable person to have dealt with all of this so calmly," Thali said. She put a hand on his cheek.

"You're my inspiration. You've had your fair share of challenges too, but I think we make a good team." Elric slid his hand to her jaw and kissed her.

A cough interrupted them, and they turned to find Sumac in the doorway waiting for them. Indi and Ana sat patiently by the door too, Indi reaching her head out to Sumac for a scratch. For a tiger that didn't like many people, she seemed to be awfully friendly here.

"Lead the way," Elric said, though Thali detected the annoyance in his voice. It had been nice to have one small moment together. It made her wonder if Tilton and Daylor had had a chance to be alone since they'd started their journey.

Chapter Twenty-Three

The next day, they packed their allotted food rations and an extra set of clothes in the bags they'd been given. Then they followed Sumac, the warrior, the wise one, and three guards into the moving box and descended. They dropped for some time before the box stopped.

"Do you all swim?" the wise one asked.

Thali looked at her friends.

Daylor flashed a grin and replied, "Absolutely."

Everyone else nodded, and they followed their hosts down a hallway and through an archway to an alcove, in which stood two guards.

"All right, the journey to the gate is not an easy one, and that is on purpose. It has been some time since anyone has laid eyes on it, so your safety cannot be guaranteed. Do you still want to go?" the wise one asked.

They all nodded, but Thali looked at them. She really, really wanted to tell them all to stay here. Only she and Alexius really needed to go.

"We're coming," Mia told Thali as if she had read her mind.

Thali nodded.

"We will descend into the pool and swim in this direction," the wise one said, pointing straight ahead.

"You will have to hold your breath for a few seconds as we descend. Then we will resurface in a cave." The wise one waited for a guard with a rope to go first. He slipped into the pool and shivered. Then the wise one followed him, holding onto the rope he'd thrown.

One by one, they strapped their bags across their backs and then dipped into the pool. Alexius went first, but Thali wanted to take the rear, so she waited for everyone else to go. She held her breath when Daylor jumped in. It didn't seem like they needed to do much swimming, but she wanted to make sure he was all right. He nodded at her and plunged under the water.

Elric went before Thali too, and they locked eyes and nodded as he slipped into the water. Nasir and Isaia insisted on going last, thwarting her plan, so they waited at the pool's edge for Thali to enter. She slipped in like she would a bathtub and immediately felt her chest seize. The water was freezing. She took a deep breath, and then with a last look at Nasir, dove under the water, using the rope to guide her as she pulled herself along. She fought to not breathe in or out. It was so cold that her body still hadn't relaxed. But moments after she cleared the building, she followed the rope upward. She could barely keep her hands on the rope it was so cold, but she ascended the couple of feet quickly and popped to the surface.

She sucked in a breath, and two sets of arms reached down to pull her up. Elric and Alexius pulled her out of the water, and she looked around at the cave. It was bare, unadorned but for tiny lights that seemed to blink on and off in the walls and a bank along the water's edge that led to a tunnel.

"The tunnel is warm, so your clothes will dry as we walk," the wise one said once all had surfaced.

The warrior had been oddly quiet. Thali wondered if they'd left their smaller sister to protect their lands and if that meant the smallest was the most powerful?

Thali looked her friends over to make sure everyone was all right. They were quiet and shivering a bit, but otherwise they had made the swim without harm.

They followed the two sisters into the tunnel, the warrior leading and the wise one walking with Thali and Elric. The ground was surprisingly even though the walls and ceiling looked to be made of rock. It seemed this space had been artificially created.

The moment Thali had stepped into the tunnel, she had felt the warm air wrap around her. She thought suddenly of Tariq, of how he could control the breeze, and wondered if someone was using magic here.

"We heat these tunnels specifically," the wise one said as she matched Thali's stride.

"Why?" Thali asked. The tunnels were clean, so Thali suspected they were maintained.

"For those who take care of this place," she said.

Thali looked around, wondering if someone was watching.

"They are very shy. You will likely not see them," the wise one said. She looked up and cocked her head as if she was listening for someone.

Only Indi, Ana, and Bardo had stayed behind. The wise one had promised Thali that they would be well-cared for, and this was not a journey her tiger and dog would appreciate given the swimming they would have to do. Bardo too had refused the moment he had known there was water. He swam well if he had to, but didn't particularly like cold water.

Thali's clothes were soon dry, and she held Elric's hand as they walked. She felt eyes watching her, but when she turned her head, the feeling disappeared. Somehow, she instinctively knew that those watching were very much like her hosts, only smaller, perhaps more octopus-snake than human. She wondered how they'd come to be.

Thali tired more with each step as they traversed the long tunnel. Once or twice they had to climb steep stairs to reach the next section of the tunnel. There, the tunnel became more and more unkempt as they ascended. More rubble littered the floor, and Thali could feel a coat of dust and grime settling on her clothes, sticking to the sweat on her skin.

The wise one grimaced. "The caretakers do not like to enter these parts."

"How much further do we travel today?" Thali asked, remembering that they were to travel for three days.

"We will come upon a large cavern soon, where we will rest for the night. When we've woken, we will travel for a few more hours. It will be much more difficult terrain, but it will not be far," the wise one said.

Thali appreciated the woman's calm, reassuring presence.

They finally came to the cavern then, but it wasn't as big as Thali had expected. She wondered if they'd been traveling underground back to mainland Cerisa.

They were all tired. Walking all day long, even with the change of scenery, made everyone's shoulders slump as they sat and ate their rations. Thali noticed that again they ate a version of seaweed and rice with beans and little chunks of who knew what, perhaps tofu. They ate silently. The food here had been dull, though certainly better than on their ship, and lacked the variety and taste of food on the mainland.

"I'll take first watch," whispered Alexius as he stood, then went to sit on a flat, raised rock. There wasn't much to see in the cavern, but at least it was warm.

Thali's friends huddled together as they lay down, but Thali wasn't sure anyone would get any sleep. Then Daylor snored and it reverberated through the cavern. Thali grinned at that as Tilton moved to shake his shoulder. Thali caught his eye and shook her head. Someone might as well sleep tonight. One person well rested would be better than no one well rested.

Alexius, do you know where we are? Are we approaching Cerisa underground, or are we under the ocean?

I believe we've traveled under the ocean. Though I do think we will eventually surface. The gate should be on land.

Then why did we not take a boat?

I'm not sure. Perhaps I'm wrong, and the gate is in the water.

Why do I get the feeling you don't like that idea?

Because I think I'm starting to guess which land this gate is connected to.

Which one?

Korsel is a land that I mentioned before. It's a land of opposites. The creatures are of mixed elements and are therefore very, very dangerous, like the creature we met. I'm starting to think that creature is connected to this gate and to Korsel. We've also stayed under the same barrier all this time. It extends under water much farther than it does on land.

Thali hadn't been keeping track of that. She felt guilty that she hadn't thought of it.

You should conserve your magic.

And you shouldn't?

I've been alive for a very long time. Trust me when I tell you that I have some pretty large stores, young one.

Thali made a face. Though it was dim and Elric had his arm around her waist as they snuggled together for warmth and comfort, she knew Alexius could see.

He chuckled, then said only, *Sleep.*

Just like that, Thali was pulled into sleep. It seemed like Alexius was becoming more powerful. And she wondered, right as she teetered on the edge of consciousness, if he was also getting more comfortable showing her what he could do.

The next morning, at least what they thought was morning, they woke and ate another rice ball filled with sticky beans and tofu before heading onward. They climbed into another tunnel and a small cavern opened again.

"Only those with magic may proceed," the wise one said. "Lorena will stay with those who remain."

The warrior parked herself with a guard on a nearby rock.

"Be careful," Elric said as he held Thali's face in his hands.

Thali nodded. She hugged him, then Daylor, Tilton, and Mia, then joined Alexius and the wise one as they stood at the entrance to the next tunnel.

Nasir followed her.

"Really?" Thali asked.

"Sorry I didn't tell you sooner," Nasir said.

"What—"

The wise one coughed.

"Not much, but just enough," Alexius said as he nodded at Nasir.

Thali turned and saw that everyone's mouths were agape. Had Nasir ever planned to tell anyone?

"Shall we?" The wise one nudged them again as she set off with two guards.

Thali, Alexius, and Nasir followed them. Thali took a step and almost fell over. She had expected the ground to be hard. Instead, it was so soft, her foot had sunk.

She took another step, then looked up to see that the wise one had pulled her skirts up, and her tentacles were gliding over the thick, muddy substance with ease.

Alexius hovered over it, making Thali think enough was enough. She used her threads then to pull herself out and hover above the ground. Alexius also pulled Nasir out of the mud. Thali threw her threads down the tunnel to a spot just behind the wise one and her guards, then pulled herself as gently as she could along the tunnel and over the mud. Thank goodness her well of magic had refilled.

The wise one and her guards moved so gracefully, they seemed to float over the mud as they slithered. She could see their tracks, but only faintly as if in sand.

Do you feel it?

Thali did feel like her magic wasn't depleting as quickly as usual. Instead, she seemed to gather more as they traveled farther down the tunnel.

It's often like this with a gate. If it's not already open, it might be leaking.

What are the odds of it being fully open? Maybe the creatures came from the north gate instead? Or maybe just a few creatures were able to slip through if this gate is simply leaking?

I know very little about the gates. That was more of a Xerus thing. I would expect to see many more creatures if the gate was fully open, and it would be odd for creatures from the north gate to have made it down here already.

Thali nodded as they continued onward. The ground began to rise, and she saw a small alcove before the tunnel turned sharply to the left.

"The entrance to the gate is just around that bend," the wise one said, pointing. "I sense magic, but no more than usual." She looked them each in the eye, then walked on.

They followed, and moments later, gathered along the edge of a chamber. The wise one poked her head in. She froze, waiting, then entered. The guards followed.

Thali took a deep breath and stepped in, then looked up in awe when four giant monoliths attracted her gaze. She stepped or rather glided farther in with Alexius. Though she tested the ground and discovered it was solid, she continued with her magic.

The magic that pooled in the room from between the monoliths relaxed Thali. The gate wasn't visible, but its magic felt wonderful, as if she had quenched her thirst. Magic felt like part of her soul now. Her threads zinged. They had been starved, but now they were full. She could feel the gate pulling her, calling to her, to her magic. She kept her feet planted where they were though. "Did the gate always leak magic?" Thali asked the wise one. "Is that how you received your gift, how your ancestors did?"

"It sustains our people. It has leaked since our ancestors came here and became what we are. We would not be if it had not leaked."

"Is that why there is a protective barrier around your island?" Thali asked.

The wise one nodded. "It is to keep the magic in instead of spilling out into the world."

Thali wondered if her world could handle the magic permeating it now from all the gates.

"We do not allow access to this room because of the gate's draw. Only I and my sisters come here, and only rarely, to ensure the gate is safe."

Thali looked around the room. It was large enough that two seal-like creatures could fill it, three if they were still. "Is this the only way in and out?" Thali asked.

The wise one nodded.

Creatures might have found another way out, or maybe some can pass through stone, Alexius said.

Thali supposed it wasn't the craziest idea. They were talking about a world completely unfamiliar to them. If Alexius described it as a world of opposites with combined elements, Thali thought her world was likely too simple for such complex creatures.

"Are you satisfied?" the wise one asked.

Thali thought it was a little anticlimatic. She had been expecting to see creatures pouring through the gate, creatures they would have to fight. Her threads told her this gate hadn't been opened all the way. That was something at least. Her brows knit together as she thought. *Could we leave a trace of magic here that would notify us when other creatures came through? Or is there a way to fortify the magic and close it?*

Not without cutting these people off from their source. I don't know if there's anything we can do to fortify it, to keep creatures out. These people need the magic to survive, though the leak weakens the gate. I think we have no choice but to leave it be, perhaps monitor it.

Thali swallowed. It was too cruel to hobble an entire population. They needed the magic.

We can leave a vessel here though. It would hold the gate's magic and might help strengthen our own. It could also offer the gate additional protection. Not a lot, but enough maybe to help keep out the worst of the creatures.

Thali nodded, only slightly. "We're ready to leave," she said.

The wise one nodded and led them out. Thali and Alexius, plus the wise one and her guards, used their magic the whole way back, allowing them to journey much faster than they had on the way there. On the way out of the chamber though, Thali had carefully knotted a thread around a monolith and pulled it with her into the tunnel. She'd grown her thread as she'd glided a few feet out of the chamber, then stopped and put a hand on a blinking rock in the wall. It had taken her only moments to fill the stone with the monolith's magic, then wrap a thread around it. That connected Thali to the gate, and the gate was stronger, more protected. She would even be alerted if something happened at this gate. As she had glided through the tunnels, she siphoned some of the magic from the source to fuel her magic, fill her stores.

The wise one had paused and looked at Thali as if she'd been about to say something, but they'd only moved on. Because the journey back was much shorter than the journey there, when they rejoined their party, they looked up, clearly surprised. Food and low tables had appeared in Thali's absence, and Elric rose from one and rushed to her. He held her face in his hands, questions in his eyes.

"I'm all right. The gate is only partially open," she said for everyone's benefit.

"You've been gone for a day and a half," Mia said.

"Time moves differently the closer you are to the gate." The wise one nodded to her sister, the warrior, who, interestingly, was sitting with Mia.

Thali would have to ask Mia for a better impression of her. "What will you do now?" the wise one asked as Thali visually checked on her friends, Elric's arm around her shoulder.

"I'm not sure, though I am sure there will be another attempt to fully open the gate. I suppose we wait until then," Thali said.

They slept, and the next day the women guided the friends back to their rooms, where they spent the next few days waiting and listening, Thali keeping an eye on the thread she'd left.

By the third day, Mia, Daylor, and Tilton had started to pace. It was getting on Thali's nerves, so she pushed all the furniture aside, and they started training, Thali focusing on Elric's training herself.

Chapter Twenty-Four

O N THE FOURTH DAY, Thali opened the door to their rooms. No one was there.

When she told the others, Mia let out a wail. "You mean we could have left this room all this time?" Mia asked.

Thali shrugged. They all dressed and ate, then set out to explore this strange land.

They decided to stay together, even though it would make them stand out. But no one stopped them. They got stares and glances, but people turned away soon enough. Thali rested a hand on the wavy, undulating wall that served as a railing keeping them from falling down the hollow middle of the structure. She leaned out over the edge, looking up and down. Suddenly, Indi's head bumped her thigh. Thali tucked her head back in just as a porpoise swam through the air in a blur. She wondered for a moment how Indi had known it was coming.

They walked along the railing on their floor first, passing perpendicular hallways similar to theirs that were bustling with people cooking or cleaning, children running, or tiny porpoises zipping. Indi, Ana, and Bardo stayed close to her, curious. She appreciated how calm they were in this new space. Thali hadn't even had to worry about what to feed her animals because whenever her food showed up, Thali also saw her animals leave and return, licking their lips.

The group came upon a sloping ramp that led them to the floor above. When they reached the next floor, Thali noticed the walls were different. In place of solid sand walls with a wave etched on top was a collection of sand dollars fused together.

When Thali cleared the ramp, she looked around. The entire space was different. Here, there were no walls blocking the outer walls of the tower. Instead, it was an open area with tables in rows, aisles spiraling outward from their pathway. "A market," Thali said. And she quickened her pace, despite more stares.

The market was like any other, with bright colors, loud voices, and intriguing wares spread out on tables. Except here, the items were organized from smallest to largest, with the largest taking the most space along the outer edges of the tower. Incredibly, porpoises zoomed by holding baskets or towing bundles with ropes, and snakes slithered along with packages in their mouths. Crabs held merchandise and waddled sideways back and forth along tables, trying to catch people's attention. Turtles swam above their heads with sand dollars in their mouths or tied to their shells.

Elric took her hand and followed her as she strolled among the tables, letting her gaze take in all the items she saw for sale.

They must have started in the homewares area because she saw familiar items: bowls, cups, rugs, and stools, all made of sand and kelp. Sea horses floated above them, bobbing up and down as if they were trying to draw her attention with their movement. One booth had jellyfish swimming in a barely visible maze, and when one was purchased, they simply exited the maze and followed their new owner home.

She continued to the next section, the others all following in her wake, where she saw clothes, simple ones like she wore but varying in color and tightness of weave. Thali turned back and looped her arm with Mia's as she knew that Mia would get sucked into the textiles.

"Where's the food?" Daylor asked as he came up behind them. They had finally made their way back to their starting point.

A young girl watched them from a stool behind a table. She wore long skirts too, making Thali glad she knew why they all wore them. Suddenly, the girl grunted softly. They all turned to look at her, and she pointed up.

Daylor led the way to the next floor with long strides. When Thali caught up, she saw the railing was different. It was a kelp field made of sand, the delicate reeds of sand almost appearing to wave in the water. It was beautiful.

Thali smelled something just as Tilton raced ahead to keep up with Daylor.

Daylor stopped then and stared down the new aisles. Sweet, salty, smoky, and pungent smells all made Thali's mouth water. Even Bardo slithered along her arm, his tongue darting in and out as he took in the smells of the food.

Daylor's shoulders sank.

"What's the matter, Daylor?" she asked.

"We don't have any money," he said. He looked so incredibly sad, Thali wanted to beg, borrow, and steal for him.

Sumac melted away from a pillar. So they *had* been watched this whole time. She pulled a pouch out of her belt and placed a few sand dollars in Daylor's outstretched hands. He dashed off right away as Sumac continued down the line.

"Thank you," Thali said.

"It's better than looking at his sad face." Sumac motioned to Daylor still running up and down aisles to see all the options.

Thali grinned.

After they had filled their bellies—and even Daylor was satisfied—Thali wanted to continue exploring. They strolled up the ramp to the next floor. This one was also open, but instead of aisles, there were chairs. The inner railing had a woven patchwork pattern that reminded her of ripples on the water but with many of them crossing over each other.

Then a horn sounded, soft and low, and Thali spun around to see that a dozen or so people had gathered with what she guessed were musical instruments. Shells of varying sizes and configurations were being held to mouths. Like most sounds here, the instruments produced a low and haunting melody that made chills travel Thali's spine. The others chose some chairs, as did Thali and Elric. But after a few minutes, she leaned over to Elric. "I'll be right back." She rose and went up the ramp to explore the next floor.

Alexius, Nasir, and Isaia followed her, moving quietly. Thali knew that eventually the tower would be level with the ocean, and she was curious to see what other surprises this place had to offer.

When she reached the top of the ramp though, she was met with several stern guards, who made a physical wall to block her path forward.

"Got it, don't go past this point," Thali said as she turned around. But as she looked to the right to see the pattern in the railing of this floor, she saw this railing was made of ordinary brick.

Disappointed, she descended the ramp and rejoined Elric listening to the performers. When they stopped, she clapped, surprising the musicians. Daylor and Tilton cheered, and the performers, bewildered, bowed as they accepted the strange acknowledgment. Thali wondered how they showed their appreciation here.

After the performance, they were waylaid again at the food market as Daylor scraped together what he could for a last snack. Some of the folks were happier to see them the second time, and Thali smiled to see them all getting along. Markets were her favorite place.

They walked down the ramps then, and though Thali wanted to keep going to see what was below their floor, her legs started to protest, so she returned with her group to their rooms.

CHAPTER TWENTY-FIVE

T HALI AND ELRIC WERE laughing as they walked past their wooden doors. They were really enjoying getting to know the people and world here. These people had such a peaceful relationship with creatures of all kinds here that Thali wished they could do the same in their home.

"I'm going to take a bath," she said. Elric smiled and nodded and went to the couch with a book.

Thali went to the bathing room and was startled to see a bird of paradise in the middle of the bathtub. It was in full bloom and growing straight up from the drain. Thali's heart leapt into her throat. She knew immediately who was trying to reach her. She walked over and found letters in yellow on the back of the green sheath.

Home, now.

Thali swallowed. She reached out and touched the flower. She hoped that was enough to let Joren know she'd received the message. It was interesting that he'd been able to get a message to her here, even though this place was so well protected. She wondered if she should reach out to Tariq but decided if Joren and Ming had news, she should just go.

Thali left the bathing room. "We have to leave."

"What's wrong?" Elric stood immediately.

"I just got a message, but please don't ask me how. We have to get back to Cerisa." Thali glanced into the bathing room. The flower had disappeared. A single petal was all that was left in the bathtub. Thali went and picked it up, tucking it into her pocket.

She went back to Elric, whose lips were pressed together. She knew it took a lot of faith in someone not to question the information. Thali stuck her head out of their rooms and saw Sumac walking by. "Sumac," she called. Sumac stopped and came back.

"Sumac, I feel I urgently need to return to the mainland. Is it possible to request your aid expediting the process?"

Sumac raised an eyebrow. "You cannot return."

"What do you mean?" Thali asked.

"Once you've entered the city, you are never allowed to leave. That is how we maintain our secrecy," Sumac said. Her expression was serious.

Thali strangely wanted to laugh but didn't think that would be a good idea. "Ever?"

Sumac shook her head.

"But ..." Thali started. She gulped. She shouldn't even have told her as much as she had. Thali nodded and returned to her rooms.

Sumac watched her as she closed the door to her own rooms. Elric looked at her.

"We're not allowed to leave," Thali said.

"Like right now? Or these rooms? Or?" Elric asked.

"Once you've entered the city, you are never allowed to leave." Thali repeated the words Sumac had said. And Thali had just told a member of the guard or army or patrol or whatever it was that Sumac was part of, that they wanted to leave. It would be immensely more difficult now.

Her ears started ringing. They had been having such a good time. The others joined them at the couches.

"What's happening? What's the matter? Did I hear that correctly? We're never supposed to leave again?" Daylor asked.

Alexius's brows were knit together.

Joren sent me a message: "Home, now." We have to leave.

It will take us some time to make an exit. Connect with him so you can get him a message. Your magic should be strong enough to reach now.

Because she needed to think, Thali went to the balcony, where she stood in a giant shell that was so thin, she could see the ocean beyond through a cream-colored lens.

Elric followed and stood next to her. "Do you really think they'll keep us here?"

Thali nodded. "I think if that's the rule they live by, it'll be tough, if not impossible."

"You need to talk to them, don't you?" Elric asked.

Thali pressed her lips together and nodded. This was the one secret she kept from Elric. "Thank you for trusting me," she said.

Elric sighed. "I just hope one day, you'll be able to leave it all behind you. When we become king and queen, I'll finally be able to slide into the role I've been preparing for my whole life, and you can stand right there with me. And we'll never have to keep anything from each other again."

Thali swallowed. It sent a lance of fear through her heart to think of never again connecting with her fellow princes and princesses of thieves: Joren, Ming, even Henrik and Makena, but mostly Garen. The lance twisted when she thought of never speaking to him—or seeing his face—again, even if it was just to know that he was safe, healthy, and well. On the outside, she smiled and nodded. "Of course."

Elric nodded in return. "I'll leave you to it then."

Alexius joined Thali on the balcony as she stared out, searching the animals nearby. Her range was farther, thanks to the magic boost from the gate. She went in search of a creature that was perhaps connected to a plant.

She found a dolphin a little farther away—surely far enough this city couldn't sense it—and she asked it to clamp down on a large patch of kelp. She needed to get Joren's attention somehow. Surely he was keeping an eye out.

Through the dolphin's eyes, she saw text appear along the flowing kelp leaves. Maybe she should have picked a better, flatter plant.

On your way?

Thali thought about what to say. How could she say it so the plant could feel it?

She found a sea slug and guided it to the stalk. She wrote one word at a time and kept it brief because the kelp wasn't particularly supportive and the slug not particularly fast.

What's wrong?

The kelp brushed the side of the dolphin's cheek as the words appeared.

Elric's parents dead.

Thali felt her heart stop. She looked again. She even called over a nearby octopus to read it again. Then more words appeared.

Attacks in Adanek. Part of palace destroyed.

You are queen. Elric king.

A gong bellowed in her chest. It rang and rang and rang, and Thali gripped the railing. Fear slashed through her next, but she stayed with the dolphin as the next words appeared.

Your parents ok.

It was selfish, but her heart loosened a little at that. Then it tightened again. It was as if Joren had read her mind as the next words popped up.

Friends all ok.

Thieves ok.

Just palace and guards.

Thali knew that was the best outcome given the situation. She'd been relaying the words to Alexius as she received them, and now she felt him join her on the balcony.

"Long live the king and queen," he said.

She finished her reply to Joren, then turned and blinked. Alexius appeared to be gone, but then she glanced down and found him kneeling. "What are you doing?" Thali asked. She looked back inside, and her gaze met Elric's; he was staring at Alexius. Thali watched the emotions cross his face, and all she could do was whisper, "I'm so sorry."

Elric's eyes went from unfocused to focused, then back to unfocused again. Sadness tightened his jaw as he swallowed. Then determination took its place. As she forced her gaze away from Elric, Thali realized her friends were all kneeling.

"Long live the king and queen," they repeated softly.

Thali's eyes found Elric's again then, and she moved silently to him. "We'll get you home, Elric, I promise." She circled her arms around his torso and shrugged herself into his embrace.

"I ..." his voice cracked then, but his arms squeezed her tight. Then he let go with one arm and guided her toward their room. Thali didn't look up but heard the doors open and close. Suddenly, she found herself sitting on the edge of their bed, Elric in her arms and her shirt getting more and more wet.

"Oh, Elric. I can't tell you how sorry I am." Thali held Elric tight.

"We have to get back," he finally said. He clutched at Thali, and she squeezed him tighter.

"We will," Thali said. She would make sure of it. Even if she had to get a great blue whale to bust through the barrier, she would do it for Elric.

Can you request an audience with the three women tonight? Thali asked Alexius. She felt him nod as he briefly showed her a glimpse of the other room, of the others all sitting on the couches, stunned, trying to take the news in.

I told them what I could.

Elric's tears stopped, but he stayed curled in Thali's arms until there was a soft knock on the wooden doors.

He sat up and ran his hands along his face and through his hair.

Thali took his face in her hands. "We're going to be all right," she said. Something had hardened in Elric's eyes, worrying her. She wondered if it would be permanent.

He nodded and the soft, sunny Elric returned for a fleeting moment. "Shall we?" He stood and straightened his clothes. There was a stiffness to his body now, as if the last remaining suppleness of youth had hardened.

Thali narrowed her eyes. She knew everyone grieved differently. She took his arm. Elric coughed before opening the doors and joining the others.

Dinner had been brought to them as usual. Instead of eating though, Thali's friends all stood and bowed, then took a knee. "Long live the king and queen," they said together. Then they rose as one. Would they do that every time she and Elric entered a room now? She certainly hoped not. Thali slid her gaze to Alexius and Mia. Mia looked concerned.

Thali let Elric go to the table first. She and the others put food on their plates, though they likely wouldn't eat much. "Is Elric all right?" Mia whispered. "I expected him to be a little more broken up," she said, eyeing him suspiciously.

"He's doing what he needs to." Thali plopped a few things on her plate as she murmured softly so only Mia could hear. Alexius could probably also hear them, but she didn't mind.

"I know he's probably been preparing for this, but ... does he seem different all of a sudden?" Mia asked.

Thali threw a worried glance in Elric's direction. "You're not wrong," she whispered before they strode apart to choose a seat.

The mantle of leadership weighs differently upon different people, Alexius whispered.

Do you think it's his way of dealing with grief? Or ...

Only time will tell, Alexius said.

Thali felt him watch Elric more carefully though as they sat and ate. As they were finishing, Sumac knocked, then entered.

"An audience with The Three has been granted," Sumac said. "I am to lead you to them as soon as you are ready."

They hurriedly tidied what was left of their meal. Thali wiped her mouth with the back of her sleeve before taking Elric's elbow and following Sumac, all her friends trailing behind. While they had been enjoyed the liberty of strolling through the city, they hadn't caught a single glimpse of The Three: the leaders of this place and the ones who had put them through the grueling challenges.

Sumac led them to the same room where they'd first met the three women. She bowed as she left them, and Thali was about to step forward, but Elric put a hand on hers and stepped forward first. The three women sat in their thrones watching closely. Thali could tell they must have been told what she wanted as their faces were stony, ready to deny them.

Elric approached their dais, and to Thali's surprise, he fell to his knees in front of them. "I come to you as a fellow leader. My kingdom has happened upon difficult times, and they are now in greater need of me more than ever before. I beg of you to let us leave. We will hold your secret at penalty of death. You have my word. But my kingdom needs its king." He looked up at them, exposing this throat.

The wise one raised an eyebrow, and the small one clasped her hands. The warrior tilted her head, looking curious.

The wise one pronounced her judgment solemnly. "You will leave immediately. And you will never speak of us. Is that understood? If word reaches us that others know of our world, or we suddenly have an influx of curious onlookers at our barrier, you will be to blame. And you will die—along with everyone you love. Do you understand?"

Elric nodded.

"We will return you to your lands via ship. And that will be all the help you receive from us, Your Majesty," the small one said.

Elric nodded mutely again.

"The others stay," the warrior said. Her gaze flicked over them as they stood there.

"What do you mean?" Thali asked.

"We have granted a king a return to his kingdom. But the rest of you must stay.

"But—" Elric said as he turned back to them.

"You alone can leave, or none," the warrior said.

Elric glanced at Thali, then back to the three women. Then he nodded.

Thali gulped. Why did it feel like a pit was swallowing her up? And why did she feel in her heart that Elric had just made the wrong choice?

Elric didn't meet her eyes as his shoulders squared, "I am grateful for your lenience."

CHAPTER TWENTY-SIX

I T HAD BEEN A silent walk back to their room. Elric would leave in an hour. Thali should be doing something, saying something, but right now, all she felt was ... what? Betrayed? Rejected? She slumped on the couch and watched as her friends disappeared into their rooms.

Elric came to sit on the low table, facing her. He took both her hands. "I had to. The kingdom needs me," he pleaded. Thali looked aside sharply, but Elric continued. "You'll find a way. I know you will. You and Alexius will no doubt burst out of here somehow. I know it. But I have to go. You leave me behind all the time. This is the same thing, and I know you'll follow. We'll just be apart for a little while. But there are things I have to go back and do. My parents always warned me that if something happened to them, there is a protocol I must follow—for the good of the people." Elric swallowed.

Thali only heard ringing in her ears. She knew what he said made sense, but she didn't feel like it did. She nodded mutely. Even if she didn't really agree, she knew Elric would fare better if he wasn't worried about her.

"The kingdom will fall to ruin if I don't go," Elric said.

To Thali's ears, it all sounded like excuses. Yes, he had been absent lately, and yes, the kingdom now lacked leadership. And yes, she was sure that she and Alexius could escape, but what about his citizens, the ones still here: Mia, Daylor, Tilton, Isaia, Nasir?

"I'll miss you every moment until you're back." Elric said. He wrapped his arms around her and kissed her forehead. He rose without another word and went to the door, putting his hand on the knob, looking pleadingly over his shoulder at Thali. Elric turned and opened the door, stopping for a few brief seconds to speak to Isaia. Then he was gone.

Thali sat in front of the hearth for the rest of that day. She felt like Elric had just walked out on her. She had always known he would choose his kingdom over her, but to feel it was harsher than she had expected.

"Hey," Mia said. She sat next to Thali, who looked up to see Daylor and Tilton sitting beside her too.

"Sorry, I—" Thali started to say until she looked up and realized she couldn't fool Mia.

"You might have to chop my head off for this, but Elric was a jerk. He shouldn't have left you behind, and you have every right to be upset," Mia said.

Thali smiled. "Thanks, but it was the right choice. I mean, Adanek truly is without a leader right now, so he needs to be there."

"You *both* need to be back."

Thali tilted her head. "Well, he more than me. Any power I have comes from him."

"Don't you have animal magic? Or did Elric gain that while I wasn't paying attention?" Daylor asked. It sounded more spiteful than anything she'd ever heard from him.

"It'll take you both to pull us—our world—out of this mess. I still say he should have fought for you to go with him," Mia said.

Tilton nodded his agreement. Daylor watched her, somber. It wasn't often Daylor wasn't ebullient.

Thali swallowed, then took a deep breath. She didn't want her friends to be so down. She would find a way to get them all home.

"You don't need to do that," Daylor said quietly.

Thali was about to paste on a smile and crack a joke, but she stuttered to a stop when Daylor put a hand on her arm, and she saw the sincerity in his eyes.

"We're here for you. We know we'll get home. Together. It's not your job alone. Not anymore. So we can take this moment to be sad," Daylor said.

Tilton reached over and squeezed Daylor's hand. Daylor scooted over and put an arm around Thali, and Mia did the same on her other side. Tilton leaned in too, and they sat squished together, staring at the hearth that wasn't really a hearth for a long, silent while.

Chapter Twenty-Seven
Elric

ELRIC FELT LIKE HE was walking away from his heart, but he had to get home. He sat, thinking, in his cabin on the ship they were sending him home in. It moved abnormally fast, and he wondered if porpoises were pulling the ship along. As they sailed, Elric recalled a conversation with his father when he was starting to learn what it meant to be king.

"Son, this next bit is unpleasant, but it's important," his father had said as he'd sat with Elric in his office. "One day, when we die—" At Elric's panicked look, he had added, "—hopefully we'll be very old. But it will happen, and when it does, you will be king."

Elric had only gulped.

"I know, it will be sad. But unfortunately, one price we pay as royalty is that the kingdom comes first. You will have little time to grieve. You must put it away and take your place. There are those at court who will try to take advantage if you do not step up quickly. They will claim you are weak or too young or too inexperienced. They will use any excuse they can to gain more power, more authority. You must step into your role smoothly and show them you are capable." His father had taken both his shoulders in his hands and looked him in the eye.

Then his father had dropped his hands and sat across from Elric. "I'm sorry you were born into this. But we make the most of what we have, and you have much to be grateful for. But this is one of the costs."

"What do I have to do?"

"You must call a meeting of the lords and make them swear fealty to you, ideally within a week of our passing. It's the best way to hold them accountable. A strong royal guard and military presence will also be useful, as would an audience of your people. The more witnesses you have present, the better." He'd waited for Elric's nod, then continued. "Then you must hold a coronation. If all is in turmoil, a small coronation in the hall with at least six nobles as witnesses is enough."

His father's eyes had softened then. "Even if you're young and don't know what to do, you must still hold regular council meetings. You must be at each of them. Listen to them talk; then choose your advisers. Choose only those you fully trust—or want to keep close. Some advisers might be mine, some may be different. You will get to shape this kingdom, my son."

Elric nodded. It had seemed unfathomable at the time to step into that role.

"If you are lucky enough to have a queen, let her help you. She will navigate court politics to your advantage, creating her own version of fealty swearing in more subtle forms," his father had also said.

Those words now felt like a knife twisting in his gut. He'd left Thali. He knew she would follow, but he knew Thali's weakest point was politics, especially at court. She wouldn't be much help, not as his father had outlined. He would have to sort it all out himself.

A knock on the door brought him back to the present.

"We've arrived, Your Majesty," the guard said.

That felt unusually fast, but he was appreciative of it. He followed the guard onto the deck and blinked when he saw the city of Lanchor before him. It looked exactly as it had when they'd left. They sailed into the dock, where twelve royal guards stood waiting for them.

As soon as they saw him, they lined up in formation, and someone shouted something to someone else who ran down the dock.

Elric hopped off the ship after a nod to the people who had brought him home. But when he turned around, they'd all disappeared. The ship had coasted away as if it was an unmanned ghost ship, no one at the helm.

The guards all sank to one knee and placed their hands to their chests. "Long live the king," they said in unison.

Elric swallowed. Part of him had hoped the information was wrong, that perhaps he would come home and would find his father having tea with his mother. But if this was how he was being greeted, then it was true: he was king now.

Elric nodded in acknowledgment and saw Amali and Derk among the guards. "What news have you?"

Derk looked away, but Amali stood, chin held high, "We are very sorry for your loss. King Devrain and Queen Adela were killed in an attack by wild beasts from above. A fight broke out between the beasts in the air, and they demolished the royal wing of the palace." Amali's face cracked then. "Your parents were found in their bed. The roof had caved in on them."

Elric clutched at his heart. His last words with his father had been hateful ones. And he hadn't been happy with his mother either.

"We lost twelve guards, but the lords have all started to gather in the palace. Your timing is welcome," Amali said. A glimmer in her eye said she had more to say but in private.

"Let's get going then," Elric said. His first priority was to show his face at the palace. Then he would learn the current state of things.

They strode to the end of the dock, where horses awaited them. Arabelle was amongst them, and Elric, a pang lancing his heart, took her reins. "Fly swiftly, sweet girl," he whispered as he waited for the others to mount. They rode out, racing as quickly as they could. Night was falling, but if they rode through the night, they would arrive at the palace by morning.

CHAPTER TWENTY-EIGHT
Thali

THALI AND HER SCHOOL friends had all fallen asleep in a pile, and someone had covered them in blankets. When Thali woke, she felt better. Shortly thereafter, Sumac knocked on the door. If she thought anything of their pile of blankets on the couch as she entered, she didn't say anything. "King Elric has arrived in Adanek. He was whisked away by his royal guards, and they rode inland." Sumac nodded, then left.

As she left, Thali glanced out the door and saw guards posted again. The women knew they would try to escape now and would watch them closely.

Breakfast arrived soon after, and Thali helped lay everything out.

Ready to discuss our options? Alexius asked.

What are the options? she asked as she handed out bowls of rice porridge.

I cannot leave through the barrier. Well, I could, but I gave them my word when they asked for a private audience with me that I wouldn't, so I can't escape that way.

Thali's heart fell. She'd been hoping he'd added a loophole.

Alexius continued. *So one option is to stay. If safety is our main concern, this is a safe place. They would shelter us.*

And the other option?

We go through the gate.

You mean the gate we don't want to open further?

Yes. We technically don't have to open it more, just slip through it.

I thought you said you suspected the gate opened into a dangerous world?

I did.

And you want to go there.

Not particularly, but I think it's our only option if the goal is to stop Rommy and save our world. The magic of these barriers is old. They will not let us cross again.

I got through once.

Yes, you got in. There's nothing in the magic that suggests you can't get in. But you definitely cannot get out.

I'd like to try.

Fine, Alexius huffed as he sat down with his breakfast. Thali knew he was exasperated with her, but she didn't care.

"Can you guys do your planning out loud?" Daylor asked as he sat down.

Thali looked up. Her friends were staring at her, making heat crawl up her neck. "Sorry," she muttered.

"I know we don't have magic, but we can help in other ways," Tilton said. He was always trying to smooth things over amongst the friends.

Thali wrapped them all—including Nasir and Isaia—in a magic bubble so they would not be overheard. Then she explained. "We can't go through the barrier to the rest of the world, but I'd like to try. Alexius says he can't break the barrier because of the oath he swore when he met with the three women privately. That doesn't mean I can't try. Alexius thinks the only way for us to get out is to go through the gate."

"The gate that we came here to check was closed?" Mia asked.

Thali nodded.

"The gate that's supposed to open to an even worse, more dangerous world than this one?" Tilton asked.

Thali and Alexius nodded.

"Wait. I thought only magic users could go?" Daylor said.

Thali looked at Alexius, but his words put her and the others at ease. "As long as you hold onto those of us that do, you can go too."

They sat back in their chairs as Nasir and Isaia joined them at the table. "We should go see that seal-creature before we go," Nasir said.

Thali thought that was a good idea. They might not be able to talk with it, but maybe they could discover a clue or learn something about the other world—if that's where they had to go. She had a sneaking suspicion they would have to despite her desire to try the barrier, but she wanted to know everything she could before dragging her magic-less friends there.

"There's something else you should know," Alexius said. They turned their attention to him again. "I know little of the world I suspect is on the other side of the gate. But there were rumors that it was also the location of an anarchist group, an ancient one. The same one who trapped Thali in her mind," Alexius said as he looked down.

She wondered what brought the pain that filled his expression as he said it.

There is something else you need to know. The one who trapped you, Xenon? Remember that he is blood-oathed and mated to Xerus? They parted poorly, but Xenon ranks highly in that group, I believe, but no one knows for sure. He and my brother met and fell in love many centuries ago. But Xenon's work now ... his beliefs ... it's why my brother still lives apart from his mate and partner despite Xenon being banished from Etciel hundreds of years ago. Xerus keeps him banished for my family. Alexius stared at his hands, unmoving.

Daylor narrowed his eyes, clearly suspecting some more mind talking, but didn't push it when Tilton put a hand on his arm. Tilton watched Alexius closely.

Thali nodded. The others didn't need to know her history with Xenon, so she kept it to herself. Instead, they huddled together, hatching plans to break through the barrier, and if that failed, to slip through the gate and hopefully go home.

CHAPTER TWENTY-NINE

T HE NEXT DAY, THALI explored. Sumac's guards tailed her, but that was all right. She and her group split up to look around some more, and they wound up back together for lunch. Afterward, they meandered to the surface outside the tower. As Thali stood on the sand looking out at the village, she realized it was quite drab. Compared to the wonders under the surface, the buildings on land were boring and plain.

"The buildings kind of look ... boring, don't they?" Mia said quietly.

"It's weird, isn't it? I thought they were marvelous when we arrived, but now, after seeing the world underneath, this is just ... plain," Thali said.

Mia nodded and took her arm as they strolled through the streets. "Do you have to be at the barrier's edge, or can you try from here?" she murmured.

"I think I can try from here," Thali replied.

Tilton, on her other side, said, "We'll create a distraction and guide you, so you can focus solely on the barrier." Tilton offered his arm too, so Thali took it.

Alexius, can they detect magic? Like if I use it to try and pierce the barrier?

Only The Three.

I'm going to try now.

All right, Alexius said patiently.

She was sometimes surprised he did not put up more of a fight when she wanted to try things herself.

"Oh, Thali, how ridiculous!" Mia said loudly.

"Yes, I can't believe you would believe such nonsense!" Tilton also raised his voice.

"Come on, let's go and see if we can change her mind," Daylor said, pushing them on.

Thali wasn't sure what they were up to, but she turned her focus inward. She wouldn't need to close her eyes, but she certainly needed to focus as much as she could. She fell into step with her friends, then grew a thread of her magic, reaching outward before she realized she should reach upward in case someone *could* see it. She didn't have to go very far up before she reached the barrier. It felt like her thread had hit a stone wall. She let her thread unravel and split into many, sliding them along the barrier looking for imperfections or holes.

Nothing. She continued with the thinnest thread she could imagine so it could pierce the barrier. If she could just get a foothold, she could widen it. If she could do this, then they need only follow through on their plan to escape.

But no matter how hard she looked or how long, no matter how thin or sharp her thread, she could not get the barrier to give.

Can I say I told you so yet?

No.

Thali tried again and again as they walked further. She sent her thread to the edges of the barrier, hoping there was somewhere she could pierce.

Nothing.

The sun sank lower and lower in the sky as she kept trying, and though her own stomach was growling, it was Daylor's howling stomach that ended her efforts.

Thali sank to the ground at the edge of their path. "I couldn't find anything," she said.

"At least you tried," Mia said. She kissed Thali's sweaty temple.

She was exhausted. Thali had not used that much magic for a long time, let alone so precisely and for so long. *I should practice more often*, she thought, thinking of Joren's subtlety. She wondered what he thought of them still not showing up. Her heart tugged when she wondered if Garen knew. He would probably find a way to bust them out if he knew, so Thali guessed he did not know. And Joren would not tell him. "Let's go back. We need to feed Daylor before his stomach consumes him," she said, offering a sad smile.

"You did great," Daylor said, giving her a side hug.

Her friends smiled and helped her up. They walked back to their room arm-in-arm; Daylor stayed at her side to support her. She didn't feel at risk of falling but maybe stumbling.

At the very least, you honed your skills today, Alexius said.

Thali was surprised no guards had interrupted her while she was making her attempts on their barrier. And when they returned to their rooms, she was even more surprised food had been laid out for them as usual. Daylor guided her to a chair before diving into the food. Mia brought her a plate.

She was hungrier than she had thought. She wolfed down her food as she looked at her friends gathered around her, eating and chatting. She smiled as Alexius came and sat on the arm of her chair. *I'm a lucky person to have such fantastic friends.*

Indeed. They remind me of my siblings.

I thought you didn't get along with your siblings.

Oh, we don't get along as well as you and your friends do, but we always came together, supported each other.

Do you miss them?

Every day.

I'm sorry.

Thank you.

Could we free them?

Perhaps.

Alexius didn't say any more.

Thali sighed and changed the subject. *So I guess we carry out the plan for the gate?* They would now have to go and do the one thing they shouldn't do. She wondered if they really could slip through without opening it.

We do. Tomorrow morning, we should visit the new creature.

Thali was too tired to respond, so she just nodded and listened to her friends discussing the customs they were learning here and basked in the calm of the moment.

CHAPTER THIRTY

T HALI WAS IMPRESSED THAT everyone was awake when she entered their common room early the next morning for training. It had been a while since she had challenged herself. She'd been so busy teaching Elric, she'd really only maintained her skills.

Alexius and Isaia came over and offered her a staff.

"Two against one?" Alexius asked, and Thali grinned. They moved all the furniture aside and started training. Nasir guided Mia, Tilton, and Daylor through some drills. Thali was surprised to see them move so fluidly, especially Mia, who knew the basics but hadn't had the same combat training as a seamstress at school as Daylor and Tilton had.

Isaia thwacked her shoulder, and Thali turned her attention back to the task at hand. Alexius and Isaia waited for her to warm up as she tested her staff, rotating it this way and that. She discovered that she quite liked this staff. When she was finally ready, she nodded to Alexius and Isaia. They started to dance around her, and Thali realized they must have coordinated this as they moved fluidly together on either side of her.

Thali grinned. She soon lost herself in a flurry of clacks as wood met wood and the *wooshing* of air as she slid and ducked and glided out of their way. Even without magic, this was her happy place.

They were all panting by the time they were done, and Thali looked up when she heard applause. Daylor, Tilton, Mia, Nasir, and Sumac all stood watching and clapping.

She bowed to them, not sure when Sumac had entered the room.

"Sifu Long has requested to meet with the new creature?" Sumac asked. They grabbed their breakfast and ate as they walked, following Sumac to the lower levels. Thali left her staff in their rooms and didn't even care that she was sweaty. When they arrived at the room with the water-filled column, Sumac stopped suddenly, and Thali looked up.

"Hello," the wise one said.

Thali bowed her head. Her friends followed suit.

"I'm sorry if we have disturbed you," Alexius said. He was surprisingly soft spoken.

The wise one glanced at Sumac, who nodded and left, closing the doors behind her. Thali stepped up to the glass just as Alexius did, and the wise one joined them. They stood watching the round column of water before them. They stood quietly and patiently, waiting for the creature to make an appearance.

The wise woman startled Thali when she suddenly spoke. "It is especially quiet after the evening meal," she said curiously. She paused, then sighed and said, "I have tried to tell my sisters that if we do not take part in progress, the world will leave us behind. Alas, they value our quiet way of life too much." She turned to Thali. "I will make sure tomorrow's supper is brought early as you requested." The wise one raised her chin and left the room.

The doors closed and Thali noticed there were no guards. "How did she know?" The wise one clearly knew their plan. There was no other way to describe what she had just said.

Alexius shrugged.

Finally, the seal-creature drifted over.

"Should I try to connect with it?" Thali asked.

"We know nothing of this creature. It's possible connecting with it will do you more harm than good," Alexius said.

"Or it gives us infinitely more knowledge," Thali countered.

"Why not ask her?" Tilton asked.

"What if … what if you offered to connect on this side of the glass? If they wanted to connect, they could, but you would each stay on either side of the glass," Alexius suggested. "Then you can pull away if you need to, and so can she."

Thali nodded. She sent her magic to the surface of the glass and split her threads, spreading them out like fingers opening and pressing on the glass. She kept them there, unmoving. It was an offer, not an intrusion. She waited a full minute before the dark shape neared and kelp—or strands that looked like kelp—spread and multiplied, much like her own threads, and lay flat along the glass.

Hello, the creature said.

Hello, Thali said. *My name is Thali.*

I am Sefarina.

It is lovely to meet you, Sefarina.

That is polite of you, Thali.

Which world do you come from?

I come from Kostiel in Korsel.

Can you tell us about Kostiel?

No, I cannot.

Why not?

We are bound by law not to reveal the secrets of our lands.

And who upholds the laws?

The Kelekona.

Can you tell us anything about the Kele … kona?

You have already met one.

How do you know?

The Kelekona have marked you. It is why I can speak with you.

Thali swallowed. She had allowed Alexius to see what she saw and hear what she heard, and now she wondered if it was time for her to have a talk with Alexius before they stepped into another world.

Is there anything you can *tell us about Kostiel?*

All I can say is be careful. Your companions' safety is not guaranteed, though the Kelekona do not like to kill unnecessarily.

Thank you. Can we help free you?

I can leave when I wish.

Thali bowed her head and turned to leave. The others followed, and she stayed silent until they reached their rooms, where she wrapped a protective bubble around them. "What do you know of the Kelekona?" Thali turned to Alexius.

Alexius's throat bobbed, but he didn't look completely surprised. "The Kelekona are the ancient society I have only heard rumors of."

"Why do you not seem surprised?"

"I—we—suspected Xenon was part of the Kelekona, remember?" Alexius replied.

"So it was the Kelekona who trapped me in my mind? Or was that Xenon on his own?"

"Every move is thoroughly calculated by the Kelekona."

"Why do they want me?"

"You'd have to ask them." Alexius looked like he was doing some mental calculations in his head.

The Kelekona had been the culprits trying to disable her, trap her in her own mind. They'd wanted to keep her locked away, to remove her as a player on the board. And now she was about to walk into their home territory. This suddenly seemed like a very bad idea. Thali sat down. "Does Xenon love Xerus?" Thali asked.

Alexius scrunched his brow, probably wondering why Thali would ask. But he nodded. "They are mates. They cannot help but love each other. It erodes each of them to be apart."

Thali thought about what it was to love. "So what if we approach Xenon with a trade. We help free Xerus and your family in return for their help?"

"That might work," Alexius said. He looked thoughtful.

"Why haven't we tried to free his family yet?" Mia asked. Her hands on her hips meant she was mad.

"It's all right. It's very complicated—" Alexius said. He looked a little stunned.

"No. It's not. Thali, we should have done that sooner, not this late in the game. Why didn't you mention this earlier?"

"I ... I'm not sure," Thali said. Maybe part of her still didn't truly believe her brother was holding Alexius's family hostage.

Xenon may not care enough to want Xerus freed. For that matter, he might just do it himself. I don't think you understand, Thali, just how lucky we got when we freed you. A moment of distraction let us slip out. But he's much more powerful than you and I combined. He has centuries on Xerus.

Does age strengthen magic?

Xenon is likely one of the most talented, clever beings in history.

So maybe it's a contingency plan. We sneak into Korsel, then hop over to Etciel and back to Adanek?

It depends which gate is closest when we get to Korsel.

Thali put her head in her hands and her elbows on the table. This was too much to think about. They would just have to worry about it when they got there.

"So our plan is to sneak in through this gate, find yet another gate to another world, then go through that gate and slip back into the human world?" Mia asked. "And that's the best-case scenario? We might have to find more gates in more worlds? Or bribe Xenon?"

Thali nodded.

"Maybe I should have stayed at the palace ..." Mia said.

Thali looked up. "You can stay here, deny you know anything of what we're doing."

"That's not what I was saying. It's just a lot. But I'm ready." Mia put on a brave face.

Thali swallowed. She really hoped they made it through.

If it makes you feel any better, humans are well below the Kelekona. They don't consider humans really worth their time—except you.

I don't know if that makes me feel better or worse.

CHAPTER THIRTY-ONE

THEIR SUPPER ARRIVED EARLY—AS promised. Thali had been a little suspicious of the wise one. Would she follow through? Had Thali truly heard her properly?

They ate in silence, then packed their things, only strapping on whatever they could carry beneath their clothes. They couldn't bring much if they were to look like they were just out for a stroll. They did manage to conceal some supplies in a bag hidden by Indi's belly fur though.

After a long, shared look, they left their rooms, three guards tailing them. Sumac was surprisingly not among them. They wandered into the city's center down the great spiral ramp, but when they were three floors down, they came upon a commotion. They couldn't see what had happened, but when additional guards ran by, their own guards looked back and forth between them and the direction their compatriots had run off in. "Stay here," one said and then they all took off.

Someone coughed behind a stack of bookshelves, and Thali turned to see a door pop open. *Follow me,* she told Alexius, then walked over to the door and through it. Apparently, they had more help than they'd realized. She strode down a dark hall until a dim light on the wall illuminated some stairs that descended into more darkness. Glancing behind her to see if her friends had indeed followed her, she nodded when she saw them, then hurried down the stairs. Partway down, she reached out with her thread, searching for the fastest route to the gate and was surprised to find they only had to keep descending the stairs. *Why did The Three take us on such a long, arduous route if there was an easier way to get to the gate?* Thali wondered, then realized perhaps they had wanted it to only *appear* it was difficult to get to, thus well protected. Thali shook off the thought. There was no time for speculation.

When she reached the bottom, she took a few steps only to find a wall. Her friends fanned out along the wall as they too reached the bottom of the stairs. Thali swallowed. Even in the dimness she could tell her friends looked nervous. As one though, they nodded. She pushed on the wall. It swung open like a door. She stopped on the threshold as her toe sank into the squishy ground. Thali used her magic to weave a solid surface for everyone to stand on. She took a few tentative steps, and when the magic carpet held and no one jumped out from the shadows, she strode to the monoliths. She looked around, surprised to see no one, no guards, no warrior sister. Then again, given the assistance they'd been given so far, maybe Thali should have expected a quiet escape.

Everyone gathered at the edge of a monolith.

"Are we sure?" Daylor asked. He looked ready to leap in but paused.

Thali looked back at the dark caves that awaited them. She nodded.

Mia took her hand, Tilton took Mia's, and Daylor took Tilton's. Thali reached for Nasir with her other hand and he to Isaia. Finally, Alexius stepped up and placed a hand on her shoulder. She felt a surge of magic from him and used it to push a thread into the opening of the gate. Then she pushed more threads in and widened them, opening a gap big enough for them all to walk through.

She went through first. The ground felt less like pudding this time, unlike her previous journeys to other worlds. It felt more like walking through milk. She felt a cool liquid wrap around her skin with each step but saw only fog as she moved.

Less than ten steps in, one foot landed on a hard surface again. She weaved threads of her magic in front of her like a shield, then wrapped it around them like a bubble as she stepped into the strange world. Who knew what they were stepping into?

Some of the fog had been trapped in their bubble as she'd weaved it and made it difficult to see, but Thali wasn't about to leave them unprotected. When everyone had finally stepped into the new world, Thali focused on trying to see their surroundings. It was bright on the other side of the fog. Thali poked a tiny hole in her bubble to let the moisture escape, then closed it back up.

"Squid turds," Thali said when she finally saw their surroundings clearly.

Chapter Thirty-Two

THALI GULPED AS HER friends formed a circle behind her and Alexius stepped in front of her.

Eight snake-like dragons surrounded them, two between each monolith, claws out. They didn't move as Thali examined them. Red, orange, yellow, they were all varying shades of those colors—except one. He stood right in front of Alexius. Thali shuddered, suddenly very happy that Alexius was shielding her from his line of sight. The dragon in front of Alexius was only as large as a person, but Xenon was seared in her mind's eye forever.

"Well, well, well. Now this is a lovely surprise," Xenon said.

She heard his voice with her ears, but it slid into her brain and made Thali freeze. When she'd been trapped in her head two years ago, this voice had been her captor, had taunted her, had shown her what real power and real magic was. She looked down at her trembling hands. Mia and Nasir squeezed her hands tighter.

"Xenon," Alexius said.

"Alexius," Xenon replied with mock seriousness. "Come, let us show you to your accommodations." He grinned, rather slyly Thali thought.

She didn't let go of her friends' hands as they were marched away from the monoliths, though she looked around for the first time since they'd arrived. Trees with skinny, stark-white trunks and black leaves surrounded them. The ground reminded her of ash as its grayness was soft and fine. It wasn't completely unpleasant.

As they walked, the dragons flanked them. The dragons marched in like-colored groups, and she wondered at their significance and why they were colored and the world was not.

"Not here," Alexius whispered. *No magic use.*

Thali was brought back to the time she had been so frustratingly imprisoned. Her world had felt much like this one looked: monochromatic.

Mia squeezed her hand, and Alexius reached back to take her other hand when Nasir let it go to rest his hands on his daggers. Alexius squeezed her hand quickly three times, reminding her of how she'd told him how Rommy used squeeze her hand three times to tell her it would be all right, to be a little more patient. Thali raised her chin a little higher as they continued through the forest, even though she felt like running back to the gate.

The trees ended abruptly then, and they stepped onto a field of white grass. Except it wasn't grass. It looked like feathers. Thali half expected her foot to sink into it as if they were walking on a living creature. But it was solid like earth and dirt beneath her feet. Strangely, the feather-grass had a stalk with thin filaments of white inside, just as feathers did.

Mia gasped and Thali's gaze shot up. They were headed toward a faded building, with many other similar buildings surrounding it. They all looked as if they'd once been black and red, but the color seemed to be leaking from them. Bleached-white splatters pocked the walls as if the monochromacity of this world was a disease.

They walked across the field of white feathers and up to the front of the large building. Was it a palace? Thali wasn't sure. The moment they stepped into the building though, she realized not everything in this world was black and white. Brightly-colored creatures wandered this way and that. Some were pastel colors, and some were bright neon, all colors she'd only seen in paintings and tapestries. The creatures streamed this way and that as Thali's group stopped on a landing overlooking the busy creatures below. Thali had half expected the place to be filled with miserable workers; instead, these creatures looked like they had purpose as they bustled about in a multitude of directions. The dragon escort hustled Thali's group along, and as they strode along beside the railing, only a few creatures spared them a glance. Then the group turned into a much quieter wing—right to the very end of the hallway. It was dark and far away from all the other doors they'd passed.

"Your accommodations," Xenon said. The dragons fanned out around a set of double doors, making Thali afraid of what they might find on the other side. But then Xenon opened the doors and walked in. To her surprise, the room was all gray, but beautifully so. Her group followed Xenon, and Thali saw a large common room filled with couches and adjoined by multiple rooms. The windows were the most impressive feature. The enormous, floor-to-ceiling windows allowed a view of the field they'd just walked through. It was like an awe-inspiring, black-and-white painting with the white sky in the background.

These were much nicer rooms than she'd even had when she'd gone to Alexius's world.

"I'm sure you'd like to rest, so I'll return for you in two hours' time." Xenon smiled again, a smile Thali did not trust. And then he was gone.

Alexius hurried to the doors and poked his head out, then back in. "Four guards."

Mia sat down on a couch and put her feet up. "I have to say, Thali, this is a lot nicer than I expected."

"Why were we so sure they would threaten our lives?" Daylor asked, sitting and crossing his ankles.

"It's *too* nice," Tilton said.

Thali agreed. They were probably being watched right now. Or maybe they'd be picked off one by one later. Xenon's voice had slid over her skin like grease, and she didn't think she'd ever be able to wash it off.

"Thali, what's wrong?" Mia asked.

Thali didn't want her friends to worry any more than they clearly already were. They were, after all, likely prisoners here. So she shook her head, pled exhaustion, and went to explore one of the rooms, half expecting it to dissolve in front of her eyes into a dungeon of cold stone. But the bed was fluffy and soft, and even her animals jumped up and surrounded her as she lay down. She was asleep before she knew it, only to wake up with a start.

She heard soft murmuring in the other room, so she went in search of a basin and water to wash up with, which she found in an adjoining bathing chamber. After a quick search of her chosen room, she found black-and-white clothes like what she normally wore and changed into them. Dressed then in clean white pants and a shirt with a black vest and her own black boots, she walked into the main room to see that everyone else had also freshened up. Alexius caught her eye and raised an eyebrow, and she nodded in response.

A soft knock sounded, and Xenon entered. This time, he was dressed almost like Xerus usually did with a long, black-tailed coat and a ruffled black shirt. "Hello again." He smiled yet again. It still made Thali's skin crawl.

"Hello!" Mia nearly sang out.

Thali turned to her. Why were her friends being so friendly to their captor?

"If you'll follow me, we have your dinner prepared, after which I thought we would chat about your journey," Xenon said.

Thali thought for sure they were walking to their deaths.

They walked back up the quiet hallway into a room that was also all gray and white and black. The food on the table offered splashes of color here at least. The food reminded her much of Etciel's: it was brightly colored, though the wrong color, and the shapes were similar to the food in her home world. Meat looked like meat, and vegetables looked like vegetables. They were just all wrong colors.

"Please, come and join us. Let us break bread together," Xenon said as he sat at the head of the table. It wasn't lost on Thali that four dragons remained on guard along the walls. Even Isaia and Nasir sat, though they sat at each end of their group. Creatures began to drift into the room, some sitting on stools, some floating in place. What surprised Thali the most though was how none paid them much attention, as if seeing humans was commonplace. Or perhaps seeing creatures of other kinds was commonplace. If Thali wasn't hypervigilant of Xenon, she would have thought this a lovely meeting of many cultures.

"Let us show our guests how to have a good time," Xenon said.

Thali turned to watch a purple hedgehog-type creature glance nervously down at his lap before taking some food and heaping it onto his plate.

As the dishes were passed, her companions helped themselves. Strangely, Xenon would receive his food last given where he sat. Thali still hadn't been courageous enough to meet his eyes though, and her hands were trembling again.

Thali was sure the food was poisoned. She glanced at Alexius, whose mouth was tight, but he had sat and put food on his plate just as the others had. Thali could feel her friends' eyes on her as they waited to see if she would eat.

Thali watched the other creatures dig into their food. A snake swallowed a pink egg whole, and a pastel-pink, antlered creature dropped grapes into their mouth. Thali swallowed, feeling Xenon's eyes on her. "Thank you," she whispered before taking a slice of meat with the utensils in front of her—sticks, just like she used at home—and putting it in her mouth. She chewed a few times and then swallowed, wondering if it would be her last bite. She could feel the blood draining from her face. When nothing happened, her friends all ate too. She was eternally grateful for the presence of her friends right now.

Laughter and chatter grew around them, and the group continued to eat, Thali only because her stomach told her it had been hours since they had last eaten.

Xenon preoccupied himself with the companions on his far side, not really turning his attention to Thali or her friends. Alexius, though, looked like he was doing what she was: waiting for the poison to take effect.

By the time small golden orbs were brought out, Thali was full. The orbs floated out and hovered above everyone's clean plate. Then before her eyes, they became smaller orbs. She watched as Xenon and everyone else opened their mouths; then she did the same. If they were going to die, they were going to die.

The first tiny orb floated into her mouth and melted. Wait, was that chocolate?

The creamy smoothness coated her mouth, and Thali's eyes grew wide as it slid down her throat. It was like she was drinking chocolate.

When it was gone, she opened her mouth again—as did the others—and again an orb floated into her mouth, coating it in sweet smoothness.

"This is the best thing I've ever put in my mouth," Daylor said.

CHAPTER THIRTY-THREE

THE NEXT DAY, THALI woke to find a piece of parchment floating above her. She plucked it down and saw a flourish of gold ink.

Join me for a tour of the gardens?

–Xenon

Thali's palms moistened. The last thing she wanted was to be alone with him.

You won't be alone. I'll be with you, Alexius said.

Thali nodded. Xenon was immensely more powerful than Alexius, but knowing Alexius was joining them made her feel better. She could feel Xenon's power now, and it made her feel like a seashell meeting a wave. Even now she trembled to think of how she had been trapped in her own mind.

Thali went out to the main room, where she absentmindedly stuffed a pastry in her mouth as a soft knock sounded. Nasir opened it, and Xenon stood there in all his argent glory. She blinked as she felt his wave of magic dwarf hers.

"Shall we?" Xenon asked, gesturing at the door.

Thali glanced back to her friends sitting on the couch. They just watched, dumbfounded. They hadn't been addressed from the moment they had arrived in this world. Now, it was like they were simply part of the room.

"I'll see you later," Thali said. Everyone nodded at her. Even Indi and Ana sunk into Mia's and Daylor's arms as Thali left. Nasir, Isaia, and Alexius, though, followed her out of the room as she followed Xenon down the pristine hall. It was all harsh white and black, yet as her feet landed on the ground, the floor felt softer than she had expected—or remembered.

"What do you know of Korsel?" Xenon asked as he walked. He sometimes nodded at those he passed or smiled and said a few quiet words before continuing.

Thali turned to look out the windows as they strode along. The view was magnificent. Swirls of grays and whites and blacks danced across the sky. "Not much," she finally replied.

Xenon nodded as they continued walking. "Korsel is a world of opposites."

Thali nodded.

"You know, you are a key player in the events about to unfold, and I could help you."

"What if I don't want your help?"

"What would you rather have?"

"Anything else." Thali knew she was being rude, but she couldn't help it. The memory of being trapped for no reason with no reprieve was still fresh in her mind.

"I see," said Xenon the man, who just seconds ago had been a dragon. He looked over at her and examined her closely. "I entrapped you because I thought that would lead us to the future, that you were the player holding us back," he said.

"And now?"

"Now, I think you're a major player in what is about to happen, and I'd rather have your ear than your hatred," Xenon said.

"What if that ship has sailed?" Thali asked.

"I have lived long enough to know that nothing is ever permanent. There will be a way to win your trust, whether you know it right now or not," Xenon said. He was just so calm, it put her off kilter.

Thali didn't know what else to say. Her nerves were fried from being hyperalert, ready for anything. She'd relaxed when he'd said he didn't want to harm her, but at the same time, she still didn't—couldn't—trust him. "What does your association do, exactly?"

"We work toward peace. Or at least, peace as we see it. Peace for all creatures."

"Then why come after me?"

"Because you broke the peace, and we thought you were a threat to the peace."

"Not on purpose."

"But you were able to, and doing so ignorantly made you even more dangerous."

"And now?"

"You know enough that not only are you no longer ignorant and dangerous, but an ally—in my mind."

"Why didn't you just teach me back then instead of trapping me in my own mind?"

"We couldn't get close enough. Remember the orange dragon that came to your home, and the green dragon that came to the palace?"

"The ones that tried to kidnap me?"

"They were supposed to bring you here so you *could* learn."

"Why didn't Alexius want them near us?"

"Alexius, as you know, was under orders, some of which were to protect you from others who might take you away."

"My brother," Thali whispered.

"He does not know of our group's existence. But he does know there are other dragons. I mean, Alexius's family is not the only dragon family in existence. And he did not know what those visiting dragons' purpose was."

Thali remembered then that Alexius had kept that secret from her—until he'd been forced to perform a blood oath to her to rescue her from her mind. But Xenon had put her there. "Did you orchestrate my ... isolation, so Alexius would be free of Rommy's control?" Thali asked.

Xenon turned to look at her, then turned back, grinning. "I'm not sure I'd call Alexius free."

"Is there a way to release Alexius from his blood oath?" Thali asked. She hadn't had much time to think about it, but it hurt her heart to think that Alexius, an immortal dragon, had tied his life to her mortal one. Even if she managed to somehow live until old age, Alexius could still live much, much longer.

"There is not," Xenon said. His pressed his lips together, and Thali thought perhaps he spoke from experience.

They walked on, and Thali was surprised to discover she felt more at ease as they did. "Why did you and the royal dragon family, Alexius's family, butt heads?" she asked. She figured she would be dead if Xenon wanted that anyway, so why not be brave?

"We do not always agree on the best course of action," Xenon said plainly.

She supposed she'd experienced that firsthand as she thought back to how she and Elric had been effectively exiled from Adanek. "What is it you want from me?" she finally asked as their building came back in view. What was it anyway? Was it a castle? A palace? A complex?

"Now that you're here, we would like to include you in our plans." Xenon said.

Thali nodded but bit her tongue. She wanted to ask what would happen if she disagreed with them, but she didn't want to put that thought in his head at the moment. Then she glanced back at Alexius. He had surely heard everything. She wondered if they could find a safe place to talk alone while they were here since they shouldn't use magic.

She also wondered if Xenon would let them go home. They were supposed to have used the gate to get home to Adanek via Korsel and Etciel. Would he help her if she asked to go home?

Xenon walked her back to her rooms, where she sat down amongst her friends and Tilton pressed a cup of something warm into her hands. They didn't ask anything of her, just continued their chatter, giving Thali the time she needed to think. She supposed there was no way around it; she had to see what Xenon wanted to do and what he would do for her friends before they could decide their next step. She turned to Alexius, wishing terribly that they could communicate in their minds. He was watching her carefully though, as if waiting for her.

As she looked at him, she felt him wrap magic around their group, a considerable layer.

It's safe now.

I've missed your advice.

You've had a lot to think about.

Will Xenon let us walk away?

I don't know. Depends on what he wants from you and how important it is.

You're sure he wants something from me?

He wouldn't be treating you so kindly otherwise.

What do I do?

Only you can decide that. Though it wouldn't hurt to hear what he has to say. At the very least, he might reveal what they have planned or what they want.

What do you *want, Alexius?*

I'm not sure. But you should think about what you want your world to look like.

What do you mean?

Three gates are open, though one only slightly. The last might soon be. It might not be realistic to sequester the magical animals again.

Thali didn't have anything to say to that. One world combined. Would humans be able to visit Korsel? Etciel? Or could only magical animals come and go? Would they pillage her world's towns? Thali felt the magic around them release. Alexius had let go of the bubble.

"Perhaps we should go into town tonight?" Alexius asked.

"Are we allowed?" Mia asked.

"There's only one way to find out," Alexius said, and Daylor and Tilton leapt up. They opened the main door for Thali, who encountered four dragons: two yellow and two orange. They turned to look at her.

"Can we go out into the city?" she asked.

"Our instructions are only to follow you," one orange dragon said.

Thali nodded. "Let's go then." She led the way down the hall to the entrance.

Xenon stood there, waiting for them. "It would be my honor to act as your guide," he said. Then he bowed. Thali was surprised he didn't have more pressing things to do but accepted nonetheless. She didn't think they were really in a position to refuse.

They walked out then, the stark white and black of their surroundings still a bit of a shock, especially the independently moving carriages rolling by.

"Why is everything but the dragons and food black and white?" Thali asked.

"Humans cannot see the colors in which Korsel is adorned without a creature's permission and assistance. The world looks black and white to you, but to us, it does not. I allow you to see the color of the food, and the creatures give you permission to see them, with my assistance. They do so like to show off."

Thali wanted to jump into Alexius's mind to see what it looked like to him but remembered that every communication could be monitored.

This is innocent enough, Alexius said.

But then Xenon said, "If you'll allow me, I could show you."

They looked at the buildings surrounding them. From the top of the exterior stairs, they could see the town below. The buildings may have been all black or white, but they came in many shapes and sizes: round, square, small, large. It was one of the most beautiful mixes she'd ever seen, even in black and white.

Mia joined Thali and Xenon. "I would like to see it."

Xenon turned and stared at her as if she was an ant that had just crawled onto his dinner plate. But his look was gone a moment later, and he nodded. Mia gasped as she glanced around.

Thali let Alexius through their thread as she saw the town before her come to life. Glints of gold and silver adorned some milky pearl buildings; others were of soft, pastel blues, purples, or pinks, and some were of bolder reds, blues, and greens. It was like a rainbow but in tones and shades, even textures.

"Shall we?" Xenon asked. He held an arm out for Thali, so Mia stepped back as Thali stepped forward. "You may feel a bit unsteady for a moment," Xenon said.

Suddenly, they were in town. She turned and saw Tilton holding onto Daylor while Alexius held onto both Mia and Daylor as Nasir and Isaia held onto Mia. Alexius looked a little miffed.

"Magic is useful to get places quickly," Xenon said. Thali wanted to ask more about how and what he had done with magic but she held her tongue. There would be time for that later. They were now in a town of black and white, and while it was prettier than most—light glowed here and there, adding gray to the mix—but nothing quite compared to how the dragons saw it. Thankfully, Xenon colored the world. Thali swallowed down her anxiety.

"There's a market down the street here. It's a wonderful place to taste the local delicacies," Xenon added.

Thali loved markets, so she calmed her breathing as she realized she would get to see another market in another world. She wondered if Etciel had markets.

They rounded a corner and found stalls lined up and down the street. It wasn't nearly as neat and tidy as some she'd seen, but there were vendors of all kinds here. And it was busy. What surprised Thali the most was all the different creatures. There were bipedal ones, some with flames for hair and some with water, ice sculptures, or greenery-like bonsai trees for hair. There were also floating creatures, small balls of pastel light, and dogs or cats made of elements. One cat creature even looked more like a floating tablecloth with a fiery nose. Then there were large creatures, ones that had to squeeze through the rows yet never disturbed anything. Some walked slowly, some glided, and some even hopped from one spot to the next. Still other creatures had legs that seemed to move backward even as they moved forward, and others had legs that moved straight up and down as they walked.

Surprisingly, no one turned to stare at them. Thali swallowed. It was overwhelming. Her friends too were all wide-eyed as they took in the market.

"Come, let us wander," Xenon said as he started to lead Thali down an aisle. While Thali and her friends did not seem to garner much attention, Xenon sure did.

"Leader," an elephant with many arms tipped their head—or was it a hat?—at Xenon as he passed.

"Leader," said a ball of light as it passed them the other way. Every creature they passed said the same.

Thali forced herself to turn her attention away from the creatures and to the tables and the wares being sold. She really didn't have a clue what she was seeing though. Some things she recognized as plates and bowls, perhaps even weapons, but for the most part, the objects were foreign. There were fire and water disks, spinning air, and rocks that looked like grills. Little pieces of what Thali assumed were meats and vegetables on sticks were cooking or sitting in ice or salt.

And there were so many shapes: round, flat things; lumpy, rounded things; and boxy, bumpy shapes. Thali didn't even know where to start.

"Is that abondi?" Alexius asked, stepping next to Thali.

Xenon nodded. "Please help yourself." The vendor—a cloud-shaped something—took several of what looked like clouds on sticks and handed them to Alexius, who gave one to Thali and the rest to each of their friends. The vendor bowed their top half when Xenon offered them what Thali assumed was coins. The vendor took only half the coins offered.

Interesting, she thought.

Thali bit into the cloud on the stick and was surprised to be met with a jelly texture as she bit down. And it was salty, but smooth like gravy.

The best way she could describe it was to call it gravy gelatin, even though her eyes told her the consistency should feel like meat.

They continued down the line, Xenon sometimes stopping here or there to buy food for them to try; other times, Alexius stopped. Dragons could definitely outeat humans.

Eventually, Thali was stuffed beyond measure. Though her stomach was full, her tastebuds were confused and overwhelmed. What they saw with their eyes did not match what they tasted, and though Thali found it exciting, it was also confusing.

Alexius handed her something that looked like a small squid, squished flat, from ... an ice grill? He grinned as he handed it to her and watched as she and the others ate it.

Thali bit into it, expecting something squishy or bouncy, but found instead that it was sweet and liquidy. She bit off another piece, and it melted in her mouth as if she'd taken a drink. It coated her mouth in sweet freshness.

"What do you taste?" Alexius asked. He glanced at Xenon, who grinned in return. It always surprised her when they were friendly to each other.

"Strawberries. But very sweet, like they're coated in sugar."

"Is that your favorite food?" Alexius asked.

Thali nodded.

Thali turned to Daylor, whose favorite food was meat of any sort. "I taste beef. It's not quite texturally right, but it tastes like the best, fattiest cut of beef you can find."

"I taste peaches," Mia said.

"I'm tasting a plum cake," Tilton added.

Thali turned to Alexius. "What do you taste?"

Alexius grinned, showing his pointy canines. "I taste fresh appleberries."

Thali turned to Xenon, who grinned again. "Jasmine flowers from the high mountains."

Thali was about to ask if he meant the ones in her world because she knew of mountainous jasmine, but a gong sounded just then.

Xenon looked up at a tower that glowed with lights. Suddenly, it popped and its lights darkened to gray. "We should get going," he said.

Alexius swallowed as if he'd heard something unpleasant, then he nodded. Many market vendors swiftly packed up as Xenon led the group into a clearing. He looked around, and in a blink, Thali was standing on the front steps of their building again.

"What was that, the gong and the light change?" Thali asked.

"It tells us it's the time of the carnivores," Xenon explained.

"What does that mean?" Daylor asked.

"That is when the largest of creatures, the predators, are welcome to roam the city, those who eat others. We have all kinds of creatures here, but killing within city walls is not permitted. Therefore, we separate the predators and the prey to keep the peace within our town. Outside these walls is a different story. Any creatures in the streets are fair game during carnivore hours, so we would have begun to see some gruesome sights," Xenon said.

"But I thought you said there is no killing allowed within city walls?" Mia asked.

"They capture their prey and bring them home, or even just outside city walls," Xenon explained. The main doors opened, and he guided them back inside. He escorted them back to their rooms with a warning. "There is only one place where the predators are not allowed to set foot, and that is here. You should not wander beyond these walls in the middle of the night. Carnivore hours end at dawn."

Everyone nodded vigorously, including Thali, as they gladly entered their rooms.

Chapter Thirty-Four

THALI WOKE UP NOT wanting to wake up. Sleep had been hard to come by. Even though they had been told they were safe inside, Thali had heard and felt the large, hungry animals that had prowled around outside, and she'd shuddered to think of what each sound meant.

She stumbled into the common area still half asleep and saw that the others looked like they must have had a similar night. They were all a little bleary-eyed, not fully awake either.

Only Isaia was bright and cheerful—well, cheerful for Isaia.

"He slept like a log." Nasir, looking only slightly less tired than she, waved a hand at him. Hopefully every night wouldn't be like that or this place would exhaust them.

There was a knock on the door, and Xenon waltzed in. The urge to flee whenever he showed up was lessening, but the instinct still made her very much awake.

Behind him followed a few trays of food that he ushered in. Alexius approached the food first, following his nose as the trays floated to the table.

"Breakfast! And then I shall show you a most fascinating place," Xenon said.

Alexius got a plate and dug in. He also grabbed a glass of green liquid.

Thali raised her eyebrows.

"You'll enjoy this," Alexius said as he pressed the green juice into her hands.

She sniffed it, then sipped. She had expected it to taste like grass or plants; instead, it tasted like warm honey and coconut.

"It's five times stronger than coffee," Alexius said.

Thali looked down at the glass, wondering at how it could feel cool in her hand but warm in her body. She nodded and drained the glass. She reached for a second one, only to have Alexius block her hand and shake his head. "Wait ten minutes first."

Thali raised an eyebrow. Her instinct was grab one to spite his warning, but she reminded herself that she was in a foreign land. Instead, she chose a pastry.

When she and the others had finished the foods they'd chosen, Xenon waved his hand, and the trays floated back out the door. Then he nodded, so they all rose and followed him down some hallways and outside. This time, they didn't *poof* to a new place but walked to another building. This one reminded her of a bunker. It was low and squat and had few windows. What windows there were sat high above the ground, higher than a tall human.

"Welcome to the registrar," Xenon said. He walked in and nodded at the two red dragons standing at the door. The dragons eyed the group closely as they walked in.

As Thali followed, she looked up to see a dragon statue standing on a square base. Within that square base was an everchanging number.

543, 544, 542 ...

"What is this place?" Thali asked.

"This is where we keep a record of all the creatures that have come to this world and all the creatures currently here," Xenon said.

Thali gulped. That meant there were over five hundred dragons in this world right now. That seemed ... overwhelming. Beside the dragon form was a griffon. "Are these ... stuffed?"

"They are magical representations," Xenon said. He waved his hand through the griffon's face, and it wafted like smoke before reforming itself.

Thali recognized some of the creatures, like a hornsnoad with its beautiful, feathery, blue wings. The sight of it made her heart sink as she remembered the ones in Alexius's world that had committed suicide after she had infiltrated their minds. The hornsnoad's base before her now said 87.

She saw a caladrius too. It looked almost exactly like the silky white chicken that had taken up residence in Densria. Its number read 0. When she came to another recognizable winged creature, she quickly looked away, though she hastened her pace when she saw the number 2 below it. Thali continued down the aisle to the far back corner, where she saw a naked human with the number 7 below it. She gulped. They were completely alone here.

As she continued to walk down the aisles, she saw creatures she'd seen at the market the previous day and marveled at their impressive detailing. Just as she was thinking she could get lost in the rows and rows of creatures, she heard Alexius and Xenon speaking softly.

"Why are you stalling?" Alexius asked.

"I'm not stalling. How dare you, brother? I'm simply sharing things of interest. She is interested, no? It's worthwhile for her to learn of all the creatures here," Xenon said smoothly.

Thali rounded the corner and confronted Xenon. "He's right, Xenon. Why are you stalling? Why keep us here? Our intention is to go through this world's gate to Etciel, then back home to Adanek. We must get moving."

"Is this not educational? Is it not fascinating? Are you not learning valuable information?"

"I am," Thali said. "But that's not the point."

"I am bringing you to the council meeting tomorrow. I thought it important for you to learn of some of the representatives." Xenon held his chin high.

"And the next day, you will lead us to the gate to Etciel?" Thali pressed.

"We will see," Xenon replied.

"That's not an answer," Alexius said.

"You'll want to wait until after our meeting before deciding your next step," Xenon said.

Thali narrowed her eyes. "We want to get home. We need to get home."

"And perhaps you will," was all Xenon said before walking away. Thali gritted her teeth.

When they returned from the registrar's, Thali spent the rest of the day pacing. She told the others about her conversation with Xenon, and they were all trying to stay calm. The truth of it was they were at Xenon's mercy. If he didn't want to show them how to get to the gate, then they would never get there—and never get home.

Mia took Thali's elbow and guided her through the building to a courtyard out back. Creatures of all kinds roamed the path, and Thali let Mia link arms as they walked. The space was grand and reminded Thali of Cerisa's training rings—if they were gardens.

"You know, this place isn't so bad," Mia said.

"It's lovely, I know, and we're being treated well," Thali replied. It was true. She'd been through harder, more trying times in worse places.

She wasn't a fan of political battles and strategies, but at least they could live comfortably, unlike in physical battles and war.

"Thali, as a kid, I remember seeing ants cross my path and wondering how it was that they didn't know about the larger world around them. They were so small, even carrying a tiny piece of melon was a gargantuan effort for them. Here, we might be those ants, but this world seems to at least respect their ants."

"What are you saying, Mia?"

"I'm wondering if it would be so bad if we just stayed here. We have food, we have shelter, and we can live productive, meaningful lives here. I saw a seamstress shop when we went to the market the other day. I'm sure we could all find things to do with our lives. We could live happily here."

"You want to stay?" Thali turned and stopped, surprised that Mia had said that.

"I'm only saying we *could* stay. There's a difference, Thali. We're dealing with dragons, creatures so ancient they probably formed the world. Even I can tell they're well organized and incredibly powerful. We might not have the option to leave if they do not wish it."

"I'll find a way to get us home." Thali squeezed her friend's hands.

"Are you so sure we'll have a home to go back to?" Mia asked, swallowing nervously.

Thali's brow wrinkled in confusion.

"The king and queen are dead. The palace is partly in ruins. What if the entire city is in ruins by the time we get there? What if it's just a fight for survival now? We could live civilized lives here," Mia explained.

"What about Aron? What about Elric?" Thali asked.

"I love Aron, but what I want might not match what these dragons want. I know we escaped from that island, but those folks were human—and we had help. Here, I saw an elephant with eight arms and watched a flying cloud cook food. I'm just saying I think we might have to consider making do with the cards we've been dealt." Mia squeezed Thali's hands back. It brought tears to Thali's eyes to think that her best friend was giving up. "I'm not saying I don't want to go home. But I've talked to the others. We recognize that we might not have a choice. We don't want you to do something reckless to try and get us home because this place ... well, it's not so bad." Mia shrugged.

"I ... I can't even absorb what you're saying right now." Thali turned and continued walking. Mia followed. As Thali looked around the courtyard, she realized if they stayed here, they'd rarely see color again.

The friends had done two full laps before Thali was ready to say anything again. "Thank you for offering me this possibility. But I will get us home," she said.

Mia nodded. "Please, promise me you won't do something stupid. We're literally amongst ancient dragons. I heard someone say that Xenon has been the leader here a millenia. Thali, *a millenia*!"

Thali nodded. Mia was partially right. Even though Thali could feel the ancient power rolling off Xenon, he seemed much more respected than he let on. She wondered if he was trying to trick her again. If he wanted to, he could trap her in her mind again, and if Alexius was trapped with her because they were oathed, she would never escape.

A shadow from above crossed their path, then Thali heard a *swoosh*, both behind and before them. Xenon landed softly in front of them in his dragon form. He was glorious. Argent scales covered his slender snake-like body, and gold ran down his back, accenting his facial features. Thali had seen the dragon paintings in Cerisa but seeing one in person was a completely different experience. He switched to his human form and offered Thali an arm. "If you'll follow me, I'll take you to the meeting this morning," Xenon said.

Thali knew the *swoosh* behind them had been Alexius, so she turned around. Isaia and Nasir were following at a distance.

"I will take Miss Mia back to our rooms," Nasir said.

Thali nodded.

Xenon continued through the garden toward another wing, Isaia and Alexius following closely.

Thali asked, "Is this a palace? Or a castle? Or a—"

"Building. Just a building. We call it Union. It is a neutral place where all are welcome to enter and find safety and shelter."

It wasn't lost on Thali that the dragons guarding this area of the building were darker. They were almost maroon red, like blood. She wished she could ask Alexius whether dragons changed colors as they got older or became more skilled, but now wasn't the time. They walked up to a large set of doors. Xenon had outstretched his arms to open them when Alexius stopped them.

"Wait," he said. He placed a hand on Thali's shoulder, and she felt her simple clothes start to change.

"Mia's request," Alexius said.

Thali looked down. She wore a floor-length gray dress that tapered as it neared her feet and had a wide cape and a tight bodice, tighter than anything she'd worn in a long time. Capped shoulders topped sleeves that draped down her arms.

Alexius sent an image down her thread, and Thali saw what it looked like to him. She was a vision in gold and red, purples and blues, pearls dotting the front and sides. Thali saw them as little white beads, but her monochromatic view didn't do the dress justice. "Mia is amazing," Thali said.

Alexius nodded. Even Xenon did. Then he raised an eyebrow and pushed the doors open.

The interior was underwhelming. It looked like any meeting room in Adanek's palace. The only difference was that instead of a large table in the middle that everyone sat around, each creature sat at their own table of a style and height that accommodated their form. There were about thirty creatures present, with some large elephantine creatures on one end and a glowing pink ball hovering on the other.

Everyone turned when Xenon entered. "Good morning. Shall we get started?"

Thali heard only clicks and high-pitched sounds at that, but when she sat in the chair Xenon gestured at, the clicks and sounds suddenly became words. She shifted to cross her legs, and again all she heard was clicks and snaps. But then she put both feet flat on the floor, and the sounds once again became words.

"Please introduce your companion," a high-pitched, soft voice said.

"Of course. This is Queen Routhalia of Adanek, Lady of Densria, Baroness of Bulstan, and Princess of the Western Thieves. She comes from the human world, and I have invited her to join us this morning so she may learn and witness, perhaps even participate," Xenon said. He looked around the room. "Are there any who object to her presence?"

The elephantine creature waved its trunk. Water circled and slid up and down in front of its face. "What is the point of her being here? There are not enough humans in this world to back her as a representative."

"Ah, thank you very much for reminding me, George," Xenon said.

Thali wanted to laugh at the very ordinary name of this very extraordinary creature in this very strange place.

"She's also the strongest magic user to appear in the last three centuries," Xenon said.

Thali's eyes widened as she turned to Xenon. She had not thought she was that powerful, and she wondered who the last magic user to be that powerful was. The elephant's feet burst into flames though, so Thali bit her tongue.

"You mean to tell me she is the one they speak of in the prophecy of the worlds coming together?" George looked at her, examining her closely. His lower half was blazing while his upper half seemed to be turning into water.

"She is indeed," Xenon said.

George was quiet. Thali hoped she had passed his inspection. The whole room stilled as they waited for him to decide his next course of action.

But just as suddenly as he had become both fire and water, he became a leathery elephant again. "Welcome then," George said.

Thali looked around the room. The creatures nodded one by one as she took each in, noting trunks, legs, tentacles, soft bodies, stoney bodies, and even some that seemed to constantly shed dirt. Of the thirty creatures she counted in this space, all had hints of at least two elements within them, whether of water, fire, earth, or air. This could be a very dangerous meeting indeed.

CHAPTER THIRTY-FIVE

T HE MEETING HAD BEGUN in exciting fashion, but as meetings always do, it devolved into much disagreement and debate, even over minor, boring details. Thali was exhausted by the time she returned to her rooms with only Isaia. Xenon had wanted a word with Alexius. She had hoped the meeting would end with them being sent home, but she was still no closer to getting them all back to Adanek.

Thali went to retrieve her bag. She hadn't brought much with her, but she always kept a small bag of possessions with her. She slid a vial out of one of the small pockets she'd had secretly sewn into the lining. One could have felt it had they touched the pocket, but no one had. She slipped it out and into her sleeve. Foxall had been wary when she had asked for it, but he'd given it to her nonetheless. She asked Bardo for his help, and he wrapped himself around the vial and her wrist at the same time.

Thali entered the main room again, and Mia hushed everyone.

"Tilton, can I ask you something about how the palace was run?" Thali asked. He nodded, and they moved off to the side while everyone else chattered and filled their plates. There, Thali held her hand out, and Tilton, as respectable and polite as he was, took it. She got Bardo to slip the vial into Tilton's. His eyebrows raised as he took it from her, then he glanced around and back at the vial. His eyes widened a fraction when he took in the milky-white substance he'd seen once before.

"If anything should go wrong," Thali said.

"Are you sure?" Tilton asked.

"I think it may be our only way out."

"Do you think he would?"

"I think if we need to, he will. He's our best chance," Thali replied.

Tilton nodded. He tied a string around his neck, then around the vial, and tucked it under his shirt.

Mutely, they rejoined the others.

Chapter Thirty-Six

T HALI STARTLED WHEN SOMEONE knocked on the door. Her friends were all out in the garden. Though they'd dropped their guard, Thali wasn't one to forget and forgive quite so quickly.

"Good afternoon," Xenon said, entering the room.

"How are you?" Thali asked.

"Well, thank you. Would you come with me to the main hall?"

Thali nodded and followed him. They strode down the hall, the tension in Thali's chest easing when they entered a busy wing. Then they ducked into a side door, and Thali blinked to adjust to the dark lighting.

She gulped. Suddenly, the door behind her closed with a thud, heavy footsteps telling her guards had arrived. Thali didn't turn to look. The sight before her held her attention.

Alexius was strung up—in an orb of swirling gray tendrils.

"What did you do to him?" Thali asked as she looked around for Xenon. Panic made her heart start to race.

"I've been thinking all this time about how to ensure your cooperation." Xenon smiled as he sat on a throne.

Thali ran up to the orb. Alexius's eyes were closed, and a fist tightened on her heart.

"Don't worry, he's not dead. I don't want you dead, after all," Xenon said.

"What did you do to him?" Thali asked again. In her mind, she gripped her threads, ready to do whatever she had to. But wait—when had her connection to Alexius changed? Now it was a milky void.

Xenon waggled one finger at her. "Uh uh. None of that. No touching your magic." He drew a slow line through the air with one sharp claw.

Alexius screamed as a large slice started to appear across his torso. Thali felt the ghost of it in her own flesh and clenched her teeth to keep from screaming.

Feeling it slice her flesh while feeling Alexius's pain was doubly hard. She looked down at her own chest, but no bloom of red spread over her clothes. She felt his pain but didn't suffer the same physical damage. Thali stuffed her threads back into her mind.

Alexius's skin knit back together, but he didn't look up, though she wished he would.

"What do you want from me?" Thali asked.

"I'm not sure yet. But I had to make sure I could get it when I am," Xenon said.

Thali walked up to him, whispering menacingly, "That is your mate's brother."

"In case you haven't heard, my mate and I aren't currently speaking," he whispered as menacingly as she had. "For now, if you would be so kind as to put these on and step onto that box there." He held two golden cuffs and pointed at a small cube that was maybe a foot tall.

"What does it do?" Thali asked.

"Well, these ..." he pointed to the cuffs, "... are to entrap you and keep you and your magic all in one tidy little space. "And that ..." he pointed to the cube, "... is a surprise."

"Why? Why are you doing this?"

"Well, I lied, you see. We're not ready for the worlds to change, to merge, and that's what you're here to do, no? Change the world?" Xenon asked.

"I don't want to change things either! I just want to get home," Thali said.

"But going home would mean facing the events there, and that has a nasty habit of snowballing into much larger issues. Your getting involved would undoubtably start a chain reaction through all the other worlds. So, we're just going to push pause on it," Xenon said.

"You can't outrun what's already happening," Thali said.

Xenon raised his eyebrows and looked at the cuffs. "Shall I bring your friends in? Or would you like another demonstration with Alexius?"

Thali clenched her teeth and went to put the cuffs on. They were like giant bangles. But the moment she slid them over her hands, they shrank to capture her wrists. They didn't squeeze, but she could feel her well of magic dry up. It left her feeling empty.

"Now the box," Xenon ordered.

Thali stepped onto the box. Like a curtain flying up from the floor, she was immediately surrounded by black. It was like when she'd been trapped in her mind, but now she saw nothing but black. She could still feel though, which she was thankful for when two hands took hers. Her first instinct was to release the dagger at her elbow, but it wasn't there.

"It's me," Alexius said.

"Alexius?" Thali asked. She'd thought he was trapped in that hovering bubble.

"You stepping on the box released me from my confinement, but I have the same cuffs as you do," he said.

He led her forward, but Thali was hesitant. She couldn't see anything. She felt like she would step out into the abyss.

"I've got you," Alexius said. He took one forearm and put an arm around her shoulders.

"Oh, this is taking forever," Xenon said.

Thali suddenly felt the world slide out from beneath her.

The emptiness and the sudden movement she couldn't see made her stomach flip, and she doubled over and emptied the contents of her stomach onto what may have been the floor. She heard it land but couldn't see it.

"Sit down," Xenon said.

And then she was sitting.

"I still don't understand what it is you want." Thali wiped her mouth with her sleeve.

"I want you under my control, that's all."

"I'm useless to you like this," Thali retorted.

"Not at all. It will be quite useful to have a queen from another world sitting next to me on my throne. Your support is very much appreciated."

Thali could feel the grin on his face.

"Tell me, do you miss your sweet husband?" Xenon suddenly asked.

Thali paused; she didn't want Elric involved in this at all, not even his name.

"I'll take that as a yes," Xenon said

Without knowing how, Thali was back at the palace. Or more specifically, she was walking through the palace. She looked to her left and saw Avery handing her some papers.

"You know what? I think we should get the other one involved too," Xenon said.

Thali watched the scene as she sat down at a desk and started to read document after document. But then she heard the clink of ale mugs and distinct chatter. She focused on what she heard and swallowed as she recognized where she was and who she was listening in on.

"Boss, Ella wants to see ya before the night's out," Fletcher said in her left ear. Thali heard Garen take a deep breath in and out. But when she looked down, she saw Elric's hands bring papers into view.

"Sure can be disorienting to watch someone's life and listen to an-other's, don't you think?" Xenon asked. She heard both him and the hubbub in the tavern at home as Garen looked around.

Alexius squeezed her hands, but she didn't have the coordination to squeeze him back. "This is cruel," he said.

"Cruel?" Xenon began. "Do you know what's cruel? Killing an entire family of hornsnoads, or creating a creature that has nothing to eat, so they starve," Xenon said.

Thali shrunk into herself as much as she could. She hadn't meant to do those things.

"Queen Routhalia has committed enough crimes to be held prisoner according to the laws of this world," Xenon said.

Thali's heart sank. Then she was walking, or it looked like she was walking, down the hall into a meeting room. Around her were the lords of the court. The moment she walked into the room—or Elric did—they started to yell at him. But she couldn't hear their voices. What she *could* hear was Garen's world.

"Boss, there's been an attack on the next town over. They wanna know if they can bring their wounded here, if we can help." Ilya's voice was gentle and soft in her ear, and Thali wanted to know what was happening.

"We'll set it up. Let Foxall know," Garen said. Just hearing his voice soothed her. But more people wanted his attention, with more reports of folks injured or market prices soaring.

Her vision swam then, and she realized she was crying. King Devrain and Queen Adela were laid out on gold-gilded tombs before her, and Thali's heart broke not to be there with Elric. She wanted to hold him, hug him, at least tell him that she was bearing witness to this with him. He just stared at his parents silently.

"Boss, there's trouble at the brothel again," Fletch said. Then Thali heard running. She heard opening doors and climbing and hard breathing as Garen ran to the brothel to handle yet another emergency.

"Sleep." Alexius's voice broke through.

The sights, the sounds, melted away. Thali found herself on a ship, in the crow's nest, wearing what she always wore when she was sailing. Then she turned around and saw Alexius standing there. He wore something shimmery, like silver silk.

"Are we dead?" Thali asked.

He shook his head, and the corners of his lips turned up. "Xenon has left the room, for the day, he says. With him gone, I can hold us in this place so you can have a reprieve."

Thali threw her arms around Alexius and leaned into him. "Thank you." Then she started to cry, and uncontrollable sobs racked her body. Alexius held her shoulders and squeezed her tight. He didn't say anything, and she knew he wasn't about to lie to her. That meant he didn't know if they would be all right. They'd walked into the dragon's playground, and they'd been ensnared.

Thali didn't even know if it was safe enough to tell Alexius of the contingency plan she'd put in place. All she could do was hope Tilton would recognize that it was time to act and that her brother would still be able to see.

She didn't know, though, if she had the luxury of waiting for Tilton to discover it was time. Would Xenon just kill her? Would he kill her friends? Thali took a few breaths to calm herself. "Mia will know. She'll know something isn't right, and she'll demand to see me," Thali whispered. Alexius and Thali sat on the floor of the crow's nest now, and they leaned on the mast in the middle. "Is this of your making? Not that I'm ungrateful, but I think I'd rather sit somewhere less cramped."

He huffed a laugh and then they were on a ship's bow.

"You picked this for me?" Thali asked.

He nodded.

"Alexius, I'm sorry your life is tied to mine. If there was a way for me to undo it, I would."

"I made the choice willingly. It's not your fault."

"Even if we get out of this, I won't live forever, and I can't even imagine how much more you could achieve if you could live on." Thali looked out and saw water and blue skies above them. Alexius was good at helping her feel calm.

"Can I be completely honest with you?" he asked as he looked up.

Thali nodded. "Always."

"My sister and my mate are both dead. I know there are some that abhor the idea of dying, and don't get me wrong, I'm not exactly about to just end myself. But knowing I can go when you go, when you're old and gray, brings me peace. I'll see my sister again, my love too."

"Do you believe as some do that they're watching over us?"

"I know it. Every time I feel a breeze on my cheek or a warmth on my shoulder, I know Brixelle is with me."

Thali nodded.

"Stay strong, Thali. Xenon returns," Alexius said.

Thali scrunched her eyes shut tightly. She saw Elric's desk, laden with papers and documents, and Ban, the stupid oaf, walking into Elric's office.

Thali clenched her teeth so hard she thought her jaw might lock. Ban's lips moved and Elric nodded. And then Elric must have spoken because Ban nodded. After Elric gave one curt nod, Ban left. Elric sat back for a moment as if in thought before being interrupted. Avery walked into the room and placed more papers on the desk. Elric's gaze went to his arm. Avery had rested her hand there, making jealousy rage in Thali. Elric moved his arm abruptly and took the papers away, then said something to Avery. She turned mutely and left the room.

Garen must have been asleep because she could only hear the muffled sounds of the tavern, the soft squeak of a mattress, and the rustle of fabric. Suddenly, a thought struck fear through Thali: she prayed he would not be intimate with someone while she was listening.

The shift of the mattress was suddenly very loud, and Garen gasped. "Thali?" he asked. Of course no one replied. "I must be imagining things again," he said before she heard him rub his head and the scruff of his beard.

Then came a knock on the door.

"Come in," he said, sounding very tired.

"Boss, the apothecary's lookin' to talk to ya," Fletch said.

"I'll be down in a minute," Garen said.

Silence fell, but Thali smiled a little to know that Fletch was still more silent than a shadow.

"Thali, I know it's silly for me to talk to you as if you're here. But at this point, it doesn't matter anymore. You're more imagination than real to me now anyway, but I wish you were here. The animals all seem so sad lately, and the world seems to be falling apart. Word even has it that Elric's facing a battle with the lords questioning his leadership and readiness to take the throne. I know you never wanted to be royal, but I also know you'd be good at it."

All Thali heard after that was the scrape of him putting his boots on and then walking quietly into the tavern. Elric was in another meeting, and it was getting so hard for her to hear one set of people and see another set, especially when those she could see kept moving so ... well, almost violently, waving their arms around and pacing.

"And how is our queen doing?" Xenon asked. His voice cut through everything else.

Thali could only guess that her face must be knotted in a painful grimace as she tried to think amongst the sounds and sights assaulting her.

"Funny thing, isn't it, to be with but not be with your loved ones?" Xenon suddenly pulled Elric and Garen away. Thali blinked, suddenly finding herself back in the room where she'd stepped onto the box and put on the cuffs. Alexius was next to her. They were both suspended in the air, in a sphere of some kind.

Xenon tilted his head. "So, how was it?"

Thali swallowed. She wanted to burst into tears. She'd never felt more on the brink of losing herself. But she swallowed again and looked Xenon right in the eye. "You've had your fun, Xenon. Now where are my friends?"

"They're safe. Don't you worry. I'm not a total monster. It would be beyond cruel to get such measly creatures involved." Xenon cast his gaze around the room as if he was ensuring that they were indeed alone. "In fact, why don't I bring them here?" He smiled. "They have, after all, been asking for you."

Xenon didn't leave the room, but somehow, just minutes later, the doors opened and another Xenon walked in. When he stepped aside, he disappeared in a puff of smoke, revealing Mia, Tilton, Daylor, Nasir, Isaia, Indi, Ana, and Bardo.

Their shocked faces told them how she must appear. Though it was only yesterday that she'd seen them, it felt like weeks. At the thought of time, it occurred to her that time might not move in this world like it did in hers. Her heart sank at how long Elric might have to wait for her.

Her friends rushed over, but they hit an invisible barrier and a dome formed around them.

"We might as well keep your friends here with you since you're so worried about them," Xenon said.

Thali felt awful. Had she not demanded to see her friends, they wouldn't be trapped in a magic dome now.

"Thali, this is not your fault!" Mia shouted. She hammered on the side of it despite Daylor trying to calm her. Tilton slipped in behind him, as did Nasir. Isaia stood behind them, observing the dome itself.

"Oops, I almost forgot," Xenon said on his way out of the room. "Can't leave you without all your friends, now can I?"

And then the voices came back, the visuals too. Elric must have fallen asleep because all Thali saw was dim light through his eyelids. She wondered if he'd fallen asleep at his desk, if he was visiting his dead parents, or if he'd made it to their bed before falling asleep.

Garen was outside. She heard the wind whistling and wondered if he was traveling or standing on a rooftop.

"Oh, since you're handling those two so well, why not add a third?" Xenon snarled.

Then Thali felt like she was walking, wearing boots and something with sleeves that were soft and silky on her skin. The body had a long stride and stood tall, shoulders back. Thali swallowed, knowing exactly whose skin she was in.

Though she couldn't physically move, she felt like she was now. Being caught between three people in three different places was more than difficult; it was impossible. She couldn't keep it all straight. Rommy paced a lot, Garen mostly sought out quiet places unless he was meeting with his crew, and Elric alternated between scrawling on paper, reading documents, and attending meetings. Thali watched and read the papers that crossed his desk. He was certainly efficient in his work, and she could see that he was between a rock and a hard place as he looked for allies and sought to solve issues.

At one point, Elric pulled a piece of parchment out, the first line making Thali home in on the words:

> *My dearest Thali,*
> *I continue to miss you dearly. I regret every day not having waited for you, having bargained for you to return with me, or having stayed with you. Though I can say that while my heart yearns for you, I am at least making progress here.*
>
> *My parents left me a bit of a mess. I understand that most of us do not have the luxury of knowing when we will die, but there is a box whose location is only ever known by the king and queen. It contains the rules, protocols, and tools for ascension. Unfortunately, my parents did not tell me its location before I left, and I cannot find it. It has caused many headaches as the lords think this is a sign that I should not lead, that my parents, because they sent us away, did not want us to lead. Therefore, they are fighting me.*
>
> *I know not where to send this, so it will never be sent. But I do enjoy these few minutes of writing to you as if you're away on a trip. I hope you will forgive me when you return. I can't even imagine what you must be facing, but I hope every day to see your beautiful face walk through the door, to hear the horns herald your arrival. I hope you return to a peaceful kingdom. That is my only motivation now: to do what I can to make sure that*

when you return, this whole thing is over and we can
rule together in peace.
Your loving husband

Something must have startled Elric because he looked up suddenly. Avery stood there, blushing. It made Thali's skin crawl to see her standing there. But all she did was hand Elric some papers and his schedule for the day. As Thali tried to peer at the papers, her attention was jolted in a new direction. She was moving in Rommy's body, entering a warm room, and sitting at a table holding something smooth, cold, and glassy.

Then came the sounds from Garen's world. The wind had stopped, and he was now in a tavern room. The sounds were muffled and quiet enough that she heard the soft footfalls and gentle creak of someone stepping on a floorboard and someone else sitting on a straw-filled cushion.

"We haven't found any trace of her, boss." Sesda's voice floated into her ears. Thali was surprised to hear sorrow lace his words. She wanted so badly to see his face. Was he truly sad, or was it an act? Sesda had never liked her, and she'd never liked him.

"Been scouring the libraries. There ain't much about the other worlds. Apparently, hundreds of years ago, one of the kings destroyed all the books from earlier times. There's nothing much older than a couple hundred years in there." Thali heard Fletch shift in his seat, and she tried to shut everything else out. What were they looking for?

"Why are you all so useless?!" Garen suddenly shouted. Then something smashed.

Thali, her real self, took a breath. She'd never heard Garen angry.

Someone took two steps toward her, and she heard the slap of a hand on leather as she heard it land on Garen's shoulder. "She'll be back, boss. I know she will. She's just out of reach right now is all."

Thali heard Garen's deep breaths. "I don't know how to help her," he said softly.

"When we do, we'll do it. You know we all will as soon as we know how," Ilya said.

A door opened and Thali heard a woman's lighter footfalls. "Why are we smashing things now?" Ella asked, the swish of her skirts coming closer.

No one answered.

"Well, I have some information," Ella said. The room filled with silent tension.

Thali focused hard on what she was hearing, blocking out the meeting Elric was at and the way her hands felt like they were gripping something hard and cold.

"Sailor came in saying he'd seen one of the fancy merchant ships—Thali's from what he described—in port in Cerisa again. They'd just arrived and were on their way back to Densria," Ella said.

"Was she ...?"

"No. They said it was a skeleton crew. Didn't say much to anyone, just stopped in, grabbed their supplies, and headed out. No royal guards."

"Rat turds," Ilya said.

"What do you think it means that they came back without her?" Fletch asked.

"I imagine it means they don't think she needs the ride back," Ella said.

"We know all this already." Garen sounded calmer than before at least.

"Her crew is family. They would not have left her in peril—unless they were unable to assist her." Ella sounded like she was spelling it out for them.

"So you're saying she's either fine or she's in danger. How precise."

"I'm saying if we can't find her and her crew returned without her, she's not in our world."

"You think she's with her brother again?" Thali heard Garen's jaw clack shut.

"If she is, there's a reason. She's seen his true colors. My guess is there's something she needs to do in the other world."

"Ming said he'd sent her to what he thought was another gate to another world. Joren was waiting nearby and got the message to her. I mean, that's why Elric is back. But why didn't she come with him?" Garen's words slowly became a whisper. Thali wondered why he was saying anything out loud at all. He was normally an inside-his-head thinker.

"Maybe she's stuck somewhere, like a hostage," Fletch said.

"But why let Elric go and not her?" Ilya asked.

Thali heard the scratch of fabric as Garen crossed his arms. "If Joren got the message to her, then they likely let the king go but not the queen. One was deemed necessary for peace, not the other."

"Patriarchies," Ella scoffed.

"So you think she's trying to get home? That maybe she had to use that gate Ming sent her to?" Ilya summarized.

Thali wanted to shout, "Yes!" so badly. It was torture hearing but not participating.

After a pause, she heard a shuffle. "You all right, boss?" Sesda asked.

"Leave me a minute," Garen said. Thali heard shuffling feet and assumed Garen's captains had left the room.

"Thali?" he said out loud after a few quiet moments. "Why do I feel like you're with me, but not completely? I felt the swell of pride in my chest just now, but it felt like your pride. You're truly with me somehow, aren't you? You were always terrible at reading lips, so you can't see through my eyes, but perhaps you can hear our conversation?"

Thali wanted so badly to respond. She *was* filled with pride that Garen had figured it out. She was also sad that she couldn't respond and didn't know what it meant that he'd been able to detect her. But she knew in her heart he would know.

"Thali, if you can hear me, then you need to know that Elric isn't doing well. His health is fine, but the lords are converging against him. He's overwhelmed, and because they can't complete some ritual—because he can't find some stupid box—the lords don't believe he should be the next king. They haven't named an alternate successor, but they want to. You can feel it in the city. The tension is turning to fear and anger."

She was being pulled away; she was pacing again. Elric was angrily waving his arms to catch the crowd's attention and trying to shout over them.

Shock jolted her as Rommy took a startled step back. But he recovered quickly.

Thali was losing herself in the different places. Garen had re-entered the busy tavern so voices were everywhere, Elric was standing before angry lords, and Rommy was overwhelmed with strong emotions if his racing heart was any indication.

She was ready to burst or to completely lose herself. She was over-loaded between what she was seeing, hearing, and feeling. Suddenly, a wave hit her, pushing her into silent blackness for a heartbeat.

Chapter Thirty-Seven

THEN THALI WAS BACK on a ship's bow with Alexius. She leaned over the railing, heaving, though nothing came out because everything was in her mind.

Alexius had his hand on her shoulder. "It's a lot to manage," he said.

"I learned some important things though," Thali said.

"I heard it too."

"You mean you can hear, see, and feel what I do?"

Alexius nodded. "I always knew Garen was a smart one and wondered if he had some magic that was just masked."

"You think Garen has magic?"

"Maybe. Or he's just completely in tune with you."

Thali swallowed. She didn't want to think about Garen any more than she had to because it might break her heart again. "Has Xenon left?"

"He has. But the others have been watching you."

"I have to apologize to them. I never wanted them to see this, to see me like this."

"But they did, and they're all still fine," Alexius said.

Thali's shoulders drooped. He was right.

"You've put something very interesting into play here," Alexius said.

"I only hope we'll survive it, that it somehow gets us home," Thali added.

"You did the best you could with what you had available. We'll make it through."

In a blink, Thali was no longer on the ship. Xenon had snapped her out of the other bodies, so she looked around the big room. Her friends sat in their glass dome, Isaia with his eyes closed as if he was meditating.

Thali looked down to see that her hands were bleeding. She'd scratched herself, and her hair was wild, pieces of it strewn all over the orb. Mia caught her eye, but Thali saw only sadness there. Daylor and Tilton were asleep, head on each other's shoulders, as they sat.

Nasir was the first to look at the door when it suddenly burst open.

"Xenon, you've gone too far." Xerus angrily strode in. It was the first time she'd ever heard Xerus raise his voice.

"Xer?" Xenon stood straighter, looking stunned until Xerus marched over to him. Xenon placed a claw delicately on the side of Xerus's face, looking into his eyes, then down his body. Thali recognized it as a mate checking to see if the other mate was harmed in any way.

"Xenon, you need to release them," Xerus said, quietly this time.

Xenon waved his hand in an arc behind him, and Thali fell to the ground with Alexius. The dome disappeared too, and her friends ran over and huddled with Thali.

"Don't move," Xenon ordered.

Thali was not stupid; the two most powerful dragons she'd ever known were in the room, and Xerus's next move might possibly end her or her friends' lives.

"What are you doing here?" Xenon asked.

"I've come to collect my family," Xerus said. "How could you have trapped my little brother like that?"

Xenon shrugged. "I was bored. Or maybe I wanted to see what they were made of. Besides, I have to keep her out of things until I can use her."

"Xe." Xerus put his hand on Xenon's cheek. Their nostrils flared as they breathed each other in and glowed. Thali looked away, recognizing the private moment for what it was.

Many, many long moments later, Xenon finally asked, "What will you do if I say no?"

"Come, let us dine together. Then we shall talk," Xerus said. He glanced at Alexius as he turned Xenon around.

Thali was surprised to see Xenon turn and let Xerus lead him out of the room. Though a dome reappeared around them all, at least they were together this time.

"Do you think he'll really let us go?" Daylor asked.

"I think we'll be out by tomorrow," Alexius said. His forehead wrinkled, and Thali wondered what his brother had communicated to him. She knew from experience the secret language siblings had. Alexius had obviously gotten something from his brother.

So they all sat there, knowing there was nothing they could do. Eventually, dinner was brought, but when her stomach growled, Thali realized that her ability to see with Elric's eyes, hear with Garen's ears, and feel her brother's body was gone. She was relieved, but she missed them. She sat with Alexius and her friends quietly, trying to collect her thoughts.

Servants slid trays to them, making Thali wonder how it was decided what could go in and out of the dome.

"Anything can come in. It's going out that's the issue," Alexius explained.

Chapter Thirty-Eight

T HALI FELL INTO A fitful sleep, visions of Elric defending her, Garen asking her to hang on, and Rommy tracing the word *coming* on her arm spinning in her mind. When she woke, she sat up quickly, tossing a bunch of cloaks and shirts from her lap, along with an irate snake who bounced off Daylor's shoulder and into his hands. Ana and Indi had tucked themselves along her sides.

She blinked, slowing her heart as she looked at her friends. They had all stripped down to underclothes. Thali looked down to discover it was their clothing that had been covering her.

"You were shivering all night," Tilton said as he offered her a drink of water.

Alexius and Daylor had their heads together, so Thali looked around the larger room. It was empty but for them. "Have they been back?" she asked.

Mia shook her head. She was mending something. How she had a needle and thread in this situation was beyond Thali. It made her realize she was wearing Mia's long-sleeved shirt. Mia's arms were longer than hers, so the sleeves had been folded back.

"Thanks for keeping me warm," Thali said as she sheepishly handed each item back to its owner. They didn't really answer her. That was odd.

Before she could open her mouth to say more, Thali felt a quick yank. She blinked and found herself in a garden. She spun around and discovered she was adjacent to the courtyard garden. It was bright out, and it took her a few seconds to adjust to the light. When she did, she saw Xerus and Xenon sitting at a small table, breakfast upon it.

"Come, join us," Xenon said. He pushed a chair back with a foot, and Thali glanced at Xerus, who seemed determined not to look at her.

Thali took a deep breath; she could do this. She sat gingerly across from the dragons as Xenon poured her a cup of something hot and slid some pastries to her. She knew her hair was a mess, and she had her own blood under her fingernails. Plus she was probably completely streaked with dirt. But that was the least of her worries. She also knew she was an ant amongst elephants without her magic.

Xerus wanted me to tell you to use him.

Alexius's voice in her mind made her shoulders relax. Then she had a thought. She kept her eyes down and hands in her lap. Slowly, she took her cup and drank the hot liquid. It tasted like bitter tea. She put the cup down and her hands back beneath the tablecloth and brushed her wrist with her thumb. "I can help you," Thali said as she sat straight up and glanced at Xerus.

Xerus stood. "I'm going to check on my brother." He stalked off.

"How long have you worked with the association?" Thali asked.

"More centuries than you know, why?" Xenon crossed one leg over the other as he sat back and looked at her.

She kept her timid posture: shoulders forward, head bowed, hands clasped under the table. Thali mustered all the strength she could and squared her shoulders. "I have a proposition that would be mutually beneficial for us, as individuals."

"I'm listening," Xenon said. His eyes wandered to where Xerus had just walked away, and Thali smiled. This could work.

CHAPTER THIRTY-NINE

THALI AND XENON WERE walking through a tall hedge maze, planning. She had swallowed her terror and stilled her buckling knees to focus on what needed to be done, and Xenon had been curious enough to listen. They turned a corner, and Thali looked up to see her brother and Xerus walking toward them. Xerus stared at Xenon, and it seemed to unbalance the ancient dragon. He stopped a step earlier than Thali. She wasn't sure if she was more relieved or worried to see her brother.

"Hello, Xenon, sister," Rommy said.

"What are you doing here?" Xenon asked. He tore his eyes away from Xerus and looked at Rommy. He appeared remarkably calm for someone who had just been caught by surprise.

"I'm rescuing my baby sister." Rommy's eyebrows shot up in a silent dare.

"And what makes you think she needs to be rescued?" Xenon asked. Thali wondered if her brother knew how dangerous Xenon really was.

"Oh, she doesn't have to be in trouble for a brother to want to step in to help, as I'm sure you've experienced," Rommy said sweetly.

"Please, stay and share a meal. Then you may take your sister home," Xenon offered.

Thali gulped, hoping Xenon wouldn't go back on the bargain she'd struck with him.

"That would be lovely," Rommy said.

That surprised Thali. Rommy and Xenon were being so cordial and polite, she wanted to scream just to bring the false pretense to an end. Xerus put a hand on her shoulder, though he still hadn't said anything to her. Nor did he even look at her, making her wonder what she had done to offend him so deeply.

"Come, Romulus, I believe we have much to discuss, leader to leader." Xenon put his own hand on Rommy's shoulders, and they continued to walk. Xerus trailed them, and Thali had no option but to follow silently. Rommy looked over his shoulder at them but continued his conversation with Xenon.

Their walk ended with Thali being led to a bathing room to change for dinner. She was clean and freshly dressed now as she was guided to the throne room, where a dining table and chairs were set up along one end.

Thali's gaze slid to Xerus. He didn't look at her, and she still wasn't sure she could trust him. But what option did she have at this point?

Xenon had his arms crossed and was still talking with her brother as she walked into the room. She watched a moment as Xenon's finger turned into a sharp claw and sliced a hole in the armpit of his own coat. He continued talking with Rommy as if nothing had happened.

"Brother," Thali said, and she went to Rommy, who narrowed his eyes just a millimeter. She circled her arms around his neck to embrace him. At the same time, Indi rubbed up against their sides as if she had also missed him. Ana did the same on their other side. Bardo slid out of Thali's sleeve as she rested her hand on her brother's chest next to the oyster shell he still wore around his neck. It was as if she were holding him still while she leaned back to look at him. She smiled at him, making sure not to look at her hand. "I've missed you, brother."

"Why did you leave so abruptly before? Because you missed your dear husband so much?" Rommy asked.

Thali nodded. "You know me so well."

Rommy's smile told her he believed her, that she had reassured him they were a team.

During their exchange, Bardo had bitten the string, wrapped his mouth around the oyster shell, and carefully slid back into her sleeve.

"Shall we sit?" Thali asked as she turned to Xenon.

"Of course, please, queens first," Xenon said as he offered her his arm. Rommy tucked one of Thali's arms into his elbow as she took Xenon's with the other. Beneath her shirt, Bardo slid across her back and through her other sleeve to Xenon's. Then the snake crawled up between Xenon's shirt and coat and down to an inner pocket as Thali watched through her mind's eye. Bardo dropped the oyster shell in, then zipped back to Thali.

It was a huge risk. But if there was one soul who would want to free Xerus, it was his mate, Xenon. And it was helpful that Xenon was likely the only one who had the magic to do so. Xenon let go of her arm as Rommy pulled out her chair for her. She sat. Bardo slithered out of her sleeve beneath the table, then down her leg and back up inside her dress, tucking himself into a pouch she'd secured to her thigh.

She looked up and was pleased to see her friends all here occupying one side of the table. Her gaze caught two familiar faces she hadn't seen in some time. Thali wondered when Jaxon and Aexie had joined them.

Thali was on pins and needles the entire dinner and had a difficult time focusing on eating. She hoped Rommy wasn't picking up on it. During the second course, she saw Xenon reach into the pocket Bardo had placed the oyster shell in; she tried hard not to look at him after that. Instead, she turned her attention to her brother, who was always the clever, quiet center of attention, and he liked it that way. Only once did Thali risk a glance at Xerus, Jaxon, and Aexie; they were unusually calm and still. She glanced then at Alexius next to her. He was watching his siblings.

Thali felt the moment the dragons were released. It felt like taut strings being cut.

She surreptitiously watched the dragons before finally dragging her gaze back to her brother as he regaled everyone with a story about discovering a creature for the first time.

Did it work? Thali asked Alexius as Bardo slid from his pouch and down her leg.

Yes.

But why has nothing changed? They're still sitting there.

Everything's changed.

She realized her mistake even as she did it. Thali touched the oyster shell that hung around her own neck. She often did that to comfort herself. But her brother's gaze caught it, and he reached up to do the same. His eyes narrowed then, and he patted his entire torso frantically.

Thali felt Bardo slither back up her leg. He dropped something into her hand under the table. She swallowed, forcing a grin as she looked at Rommy. "Brother, you've gotten slow." She dangled the oyster necklace from her hands.

Panic flew through her brother's eyes, but he masked it with a grin. "And, sister, you've improved your sleight of hand." Rommy stood and snatched the oyster from her. He tied it back around his neck and tucked it under his shirt, patting it.

Thali held her breath. She hoped her brother believed her, believed she was just playing little sister. If he suspected she had helped free the dragons from his control ...

"This little thing is no more than a trifle anyway. You should learn to steal something more valuable," Rommy said.

Thali's eyes narrowed. Did that mean he had figured her out? She couldn't tell.

"Even if you should break the bond I created with the dragons, I still hold the ultimate control over them," Rommy warned as he sat back.

Thali gulped. So he did know.

Rommy took out a second chain, one that was much longer than the one holding his oyster shell. Thali hadn't known it was even there.

On it dangled a large sapphire the size of her fist. Inside—she had to focus to see it—was a small blue dragon.

"Papa," Aexie whispered.

Now Thali realized where their father was. All this time, her brother had trapped the dragons' father, the king of dragons, in a gem. So she had failed. The dragons may not have a magic tether controlling them anymore, but Rommy had their father. Nothing had changed.

"Thank you for your hospitality, Xenon. I look forward to our future cooperation, but I think we've had enough visiting for now. We should be leaving," Rommy said, glancing at Xerus.

Xerus closed his eyes and rose, following him mechanically. A magical doorway opened next to Thali's brother then, and Jaxon and Aexie stood and headed for it.

"Come, sister, I believe you and I have some things to discuss," Rommy said. He dangled the gem one last time before stuffing it back under his shirt.

Thali was confused. Why would she go back with him?

Rommy raised an eyebrow. Then he took a pin from his pocket and stabbed it into the gem. Alexius and his siblings all gasped as their hands flew to their left shoulders. Rommy raised an eyebrow in challenge. "As I said, there are things we must discuss. It's time to go." He held his hand out to her.

Thali felt Alexius's pain in her own left shoulder, so she stood up stiffly and followed Rommy. Indi and Ana were right there with her.

To her surprise—though she knew she shouldn't be—her friends followed with Alexius.

"You won't need them," Rommy said, glancing at them.

"Please, brother, let them come with us," Thali said. "I missed them too much last time." She tried to infuse as much pleading as a little sister could.

After many moments, he finally nodded.

Aexie walked through the portal first, followed by Jaxon. As Thali took her brother's hand, she sent her friends and animals through. Only then did she walk through herself. She looked over her shoulder at Xenon. But he only had eyes for Xerus as he held the portal open. Thali extended her hand to Xerus. It took him a breath or two to break eye contact with Xenon, but he took Thali's hand and they stepped back into Etciel.

Thank you. A deep voice floated through her head, and she knew it to be Xerus.

I'm sorry I couldn't do more.

We will find a way. You've given us our freedom, and we will not squander it.

Thali didn't know what to say to that. Were they not exactly where they were a year ago? She was back with her brother in Etciel, and they were all still under Rommy's control.

Alexius added, *You forget that you didn't know then what you do now. You know his plans, and my siblings are no longer under that spell. Xerus is much cleverer than any of us, even all of us together. You'll see. You've given them a fighting chance. Thank you.* He put a hand on her shoulder.

Suddenly, they were all in a hallway, the library to one side and another hallway leading to her old rooms to the left. *Xerus must have blinked us here,* she thought.

"Dinner at the normal time?" Rommy turned and asked.

Thali smiled and nodded. "I think I'll go clean up and rest awhile. I'm still full from lunch," she said.

Rommy's eyes narrowed a little. She hoped he would not question her. He smiled and nodded though. Thali and her entourage left the dragons and headed to her rooms. She was surprised to find them exactly as she'd left them, right down to the fresh flowers on the table.

"What now?" Nasir asked as he took a seat at the table, as did Thali.

"We wait," Alexius said.

Mia crumpled onto the couch with Tilton and Daylor, and Isaia and Alexius chose the opposite couch. The animals tucked themselves between the humans.

How could I have come so far only to be back where I started? Thali wondered, feeling defeated.

Chapter Forty

*Do you think he'll **let me go home?*** Thali asked Alexius.

I think he may let you take the others back.

And if I stay there ...

He'll come to fetch you eventually.

Then we'll need a plan.

Alexius nodded a little. Not that it really mattered if Rommy forced her to return to Etciel. She looked at her friends. She didn't care so much if she was stuck in Etciel forever, but she would get her friends home. Taking a deep breath, she said, "It's safe to rest here. We'll go home tomorrow, I hope." She looked at her friends' tired faces. Maybe they should stay longer and rest, recover.

"What state do you think our home is in?" Tilton asked.

Thali had no idea. She didn't know how much time would have passed in their home world by the time they returned. It could be days, weeks, or months. Some instinct told her it was maybe months, but then she thought, *What if years have passed and we walk into a peaceful kingdom again to find Elric has found himself another queen?* Thali swallowed.

"We'll find out soon enough," Mia said.

Thali knew Mia was staring at her, wanting to have a private conversation, but she wasn't ready for Mia's questions. She was barely ready to face herself right now.

"First though, we all need to bathe," Mia finally said. Daylor sniffed himself and made a face. The others slowly nodded, then stood.

"If you'll follow me," Alexius said, going to open the main door. Aexie was there. "Aexie will take the ladies to separate bathing pools."

Alexius nodded at Aexie, then left with the men. Isaia paused though, looking unsure.

"I'm safe with Aexie," she said as she nodded to convince him. He narrowed his eyes but finally acquiesced.

Mia and Thali followed Aexie down a familiar hallway, then a less familiar one.

The dragon stopped and said, "We normally all bathe together, but Rommy says humans are more conservative, so through these doors, you'll find alternate pools big enough for each of you," Aexie shrugged as she pushed the golden doors open.

Steam and humidity hit Thali as she walked in, reminding her very much of the hot pools in Bulstan, only much bigger. Here, the room was cavernous, and there were multiple pools.

"This used to be open to the public. Anyone wanting to bathe could come here," Aexie said. She closed the door and disappeared.

Thali used her threads to ensure she was truly gone and felt the dragon walking away. She nodded at Mia, and they walked further into the room until they found a pool tucked into a small alcove. Thali dipped her hands in. It was warm but not scalding. It would do. She stripped out of her clothes and sank into the pool. Mia did the same.

"So, are we going to talk about it?" Mia asked as she looked at the ceiling.

"Talk about what?" Thali asked.

"Oh, I don't know, maybe about how Elric chose the kingdom over you, about the secret city that seems like a perfect fit for you, about the crazy dragon that you're now working with despite him trapping you in who knows what kind of torture, and hey, how about the deranged brother now back in your life?" Mia asked.

Thali couldn't help but laugh. It just bubbled out of her.

Mia stared at her.

"It really is a lot, isn't it?" Thali asked.

Mia nodded, finally laughing too. Then she asked, "Have you processed any of it?"

"Of course Elric chose the kingdom. That's his responsibility. He had to."

"Just because he had to doesn't invalidate your pain at his decision. You wouldn't have made the same choice," Mia said. She started to say something but stopped.

Thali thought about what Mia had said. It was true; she felt betrayed. But would she really have made a different choice? Hadn't she run off to save her kingdom after Bree had gotten hurt? "I don't know if I would have made a different choice," Thali finally said.

"You already did. You could have left us three times now since our little chat. And yes, you did pick wrong before, but you didn't abandon us in a dangerous place. You left us in a safe place. We chose to sail into danger."

Thali didn't know what to say.

"I can see why your parents were hesitant for you to become royalty. Maybe I was too enamored by the glitz and glamour—not that there's been as much of that as I would have thought—but sometimes I wonder what would have happened if you had stayed with Garen," Mia said. The last part ended in a whisper.

Thali looked over at Mia, then slipped under the water, unable to face that pain. She almost *had* chosen Garen when she'd escaped this place the first time. And now she was back. Despite all his efforts to get her home, here she was, back in this place again, maybe stuck forever. Thali only resurfaced when she finally needed to breathe.

"I mean, what can Elric really do with creatures running amok in Adanek?" Mia asked.

"Ask them not to?" Thali asked quietly, though even to her ears it sounded silly.

"I know you don't want to have to demand anything of the animals—magical or no—but if it comes down to it and you have to choose between the people you love, the kingdom you love, and them, which will you choose?" Mia asked.

Thali sank into the pool, completely immersing herself again. She somehow both knew and didn't know. Anytime that thought pushed into her head, or even dangled in the very back, she pushed it away and built a wall in front of it. She didn't want to think about it.

Mia must have sensed her tension because she dropped the topic, then sighed and stretched out in the hot water as Thali looked down and saw the dirt lifting off her and into the water. It figured that Etciel's pools had magical cleaning properties.

Hours passed before Thali finally rallied enough courage to seek out her brother. She went to the library first. That was where she would have been, so Thali figured he was either there or in the office he shared with Xerus—or had taken over.

She sent Alexius a quick message down their thread to let him know she was going to see Rommy. Then taking a deep breath, she opened the library door. Her brother sat at a desk, scribbling away, simultaneously checking a book beside the paper.

"Hi," she said.

Rommy didn't look up or stop scribbling. "One sec, Rou."

Thali went to the center bookcase and saw that seven books had popped up. She took one and nestled into the floor cushions with it. She may as well relax while she waited for Rommy to finish whatever he was working on.

Finally, he put his quill down and stood to stretch.

Thali closed her book. Rommy stayed where he was, so she dove in. "Rommy, I'd like to take my friends home."

Rommy looked at her. "And will you come back?"

"I will if you ask me to," Thali said. She rose and took a few steps closer to him. Her body hesitated, but this was Rommy, her Rommy. He was confused, mixed up in a mistake that had gotten out of control. But he was still her big brother.

"I shouldn't have to ask, Rou."

"What you want, Rommy, it's going to hurt a lot of people."

"Not if they stay out of our way."

"But you're asking for the world to just ... bow down to you. How do you plan on doing that? We're talking about real people here, people with families who need food and shelter and protection." Thali tried to keep the pleading out of her voice, but she failed.

"We'll figure it out. All the worlds could be united, share food and resources. We could live for the betterment of all. We could make sure that happens."

"It's a beautiful thought, Rommy, but what about the magical animals? Why are they attacking? You're scaring people, hurting them, killing them," Thali said.

"If they're scared, then we offer them the solution: you. You can control the animals, and the people will adore you, then me by association. Then they'll do as we wish," Rommy said.

Thali's heart sank. She had hoped her brother hadn't sent the creatures, had hoped the attacks were unrelated. "And what of the magical creatures themselves?"

"What about them?"

Thali didn't want to start a fight, not when her friends' lives were hanging in the balance. "Rommy, what is it you want from all this? Rania is waiting for you." She stepped closer still and put a hand on her brother's arm.

"I need to be able to offer her the world first. I'm so close, Thali."

Thali nodded, then grinned. "Will you come show me what books are on your mind?" She guided him over to the magical bookcase. It wasn't large because it didn't need to be. It would only bring up the books you wanted to read. It was a bit of a competition amongst the dragon family to see how many they could summon at a time. Jaxon had the least at three and Xerus the most at thirteen.

"Sure, Rou. I don't have anything else to hide from you," Rommy said. He neared the bookcase as Thali stepped out.

She eyed the books that popped up. They were all of war strategy or memoirs of great leaders. There wasn't anything fun in there at all. "This tells me you need some fun," Thali said as she pointed at the books. She was surprised to see ten titles appear. But then, she really shouldn't be. Her brother had always exceeded her successes, and this was the same as every other area of her life.

"And what should I read then? Those cheesy romance books you and Aexie and Jaxon seem to love so much?"

"Maybe? Maybe it would give you some inspiration about how to woo Rania another way?" Thali fell back into her cushions, her brother across from her now.

"Thali, this is the way it has to be. I know it. I can feel it. We're so close. I put these plans in place years ago, and we're moments from achieving them."

Thali swallowed and looked away. She didn't see how she could be a good sister and a good ruler at the same time.

Rommy ran his hand through his hair. "Why don't you take your friends back to Adanek, visit your husband, and come back in a week? We can talk about our plans then."

Thali nodded. She wondered what would happen if she didn't come back.

"Jaxon will come with you," Rommy said as she rose and went to the library door. "To keep you safe."

Thali swallowed. To keep her safe or to make sure she returned?

After their forced attendance at dinner, Thali and her friends huddled together in her rooms. They'd spent a lot of time together like that in the last while, all crammed together in one space.

"We'll go home tomorrow, with my brother's blessing," Thali said.

Mia asked, "And when do you have to return?"

"How do you know I have to return?" Thali asked.

Daylor raised both eyebrows. "I'm not the sharpest tool, but even I can see your brother has a hold over you, even without the dragon in the gem." He whispered the last part.

Thali crossed her arms. "What do you mean?"

"You're a different person with him, obedient and fawning. You look to him for reassurance. I've never seen you do that." Daylor sat back and crossed his arms.

Thali huffed out a sigh. "I have to be back in a week, our time."

"And how are you going to explain that to Elric?" Tilton asked.

Thali shrugged. "I'll just point to the hulking dragon acting as my babysitter."

"Jaxon is coming?" Alexius asked. "He won't exactly fit in."

"I don't think my brother cares."

"I thought we released the dragons? Why are they still doing his bidding?" Tilton asked.

"Did you forget Rommy has their father in that gem? They have to bide their time."

"Right," Tilton said, understanding dawning in his eyes. "So if we can get the king back, we'll have dragons on our side?"

Thali narrowed her eyes. "We're leaving tomorrow for Adanek—home. Remember? The place we've been trying to get back to for who knows how long? We can't worry about that."

Tilton deflated. "You won't let us come back here with you, will you?"

Thali shook her head. "I'm going to try to not return here. But if I have to, I can get in and out faster."

"But you'll bring Alexius?" Isaia said. He'd sat quietly in the corner until now.

Thali nodded.

"Why not us?" Isaia asked as he glanced at Nasir and back.

"It's faster if just I go. Alexius has his own magic," Thali said. She wasn't sure where the disconnect was.

"Will you bring them?" Nasir glanced at Indi and Ana sprawled under the table, sleeping.

"Maybe. I don't know. Probably not. I want to get you all home safely and check on Elric. I haven't thought beyond that." Thali crossed her arms. She was done explaining.

CHAPTER FORTY-ONE

THOUGH IT WAS THE last thing Thali wanted to do, she went to find her brother. The sun was setting, but she wouldn't sleep until she had tried. She found Rommy in his office.

"What do you need?" Rommy asked.

"How do you know I want something?" Thali asked.

"I've known you way too long to not know when you want something from me."

"I just want a guide to go to the Forest of Whispers," Thali said.

"Why would you want to visit the Forest of Whispers?" Rommy asked.

"Elric needs help. He needs to find a box that belonged to his father, except his father didn't tell him its location before he died." Thali thought honesty was the best policy here.

"You want to go to the Forest of Whispers to find Elric's parents and ask them where this box is?" Rommy asked.

Thali nodded. She hoped it didn't sound as crazy as she did.

"All right, I'll have the carriage brought around. Maybe Xerus can come help us navigate the forest." Rommy stood, and Thai followed him out of the room.

Thali wasn't surprised that Rommy had dropped everything to help her. When she thought back to her childhood, she remembered he'd always been like that. He could have been in the middle of a drawing and would still have closed his notebook and jumped to help.

"You're a great brother," Thali said as they walked down the hall together.

"You know it," he said as he turned to grin at her before continuing onward. He poked his head into a room she hadn't seen before, said a few words, and then they headed for her rooms. "Grab a cloak and I'll meet you out front?" Rommy asked.

Thali nodded. She had thought she'd be going alone—well, with Alexius—so this might make for a crowded carriage ride. She ran in, grabbed her cloak, and explained to Mia, who was drinking hot tea by the hearth.

Mia shivered. "Sounds too spooky for me. If you see any of my passed relatives, tell them I said hi." She waved as Thali ran out the door.

Nasir and Isaia shadowed her. That worried her for a moment, but as she stepped outside, she saw a larger carriage than she'd ever seen. At least they wouldn't be squished.

The door swung open, and Rommy held a hand out. Alexius and Nasir entered behind her. When she sat down, she saw Xerus was already inside. Isaia was the last to climb in and sat next to Thali as Alexius sat next to his brother.

"The Forest of Whispers is a daunting and confusing place," Xerus said as the door closed, and the carriage rumbled off.

If it had just been the two of them, Thali would have made Rommy sit on the roof of the carriage with her so they could see the world around them as they traveled. This world had such an incredible landscape. "How far is it?" Thali asked.

"About an hour," Xerus said.

Thali wished for snacks at that, and Rommy pulled a basket from underneath his seat. "I know you never go more than a few hours without snacks. Here," he extended the basket, and Thali took what looked like a muffin.

As she held it in her hand, it changed color. "Is it supposed to do this?" she asked.

"Yeah, it's just trying to figure out what it wants from you in return," Alexius explained.

Thali tried to think of something, anything it could want.

Rommy chuckled. "It's best if you concentrate on what you want to give it."

So, Thali focused hard on thanking it, being grateful for it. Finally, the muffin stayed blue. They all ate their color-changing muffins in silence, and Thali looked out the window. Her mind had a hard time believing what her eyes saw. They passed rolling hills of blue, skies of orange, and the glistening Lake of Reflection. When she saw the shock of yellow trees, she started to feel nervous.

"It's best if you either control your magic and keep it wrapped up tight or stay with the carriage," Xerus said as he started to unbutton his jacket.

Rommy saluted. "I'll stay here then."

Thali wondered if her brother had magic or if he just preferred to stay out of the forest.

"I will as well," Nasir said. He had surprised them already with the knowledge that he had a little bit of magic – just enough to get what he wanted usually. Alexius had thought it fascinating.

Thali asked, "So how will we find the tree?"

"We?" Xerus asked. "It's up to you to find the soul you wish to connect with."

"How does one find the soul they want to connect with?"

"Think of them, keep them in your mind, and hopefully the forest will guide you to where they rest."

"What if they aren't here?"

"There are no guarantees in the Forest of Whispers," Xerus said.

Thali nodded. The carriage stopped, and the door swung open to reveal an exquisite forest of yellow foliage: golden yellows, corn yellows, light and buttery yellows. The trees all had stark red bark. Thali thought it looked beautiful as she stepped out.

"Do not let yourself be pulled into a soul that is not familiar to you, and above all else, do not touch the trees," Xerus instructed as he came out and stood next to her. He seemed so much taller than she remembered. She wasn't sure if he just seemed more intimidating or she hadn't given him the respect she should have.

"I'll be right here with you," Alexius said.

As she looked at Alexius, she saw Xerus look at his brother with interest, making Thali want to know why.

Isaia also hopped out of the carriage. "I don't have any magic. Is it all right if I go?"

Xerus nodded. He started off into the forest. The moment they crossed the treeline, the world felt muffled and hushed. It was quiet, unearthly quiet, like their every footstep was muted. She knew she should be louder as her feet crunched on the leaves, but she wasn't. It was as if she walked in slippers.

Xerus didn't speak, making Thali think voices must get sucked into the void of whatever was absorbing the sound. He tapped his temple, reminding Thali of what she had to do.

She nodded. She closed her eyes and thought of Elric's parents: the beautiful and serene Queen Adela and the charming King Devrain. Her heart hurt to know they had passed—and had passed not believing their own son. She was wondering how Elric was doing when she felt

Alexius's warm hand on her shoulder. *Right,* she thought, *focus on the king and queen.* So she refocused on them, thinking of every moment she'd had with them: on the steps of the palace, in the queen's study for tea with Thali's mother, the time the queen had taken her aside just before they'd left and told her she believed her, had faith in her.

She thought of how Queen Adela held herself, how tall and proud she was, and how she commanded a room without trying. It saddened Thali to not have learned those secrets.

Then she heard their voices or—no it wasn't their voices. It was a quiet hum. Thali's brows furrowed as she tried to concentrate on the sound. She turned and started moving toward it. She opened her eyes as she held onto the hum and followed her feet down a narrow path. Alexius, Xerus, and Isaia followed. Whenever the humming stopped, she backtracked until she found it again. It was a difficult, indirect path she walked. She even recognized a couple of large boulders that they'd passed a few times as the hum led her on a zig-zag path.

"I think we're almost there," Xerus said.

Thali looked up and saw that a part of the forest ahead of them looked brighter. It wasn't that more light shone through the canopy but that the yellows of the leaves were brighter here. The reds of the trunks were crisper. And the humming was getting louder.

She finally stopped in front of what looked like a giant red oak tree with yellow leaves. One branch intertwined with a smaller, slighter tree next to it. "What do I do now?" Thali whispered. She wanted to put her hand on the tree; it was as if it called her to do so. But she had been told not to touch the trees.

"Do what you feel like it's asking you to," Xerus said.

"I feel like it's asking me to touch the bark," Thali said.

"Then touch it," Xerus said. He sounded frustrated.

"But you said not to," Thali said.

"We will ensure that you do not get absorbed into the tree. Just be careful. Keep your magic wound up tight unless it asks you to release it," Xerus said. He took a breath and regained his calm.

"Thank you," Thali said. She glanced at Alexius.

He nodded confidently. She knew he was as confident in his brother as she had been in hers, but she was beginning to wonder if Xerus deserved Alexius's unquestioning loyalty.

Thali turned instead to the tree before her. She would have to think about the dragons' relationship another time. Turning inward to the soft humming in her chest, she raised her hand and approached the tree. The moment she touched the surface, fingers splayed, she was transported to the sitting room in the king and queen's chambers. The last time she'd been here, she'd been with Elric, but when she turned, she didn't see him there. Instead, she saw the queen in a robe before the fireplace, her feet on a foot stool. Her husband's arm was around her as they sipped their drinks.

Thali swallowed. It looked like an intimate moment. At the same time, she wasn't sure if she was really here or if they were relaying a memory to her.

"Do you think we did the right thing?" King Devrain asked as he stared at the fire.

"I think we did what we could to maintain peace in the kingdom. I don't like that you sent Elric away, but if anyone can keep him safe, it's her."

"You really think magical creatures are coming to attack our people?"

"Why would she lie about that?"

"It's just ... overwhelming. When I think of the drawings I saw in books as a child of unicorns, pegasi, griffons—I try to tell myself they're not truly real. They're myths, stories made up to teach children how to behave." King Devrain put his glass down.

"I think sometimes we want peace so much we ignore what's going on under our noses," Queen Adela said. She took another sip of her drink, and they were quiet for a moment. Thali admired their quiet moments. They weren't awkward or angry, just filled with space and time to think.

"Perhaps. But it's kept the peace for us until now," King Devrain said.

"Perhaps. But can you really say you know what's going on beyond these walls?"

"I know my kingdom." King Devrain pushed his lips out into a pout.

"I know you know your kingdom. But do you really know its true goings-on? For all that we've focused on food prices and sufficient resources and inflation because there are so many more people in the city with all the attacks elsewhere, have we listened to the stories of these attacks? Have we heard what the people have seen in the rest of this kingdom?" Queen Adela asked.

"Isn't it wise to focus on the practical, the basic needs?"

"Yes, in general. But if Thali is right and these attacks continue, more and more people will come. The market won't keep up, and nothing we do will help. No one will be able to afford the food and supplies they need if we don't get to the heart of the matter first, treat the cause, not the symptoms."

"Then we bring in more resources now and head it off at the pass. I'll send a letter to Lord Ranulf. I'm sure he can ensure that the merchant guild brings in more to help with the increased population," King Devrain only said.

"Yes, dear," Queen Adela said sadly.

After many long, silent minutes, King Devrain said, "I miss him already."

"I do too. And if I'm being honest, Routhalia brought new life to the palace. With the tiger and dog—and did you know she has a snake that usually rests in her sleeve? The court ladies have all been scrambling to acquire more pets: birds, dogs, anything. It's a whole trend," Queen Adela said.

"Would you like a companion?"

"I would perhaps like a small creature."

"Like a rodent?" King Devrain asked.

"Maybe a rabbit. One sometimes seeks me out when I walk in the gardens."

"Would you like me to trap it for you?"

"Perhaps. I will try to catch her this week, and if I can't, then perhaps we can leave her some enticement," the queen said.

"I didn't know you had an animal friend like the princess does." King Devrain pulled away from her to look at her.

"You don't know all my secrets." Queen Adela raised her eyebrows.

"And yet, you know all of mine," King Devrain rubbed the tip of his nose to the tip of hers. The queen smiled and tucked her head into his neck.

Thali tried to speak, but she couldn't open her mouth. She could feel she wasn't here much longer, and she needed to know where the box was, the Box of Ascension of whatever it was called.

"I still think you should have told him where the box is," Adela said as she and the king stared into the fireplace.

"You really don't think we'll survive the next few months?" King Devrain sighed and glanced at the upper right corner of the fireplace. "It'll be here when he needs it," King Devrain said. "And I'm sure it won't be for some years yet."

"Me too," the queen said. "I want to see some grandbabies."

King Devrain laughed then.

"Can you imagine the relationships we'll have once Routhalia takes over trade and commerce? It brings chills to my spine," King Devrain said.

The picture faded then, but as she started to turn away, a single thread reached out to her. She couldn't stop her own thread from connecting with it.

Tell him we're sorry and that we love him. And then the thread dissolved. Thali nodded and pulled her hand off the tree. She stepped back to look at the two trees with new eyes.

She had to go back to Adanek and pull out the box, but she also had find this rabbit in the garden. Thali's instincts told her it was important.

"Did you get what you needed?" Xerus asked.

Thali nodded, and Alexius offered his arm. She took it, and they walked back to the carriage. Connecting to the trees had taken more energy than she had expected, and she felt unsteady on her feet. On their walk back, other threads reached for her, so she put her walls up and kept her own threads tucked in tightly.

"Are all these human?" Thali asked.

"Many are, yes," Alexius replied, "but they are the mortal made immortal. For here, trees are always alive and well."

His reply sounded formal to her. He hadn't been his usual, joking self since they had arrived in Etciel, so Thali wanted a moment to privately talk to him.

Xerus walked far ahead of them, so maybe that was why her next words rushed out of her mouth. "Will you and I be trees here when we pass?" Thali asked.

"Perhaps. I believe you will. It's a little more difficult to know what will happen to a dragon's soul, for I was supposed to be immortal," Alexius said.

Thali saw Xerus stumble before he regained his balance, and she swallowed and stopped talking. They walked the rest of the way in silence, and continued their silence the whole rattling carriage ride back.

Now that the surprise of the odd-colored landscape had faded, she realized the hills and fields were empty, some overgrown. She wondered where all the citizens of Etciel had gone.

Her brother kept a close eye on her, so she couldn't ask. Xerus's demeanor had become stiffer in Rommy's presence, so asking him was out. And Alexius was busy watching her brother with as much care as her brother was watching her. It was another question she had to file away for later.

Chapter Forty-Two

THALI STOOD WITH HER friends, her animals, and Jaxon before an ornate wall mirror. Her brother stood watching, as did Xerus and Aexie. She had to keep up the pretense, so she plastered a smile on and went to embrace her brother. "I'll see you soon," she said. He squeezed her tight, and for a moment, it felt like she was comforting him.

Alexius and Jaxon watched Xerus and Aexie as they nodded at each other, clearly finishing a conversation in their minds.

"Well, shall we?" Thali turned and asked before stepping up to the now misty mirror. Jaxon glanced at it, and the mist started to swirl.

"Safe travels," Rommy said.

Alexius went first, followed by Thali with her animals, then Mia, Daylor, Tilton, and Nasir. Isaia and Jaxon stepped through last. Though they didn't blink there, the trip felt faster this time. Thali wasn't sure if it was because of something Jaxon did when he'd made the portal or something else, but she felt like she had only taken a few steps before they were pushing a door open.

Alexius coughed as Thali walked through after him, and she stopped abruptly when she saw they were not alone. They hadn't stepped into her bedroom or her study or even her armory but the main hallway to the public gallery. And none other than Lord Bannick and his sister, Lady Gabrielle, were watching them.

"Where have you been?!" Lady Gabrielle shrieked at her.

Thali was so shocked at the pitch of her voice that she took a step backward. Daylor caught her, but Ban was quick to jump in.

"Everyone's been waiting for you for ages," Ban said. He stepped closer, leering and invading Thali's personal space until Isaia stepped in front of Thali, pressing his dagger to Ban's chest and making him back up.

Thali swallowed. She needed to handle this herself. More members of the court started to file out of the public gallery, and they would all witness what she did in this moment. "I am your queen. You will show me the respect due me and tell me where my husband currently is." Thali pulled her vest down and held her head high.

Gabrielle and Ban glanced at the crowd gathering outside the gallery, then back to Thali. Ban was smart enough to dip into a bow and mutter an apology, and his sister did the same.

"He's in a meeting, Your Majesty," a runner offered.

"Will you tell His Majesty that I have arrived and will await him in our rooms?" Thali asked. The runner nodded and scurried away as she haughtily turned on her heel and strode toward her chambers. She was glad she finally knew the palace well enough now that she knew where she was going. Isaia and Nasir fell into step, and as she turned down another hallway, Derk and Amali joined them. They looked well rested and a good deal cleaner than she was, but they fell into formation around her. The group made quite the exit until they could no longer see nor hear the nobles. Daylor, Tilton, and Mia trailed behind, but Thali did not speak or look anyone in the eye until she'd made it to her rooms.

She stopped outside and bade everyone but Amali and Derk to come in. She felt bad as she saw Stefan jogging down the hallway toward her, but she closed the door anyway.

"Not a word about my return to Etciel to anyone, understood?" Thali looked at them all fiercely. "I'll figure this out. For now, take up to a week off to recover and recuperate. I don't want to see your faces for at least forty-eight hours. Is that understood?"

They started to argue, but when she put her hands on her hips, they gave up and nodded.

"Good," Thali said. "I'll have them send you supper and all your meals for the next two days. Now go bathe and sleep."

They all nodded again, looking intimidated by Thali for the first time.

Thali softened. "I love you all. Thank you."

They grinned, and Mia, Daylor, and Tilton hugged her. Then came a knock on the door.

"Come in," Thali said.

Elric opened the door and just stood there.

Thali hardly registered her friends scattering like mice. She only saw Elric. Did he look older? Surely those lines around his eyes weren't there before. Suddenly, he rushed in. He wrapped his arms around her and lifted her off the ground, spinning her around before planting her back on her feet, taking her face in his hands, and thoroughly kissing her. She felt the sunshine flood every dark doubt and scary thought as she lost herself in his kiss.

"I am so sorry I left you. I should have discussed it with you," he said.

Thali shook her head. "I understand that your first duty is to the kingdom. I was hurt, but I think you made the right choice. I'm only sorry it took us so long to return."

"You're here now, so that's what matters."

"How long has it been?"

"Two months," Elric said.

"How is everyth—" Suddenly remembering her adventure in the yellow forest, Thali stopped mid-sentence and walked out of the room. Elric and their complement of guards followed mutely. She stalked into the king and queen's old chambers, or what used to be their chambers. She stopped abruptly when she saw the gaping hole in the palace. She pushed the thoughts of what had happened away and went straight to the fireplace. Thankfully, it was still intact. She examined it for a minute, looking carefully at the stonework in the hearth.

"Amali, can I borrow your dagger?" Thali asked, and the guard dutifully stepped forward and handed Thali her dagger. She would use her own, but it was the one from her Uncle Renshu, and she wasn't sure it would survive what she was about to do with it. "How strong is it?" Thali asked.

Amali raised her eyebrows and glanced at the fireplace. "Should be indestructible."

Thali started removing the little statuettes on the mantel. "Elric, have you ever thought it strange that your parents' fireplace is the only one in the palace with a mantle? It just doesn't fit the castle's design," Thali said as Amali helped her move the little figures.

Elric stood stunned as if she was a crazed animal he wasn't sure he should approach.

Once all the objects were cleared off, Thali ran her fingers along the edge of the mantle. Then she smiled. She shoved the dagger into a spot of newer mortar. It wasn't timeworn like the rest. She stabbed at it a few times, and the mortar came out in one large chunk.

Then she stuck one hand into the hole she'd made, grabbed the mantle, and tried to rip it off. It didn't budge, so she bashed the underside of it with the hilt of the dagger a few times. Amali caught it as it suddenly fell. Thali turned it over. The mantle was hollow, and hidden inside was a box. She pulled the box out and handed it to Elric. "I believe you were looking for this." The royal seal—a dragon and a lion, paws together, in a shield—was emblazoned on the lid.

"How..." Elric asked. He opened the box and gasped. "Derk, find Avery and tell her to call a gathering of the lords immediately." He glanced at the hole in the roof and winced. It was dark outside. "I don't care what time it is. We meet as soon as possible." At Derk's nod, Elric turned to Thali. "I have so many questions, but this ... thank you." He scooped her into a hug with one arm, the other still clutching the open box, and kissed Thali's forehead. "I ... I have to go prepare," Elric said, then he looked at the contents of the box again.

"I'll see you in an hour," Thali said. She still had one more thing she wanted to do. "Also, sorry about this." Thali motioned at the mess she'd made of the chambers.

"It can be fixed," Elric said and then he turned, gave her a quick kiss, and hurried off.

Thali then went into her mind, into the threads of the animals nearby. Other than birds, she sensed no others, so she went wider. She dipped into the gardens and looked for a rabbit.

Without warning, she spun around and walked out of the room—leaving the mess behind—down the hall, and into the private gardens. There, she stopped in her tracks. This was where she'd seen a dragon for the first time, where Elric had proposed, where her aunt had died. Thali swallowed hard. She cast her threads out, looking for the soft, snow-white thread of a little rabbit. There were seven in the garden, so she spent a quick moment looking through their memories. They all had memories of the queen, but she needed to find one in particular. If the queen had kept a rabbit, she would have spoken to it, and Thali felt like the queen had shown her that memory for a reason. She just needed to find the right rabbit so she could figure out what the queen had wanted to tell her. Thali's breath hitched as she remembered that *she* was queen now.

She sat down on the bench that so many of her memories were tied to. Her guards melted away, giving her space, and she scanned the rabbits' memories. All their memories showed that whenever the queen came to the garden, they would all come running to her. She would sit on this bench and ask for lettuce and carrots with her afternoon tea. Then she'd put the treats on little saucers beside teacups of water and put them on the ground for her tiny friends.

Thali hadn't known that the queen had been so fond of rabbits. Finally, when Thali came to the sixth rabbit, she saw different memories. She reached down, picked it up, and held it closely. She saw that this rabbit, after a time, would hop up a few strategically placed stones behind the bench to join the queen. Then into her lap the rabbit would go, and the queen would whisper to her.

Thali had to focus carefully on what the queen had said to the rabbit. After all, rabbits did not understand human language, so their memory of it was difficult to understand.

"Well, little one," came the queen's voice, "You will become a very important messenger for me. I know that our dearest new princess—well, I hear—that she speaks to animals, so this makes you *my* very important messenger, you hear? I think the king made a mistake sending Elric and Routhalia away. I think he simply wanted peace, so he couldn't acknowledge what was happening. For you see, it is much easier to remain static than to do something different, to change, and especially to go to war. But I have known this about him for a long time. That is why I encouraged Elric to lead our military."

The queen stopped to pet the rabbit soothingly. "So, now I need Routhalia to know that I have not been as idle as my husband. I have long been setting up a network amongst the women of the world. We keep each other informed by sewing letters into the textiles we trade, the embroidery and tapestries. I have learned that the rest of the world is not being attacked at the rate our kingdom is, though the frozen North has indeed seen more activity. Meat has gone missing there, and here, we have mysterious disappearances and even some strange happenings in the brothels in town. Now, I know it might seem distasteful to communicate with brothels, but I'll tell you, those women know more about the world than anyone else. On the darkest night of every month, I go through the secret passageway in the dungeons to a hidden courtyard covered by trees. There, I meet with a woman from the brothel, and she tells me the news of the city." She cooed to the little bunny, and Thali wondered if the queen truly thought Thali would get her message or if she had given it a shot out of desperation.

Thali looked up at the sky. The stars were all out, as was the moon. She tried to do some backward math and realized that the darkest night would not be for another two weeks. Thali bit the inside of her cheek. She did not have to go on the darkest night. She already knew someone, someone Thali guessed was the queen's informant. Had Ella ever told Queen Adela Thali's real position? And was there a way to contact her without Garen knowing?

CHAPTER FORTY-THREE

T HALI FINALLY THOUGHT OF a way she could get Ella's attention without involving Garen. She went back to her rooms, where Elric was preparing. He didn't look up when Thali walked in, and she didn't have long if she wanted to make it back in time for his meeting with the lords. She found Mia, of course, in her closet reorganizing, even though she was supposed to be resting. "I need to pass as a man," Thali said.

Mia looked up, and without raising an eyebrow, she nodded. Then she pulled out the trunk she so affectionately called 'Thali's man clothes.'

"High, mid, or low class?" Mia asked.

"One who goes unnoticed in a brothel," Thali said.

Mia's eyebrows did shoot up then, but she nodded and pulled a few things together. "Wear your old black boots, the ones I keep saying are overdue for replacement."

Thali went to her armory, where she thought she'd hidden the boots from Mia, and came back with them. Mia already had an outfit laid out, so Thali slipped it on.

Then Mia disappeared through the servants' door and returned a few minutes later with a plain brown cloak. "One of Aron's," she said as she draped it over Thali's shoulders. She pinned Thali's hair up so it stopped just before her shoulders. Mia took a hat from a stool and pinned it on top of Thali's head. She pulled the hood up. Mia put her hands on her hips as she focused on Thali's appearance. "Shall I call for your guards, or is this a solo thing?" Mia asked as she fastened the hood of the cloak so it wouldn't move in a breeze.

"I'll be safe," Thali said.

Mia looked at her. "You know what you're doing?"

Thali nodded. Mia looked her in the eye for a moment longer, then nodded. "If you're not back in one hour, I'm sending Alexius, Isaia, and Nasir."

Thali nodded again. She kissed Mia's cheek and slipped passed her out the door. She bade her tiger and dog stay with Mia, and they started to pace. She kept Bardo with her just in case. He was more easily concealed. She had to blend in as much as she possibly could.

Thali wasn't as familiar with this city as she was her own or even Lanchor. But she knew she could find who and what she needed. She slipped out a side door in the castle walls and into the streets. There, she started to stumble on purpose and swiped a bottle she found on the road. Pretending to drink from it, she followed a few men who were also stumbling around until she reached a well-lit tavern. Music flowed from it, and people spilled out in various states of dress—or undress. It was later than she had thought.

Ever since she'd discovered that Garen had moved his operations here, it had made her nervous. So as she traveled through the alleys, she used her threads to search the rooftops so she could slip through undetected.

Her stumbling was enough to catch the attention of a younger woman near the tavern. She placed a hand on Thali's arm and rubbed it upward to Thali's shoulders. She was glad in this moment that she was at least muscular enough to pass as a man—or so she hoped.

"Looking for some fun tonight?" the woman asked.

Thali kept her hood up but nodded. She slipped a couple of silver coins into the woman's hand. The woman smiled, took Thali's gloved hand, and led her into the brothel. They passed some occupied couches that

Thali didn't look at too closely. The woman led her quickly away, but Thali still glimpsed the men and women in various positions out in the open. Thali was surprised at how far into the building they were going. But then they walked through an open door, and she saw a beautiful set of gold-painted wooden chairs and a table.

And Ella.

Ella rose from her seat. "What's this?"

Before Thali knew what was happening, the woman from outside undid Thali's cloak and spun it off her, pulling her hat from her head—with the pin—and closing the door.

"My queen and princess." The young woman took Thali's hand and kissed it, then draped the cloak and hat over a chair and disappeared through a side door.

"Well, so much for my disguise," Thali said.

"It probably fooled most, if that makes you feel better. My girls are especially well trained." Ella curtsied briefly, then rose. She retrieved a tea set from a table along the far wall, put water from a cauldron on the hearth carefully into the teapot, added tea leaves, and brought it all to the table. All that she did while facing Thali, so she could see every movement. Ella was being cautious.

"Did you meet with the queen every month?" Thali asked.

"I did," Ella said. She finished pouring the tea into two cups and handed one to Thali, gesturing for Thali to sit.

"Does he know—" Thali started to ask.

Ella shook her head. "He won't know about this either if I can help it," Ella continued.

Thali raised her eyebrow, wondering why.

"No offense, but I hate seeing him mope around like a sad puppy for weeks after he sees you." Ella crossed one leg over the other. She wore only a robe and undergarments, yet she looked more elegant than Thali had ever felt, even as a princess.

She nodded. She hated that she caused Garen so much pain, but part of her heart's tension eased to know that he still cared for her.

"You want to know what I told the queen?" Ella asked.

Thali nodded.

"I told her everything you already know. Sometimes I just passed on information the boss shared with us. Sometimes I tried to pass on details of events she could do something about."

"And did she take action?"

"After I told her how the fights in the tavern were increasing and that they leaked over into my business, within the week, more guards were posted around here. And they didn't tolerate violence."

"So she helped."

"However she could."

"What do you mean?"

"As queen, her powers were limited. You know this. Males in this world are superior. Females, even partners, always have only what power is left over." Ella placed her teacup delicately back on her saucer.

Thali was reminded to be as queenly as she could because she was, in fact, queen now. She thought about Ella's words. In her parents' relationship, her mother had often taken the lead, though many times, her father did. As a child, Thali had always thought it was because her parents were equals. But now Thali was realizing that her mother might have had to step back in some instances because she was a woman.

"You are as much our princess as you are our queen," Ella said.

Thali returned from her thoughts and realized Ella was looking at her earnestly.

Ella's gaze flicked to the spot where her medallion hid. Ever since Garen had accused her of not wearing it and breaking her promise, she'd always kept it on her. Sometimes it was more concealed than at other times, but it had become part of her outfit every time she left the castle, and often within. Thali had realized it was a good way to see who knew what because their eyes would often give them away.

"I don't know what that means," Thali finally said quietly.

"It means you have loyal people willing to help you, to fight for you. You don't need a man to ask for you," Ella said.

Thali nodded slowly, letting that sink in. "Do you have news for me today? Anything I should know?"

"I'm not sure it's new information to you, but the lords have made things difficult for the king. They have not accepted him as they see him as a child. The younger lords, those who have taken over from their fathers, support him. But the older lords, which unfortunately are in the majority, are not only openly questioning him but whispering in dark corners and to their wives about how he's just a baby."

"What do you think will ameliorate that?" Thali asked Ella.

Ella looked surprised to be asked that. "They'll come around in time, but he needs to bring the scepter out. I think looking like a king—with the crown and everything—might help. Also, maybe growing a beard?" Ella said.

"A beard?"

"It will make him look older than his childhood self. It might be enough to remind people that he's a man now." Ella sat up straight.

Thali nodded.

"Word from the other kingdoms is that more creatures are out and about, in the waters as well as in the air and on land now," Ella said.

Thali nodded; she knew that. She wondered if she should tell Ella what had happened on the island she'd escaped from. She opened her mouth, then closed it not knowing where to start. Ella waited patiently. Taking a deep breath, Thali dove in. "We have just returned from a world called Korsel. It is well guarded and magical. We went through a gate in Cerisa," Thali said.

"Do you know the names of all the other worlds?" Ella asked.

"Etciel is where I've traveled to the most. The first gate that opened led there. A second gate was opened in the Far North. That is the gate many of the newest creatures you see flooding our oceans come from. I have a source that tells me it's most likely called Aeceal. There is also a third gate in Bulstan connected to a place called Vancel, but it is the most well-protected gate, the only one not open,the fourth one, is in Cerisa and it is only leaking. That's what allowed us to slip through." Thali thought of Tariq then and wondered how he was doing. Being spread so thin already, she was at least glad he had Bree at his side. She knew she should probably check in with him now that she was back in their world.

"Do you know what creatures live in Vancel?" Ella asked.

"From my understanding, bipedal hybrid creatures. They are not well liked among those in Etciel, but they're strong and powerful."

Ella opened and closed her mouth, so Thali waited for her to go on. "Do you ever wonder, given that all these other worlds have creatures so strong and so powerful, how it is that we've survived as such weaklings?"

Thali nodded. "I think we were lucky that they were sealed in their own worlds, away from us. Though sometimes I wonder if that's not why we've become so weak. Maybe there was more magic when we had need of it."

Ella nodded slowly, looking thoughtful. Then she continued with her own report. "Cerisa is unhappy with Adanek," Ella said. Thali raised her eyebrows at her, so she continued. "The women there are reporting that there is much disgust for Adanek, and many here believe that they opened that gate, that they did it to hurt us," Ella said.

Thali was incensed and wondered if Prince Feng, or even her grandmother, was fanning the flames of those untrue rumors. Then she thought of something. "Wait, they know about the gate there?"

"They only know of *one* gate open. I don't know if anyone really knew where it was," Ella said.

Thali nodded curtly. She couldn't help but glance at the door. Was it appropriate for her to ask how Garen was? She wanted to know. Part of her hoped he was here, part hoped he was not. For if he was here, it would hurt them both. She knew he deserved better, that she was petty for wanting to see him, but at the same time, she needed to see that he was all right. And to see him happy would settle something in her.

"He's all right," Ella said. Her eyes bore into Thali's as if she were reading her mind. "I don't think he'll ever get over you, but he's finding what happiness he can." Ella continued. She narrowed her eyes, and Thali had to look away.

Emotion bubbled up in her throat, and she thought back to the moment as they walked through pudding to escape Etciel. She would have lived in pudding for him.

"He's never shared why you can't be together, but I can see it's because you're needed elsewhere. Though your resources are limited as a woman, they are much more abundant than they would have been if you had been part of only our world." Ella swallowed, looking uncomfortable for the first time.

"Thank you," Thali said. She meant it. Knowing Garen was all right would have to be enough. She knew that every time they saw each other, it was like ripping the fresh scab off a wound that needed much more time to heal.

Thali stood. She heard the soft cheep of a bird in the corner of Ella's room, and she went to it. She connected with it from habit and saw that she lived a happy life. She was much loved here by all the women, who all called her Rosita. So Thali asked Rosita if she could move her thread to an inner door in her own mind. When the bird accepted, Thali transferred the thread to the room she'd created in her mind for familiar animals that weren't part of her inner circle like Indi, Ana, and Bardo.

She turned to Ella. "If you need to send me an urgent message, please ask Rosita. She can reach me. If you tell her or show her a message, I'll get it," Thali said. She offered her finger as a perch, and Rosita hopped on gladly. The beautiful cockatoo rubbed her head on Thali's fingers before hopping back to her perch. "She loves it here, by the way," Thali said. "Though she'd prefer you spritz your perfumes farther away from her. They irritate her beak."

Ella nodded. She didn't look surprised like most often did, and Thali realized she was a little sad that she rarely saw that surprise from people now. "If you'll follow me," Ella said, pushing aside a tapestry.

"Thank you," Thali said as they descended a sharp, narrow staircase.

"This will lead you to the back of the building, away from the street. If you go left out the door and then right, it should bring you back to the palace kitchens."

Thali nodded as she swung her cloak on. Ella helped pin her hair up in her hat.

Ella opened the door and waited while Thali stepped outside and disappeared around a corner.

Chapter Forty-Four

THE ALLEY WAS QUIET at this time of night, so quiet the hairs on the back of Thali's neck prickled. She placed a hand on her dagger when she heard someone sniff from behind her. He wasn't close, but he had sniffed loudly enough to let her know he was there. Then at least three sets of feet began following her. She looked up and saw that the palace was still far away.

Part of Thali was itching for a fight. She could channel her frustration and anger into slicing these pieces of squid turds into tiny, unrecognizable shards.

Then a warm hand held hers.

"There you are, darling." That smooth, low voice spun her around, and that warm hand she knew so well sent tingles through her body. The hand wandered to her shoulder and guided her to sway as if they were both drunk.

"Let us stumble home, sweetheart. Down this alleyway here is a shortcut," Garen said loudly enough that the three men—maybe five now—could hear them.

Thali was too shocked to do anything at first but follow. Then she leaned into him. "They're not yours?"

"We've had some uninvited guests lately, but don't worry. They'll be taken care of."

"Can't we 'take care' of them?"

"I will not risk you," Garen said.

"Are you saying I'm incapable?" Thali asked. She didn't know why she was being irritable and combative, but she couldn't help it.

He led her around a corner where too many people were standing, clearly waiting. She recognized Ilya and placed a hand on his crossed arms as she passed by him. He smiled at her. Then they were out back on the main street.

"Ella should have sent you with protection." Garen scowled.

Since they weren't in danger, Thali stopped and put a hand on Garen's arm as she turned to look at his face. From her periphery, she saw the quiet shadows of Garen's people taking care of the men who had followed them. Part of her hoped they eviscerated them and left the pieces hanging for all to see, and part of her hoped they would show the miscreants mercy. "It's not her fault. It's not like I can't take care of myself."

"Just because you can doesn't mean you should have to," Garen said. He covered her hand with his. "Will you tell me why you went to see Ella?"

"Are you asking or commanding?"

"I cannot command you to do anything," Garen said. "Nor would I even if I could," he said so softly that Thali wasn't sure he'd said it at all.

She was getting lost in his eyes. Drowning in their ocean, she saw whitecaps in the blue waves of the deep sea of his irises, or was that her imagination?

Someone coughed next to Thali, and she dropped her hand from Garen's arm. His arms fell to his sides; then he turned and disappeared. Thali had to blink hard to come back to herself, then she saw Nasir and Alexius standing there.

"We were sent for," Alexius said. He tried not to look her in the eye.

"I'm fine," Thali said. The alley had quieted, and she slowly oriented herself toward the palace. Before they turned the next corner though, Thali glanced over her shoulder and up to the rooftop, where a figure backed into the shadow. She felt warm and fuzzy inside but also settled in some way.

They were just reaching the palace gates when a commotion made her stop.

A dark, buzzing cloud was approaching the city, and when Thali squinted, she saw that it wasn't a cloud but a great group of creatures. She tried hard to see what they were.

"We have to go," Alexius said. He sounded scared.

"What is it?" Thali asked.

"Liozardillos," Alexius said. "I thought they were extinct. But we need to take cover, now." He wrapped his arms around Thali's middle, and they dashed into the guardhouse just as the guards ran out to protect the gate.

As soon as she, Nasir, and Alexius were inside, Alexius waved his arms, and swathes of light wrapped around them and expanded.

"What are liozardillos?" Thali asked.

"They have a lion's body, an armadillo's back, a crocodile's jaws and tail, a reptile's claws, and ... wait, they breathe fire?" Nasir said as he peered through a crack in the wall.

Thali went over and pressed her eye to the crack too. The creatures were huge, as big as Alexius in his dragon form. They were breathing fire and ... a liquid that caught fire when it came into contact with the buildings. People ran screaming hither and thither, some on fire.

"A dragon is afraid of liozardillos?" Thali asked.

"They thrive on destruction. Their power grows with fear and chaos," Alexius said. His brows were furrowed, and he didn't seem as keen as she and Nasir were to see what was going on outside.

"You don't want to see what's going on?" Thali asked as she backed away from the crack and turned to Alexius.

He swallowed and shook his head. "They leave cities the same way each time: burnt to the ground. Centuries ago, they ran rampant in part of Etciel. It took a team of twelve dragons to round them up and kill them. My father severely restricted their territory after that. I don't know how they got out. But it doesn't bode well if they're here now."

"I have to do something," Thali said. She pressed her face to the crack. There were people out there.

"I've put protections around the houses, and illusions. They will look destroyed as the creatures fly by, they'll even feel hot, but everyone inside will be safe."

Thali hoped and prayed that Garen and the others were all inside. She reached into her mind and saw the glittering, putrid, yellow-green threads of the liozardillos. Their threads were encased in something hard and clear, and she couldn't connect with them.

Come back to me, Rou, her brother's voice said in her mind. The liozardillos disappeared.

"They've disappeared," Nasir said.

Alexius looked up suddenly. "They've been pulled away."

Thali pushed the door open and saw guards running toward the gate. She turned to the city. It was all ashes and smoldering flames licking the sky. Everything not in flames was brown, gray, and black. Thali's heart sank. There was nothing left of the city. A tear rolled down her cheek.

Then Alexius put a hand on her shoulder, and he lifted his magic. The city came back. It was darkened by ash, and a few buildings closest to the gate were smoldering, but the rest of the city was all right.

"I'm sorry, Alexius," Thali said. She turned to him and hugged him, realizing the illusion had not been his imagination but a memory that he'd overlayed onto the city.

He nodded, and suddenly Isaia appeared. They all ushered her back to the palace.

There, she blinked. "Alexius, do you still have an illusion covering the palace?" Thali asked. Before her, a huge section of the palace lay in ruins, as if dragons had landed on it.

"No, I've lifted them all," Alexius said.

"Your Majesty, that's the leftover damage from the battle that killed King Devrain and Queen Adela," said a royal guard who had joined them at the entrance and was now trying his best to get them moving.

Thali swallowed. She hadn't seen the palace from the outside until now. She was heartbroken. The smoke and flames were long gone, but the castle had missing chunks like a child had knocked blocks over. Ragged edges and blackened stone told her where there had been flames.

Even the barrier isn't perfect. Alexius said.

Thali nodded. More determined than ever as she strode back into the palace.

CHAPTER FORTY-FIVE

T HALI DIDN'T WANT TO deal with the nobles, but she had to, for Elric, for the kingdom. Once back in her rooms, Mia helped her dress in her finest queenly outfit in the purple of Elric's family crest. When Thali glanced at the mirror, she blinked: she truly looked like a queen. It was a purple gown that faded to red halfway down her skirts, with a boat neck and an overlay of crystals. It was the spakliest dress she'd ever worn. "Wow, Mia."

Mia beamed. "A dress fit for a queen."

Thali hugged Mia, then hurried off to join Elric in a room adjacent to the public gallery. She hoped this would be over quickly.

"You look stunning," Elric said as she took his hand. He was dressed in his most royal outfit too. He carefully placed a silver crown on her head; it matched his own. Three gems inlaid in silver filigree was both beautiful and imposing. This would be a moment.

"Ready?" she asked. She glanced at the box Avery held.

He nodded and reached into the box. He brought out and unfolded a belt of gems. It looked heavy. He placed it across his torso, Stefan helping him buckle it at the back.

Thali looked at the gems. They shone differently than she had expected. She blinked as Elric took out a wand with a ball on top, both completely encrusted in diamonds and plated with gold.

He took a deep breath, then held his arm out.

Thali placed her hand lightly on his arm, not weighing it down so as not to make this more difficult for him. "Wait," Thali said. She swallowed, then called Bardo out from a pocket in her skirts and asked Indi and Ana to step forward, Indi closest to her and Ana next to the tiger. Finally, she called for one more friend.

"Stefan, could you be a dear and open the door?" Thali asked, and Stefan did so. Arabelle trotted into the room to everyone's surprise, and she chuffed into Thali's hair in greeting before standing behind her. Thali glanced over her shoulder; Nasir, Isaia, and Alexius all stood there in their most formal uniforms, but it was Alexius whom she made eye contact with. He nodded.

The doors opened, and they walked into the gallery. Thali held her head high. It was time to play queen.

The chatter in the room stopped. Thali knew she wouldn't see a single friendly face, but while she'd expected to see mostly lords here, the ladies had come as well.

Gabrielle fanned herself with her eyes cast down in the most pathetic of bows, while many of the lords bowed at the waist.

A scoff to her left caught her gaze. It was none other than the same councilmen who hadn't believed her, who had caused her banishment.

Thali rallied despite them. "I have heard rumors that my husband, the king's, right to rule has been questioned by the very nobility that benefit directly from his leadership," she said.

Whispers washed through the crowd.

"Who would question my lord and king?" Thali demanded.

The scoffing councilmen and two older lords stepped forward.

"How do we know that is the same scepter and belt that has been passed down through the monarchy?" one asked.

"You may examine it," Elric said. He beamed at her, and she hoped it was from pride.

An older lord approached and looked closely at the scepter, at the belt across Elric's torso. "You have my fealty. These are the true belt and scepter," the lord announced.

He must have discovered the few imperfections in the belt and scepter that Elric told me about. They made them authentic, Thali thought.

"Thank you," Elric said.

The lord melted back into the crowd.

Councillor Liman, of course, looked her directly in the eye. "How is it that *children* will rule this kingdom? How will *children* protect us against the terrifying creatures that attack us from above?"

I think it's time to show them who you really are, Thali said.

Happily, Alexius replied. The lords hurriedly shuffled back when he popped into his dragon form. The crowd gasped. Some lords and ladies even fainted. Thali felt the dragon's warm breath over her head and grinned at how Alexius must be staring down the room.

"Does that answer your question?" Thali looked at the councilman.

He too melted away mutely.

Elric glanced at her and raised an eyebrow as if to ask if she was done. At her nod, he said, "This will be your last opportunity to swear fealty." His voice rang clearly and loudly through the hall, and the lords all shuffled into a line with their ladies. They bowed or curtsied before Elric one at a time, announcing their names and houses as they went.

Thali was glad to see the rest of the noble families step forward and promise their loyalty. She was also glad for all Ana's staring, Indi's claw licking, Bardo's tongue flicking, Arabelle's stillness—and the steam coming from Alexius's maw. Maybe being Queen wasn't so bad.

Thali had given up on sleeping. She didn't hear the door open as she finished the letter she was writing and sealed it, placing it on the stack on her desk. Then she moved the pile of letters on the silver plate her mail usually arrived in and hoped it all made it safely into the intended hands.

It wasn't until Elric placed a hand on her shoulder that she realized he was there. She turned to face him. Part of her hoped she could leave without a fight. But he stepped in front of her, holding the bag she had just finished packing. "Where are you going?"

"I'm going back to my brother."

"Why?" Elric's jaw snapped shut. He was angry.

"That devastation out there, I can't let that happen. I must convince my brother to change his mind."

"And what if he doesn't? What if your brother turns on you because if you're not with him, you're against him?" Elric asked.

Thali paused and looked up. "It's my brother. Rommy wouldn't hurt me."

"Until he does, even by accident."

Thali didn't meet his eyes. She could hear Elric grinding his teeth.

"Will you at least take some guards?"

"I'll take Alexius and Nasir, Isaia and Jaxon," Thali said. She felt Elric's tension release a little bit.

"I really don't think your brother is going to listen to reason," Elric said.

"I ..." Thali looked up and saw Elric's eyes weren't hard and angry as she'd expected them to be; they were instead soft and sad. "I have to try. And if I can't do that, I at least have to try to free Alexius's father. I don't know how yet, but if we can free him, then maybe there won't be a war."

Elric looked out the window. Thali sat down on the bed. "If I commanded you to stay, would you?" he asked, still facing the window.

Thali froze. What were the repercussions if she disobeyed her husband, the king?

"No, I would still go," Thali said.

Elric sighed. "I always thought that once we were married, we would never be parted again, that I would dine with you every night and every morning, wake up to you at my side, help the people with you next to me. And really, it seems like you've left me more times than I can count," Elric said.

"I'm sorry. I want to come home and live here peacefully. But isn't it worth it if we stop a war?" Thali stood up and strode over to take Elric's hand.

"As a king, I say yes. As your husband, I wish you'd let Alexius go instead."

"I need to go. If anyone can stop this, it's me," Thali said. She turned and grabbed her soft silk pajamas and threw them into the bag on a last-minute impulse. There were a few things that she enjoyed about the luxurious princess lifestyle. "You're not going to try and stop me?" Thali looked up carefully.

"Even if I locked you in this room or locked you in a dungeon, or even in that magic-sucking room, you'd only resent me for it. That's not the relationship I want. And I would rather you were absent *for* the kingdom instead of just plain missing," Elric said. He sighed as he sat down. "I hate that you're going. Don't get me wrong. I want to go with you—not that I can do much to help. I learned that in Cerisa." He laughed. "I knew when I fell in love with you that you would be a very different queen. I thought you might throw some trends out the window, maybe get all the ladies at court wearing trousers, but I never imagined you'd leave our world quite so often." Elric smiled a tight smile.

Thali took both his hands and nudged his legs open so she could stand between his knees. "I'll be back, I promise. If I can't convince him, then I'll free Alexius's father and come back to you, to Adanek."

"Promise?" Elric asked. His voice broke into a whisper.

Thali nodded, then bumped her forehead into his.

"Always bumping into me." Elric smiled. He took her face in his hands and kissed her deeply.

Thali felt the love, the desperation, the sadness in that kiss. She let them linger in that kiss until a knock at the door sounded.

"Come in," Elric said as Thali cleared her throat and straightened her tunic.

Nasir and Isaia walked into the room in full armor, Alexius right behind them with Jaxon.

"All right, first, lose the armor. We're not storming the castle," Thali said as she saw they were battle ready.

Isaia and Nasir looked at her and then at each other.

"Seriously. We're going to try and convince my brother peacefully. Not like that."

Elric nodded, so Alexius helped them remove their armor. Once they were more plainly dressed, Thali nodded.

"Nasir, Isaia, if you come back without Thali, I'll kill you myself. And Prince Tariq has said the same, so you'll be dead twice." Elric warned, looking them straight in the eye. They nodded. "Alexius, please protect her, keep her safe, in body and mind." Elric sounded more pleading than threatening that time.

Alexius nodded.

"It was nice to meet you, Jaxon, but you'll forgive me for saying I'm glad you're returning home," Elric said, and Jaxon just grinned.

Thali thought, *Rommy, please hear me out. Please, please let this work.* She closed her eyes and imagined the black-and-white tiled sitting room with the great fireplace. She drew her magic to that place, then she imagined the door. By pulling on the door with her threads, she made the door swing open, and Thali opened her eyes to see her imagined sitting room on the other side of the mirror.

Alexius nodded and walked through, Nasir and Isaia following. Elric grabbed Thali's hand and cradled her face once more. He kissed her; it was soft and sad and warm and tore at her heart. She wanted to stay with him, stay here. She didn't want to face her brother, possibly fight him, possibly anger him.

"You are strong, and you can do anything. So do what you must and then come back to me," Elric whispered as he rested his forehead on hers. They stayed like that for a moment more; then Thali pulled away. Elric stayed rooted to the spot as she walked through the doorway, then turned back to him. She had a job to do. Jaxon walked through last, and she slowly closed the door to their bedroom.

Immediately, she took a deep breath. Being in Etciel was like coming up for air. Magic surrounded them here; it wasn't the finite resource it was in her world.

When Thali opened her eyes, she swallowed. Xerus, Aexie, and her brother surrounded them, and they did not look friendly. She looked at her brother, whose expression held a question with his raised eyebrow.

"Rommy?" She swallowed her fears and opened her arms.

Rommy cracked a smile, took the two steps to her, and embraced her. Thali relaxed as she felt the familiar, warm embrace she'd grown up with. Her brother was in there somewhere. She just had to get him to come back permanently.

If you enjoyed this story, consider subscribing to my newsletter to join my animal loving community and keep up to date with book news!

Visit: https://geni.us/camillatracynewsletter

or scan this QR code:

Note from the Author

I T'S REALLY DIFFICULT FOR me to believe that this is book five. There's only one more book to Thali's story! Kind of. Next up is a prequel of short stories that will introduce you to some of Thali's friends before she went to school in Lanchor. And then book six!

In order to publish this many books in such a short time (six books in 17 months), I had to save up a few before I started publishing the first one. Now you've caught up! The last book is half written but it's very exciting that we've finally converged!

Visit my website at CamillaTracy.com or scan this QR code:

Camilla Tracy
camillatracy.com

CONTINUE READING...IN ARMOIRE OF ADVENTURES

We'll be diving into Thali's past – stories from the decade before she arrives at school in Lanchor (or the first book) to meet some of her friends that may come back in the final book!

Coming in Spring 2025

Visit https://geni.us/ArmoireofAdventures to buy or scan this QR code

ACKNOWLEDGEMENTS

A LWAYS FIRST AND FOREMOST, I'm so grateful to you, dear reader, for choosing this story to read and I hope you're entertained. There's a theme of friendship in this book, and that's where my thoughts are in these acknowledgements.

As this is in the process of being published, I've broken my fibula in a very ordinary way. The outpouring of friends that have checked in, offered assistance and support has been truly heart warming and I'm so very appreciative of your time.

Thank you to Char. You were one of my first cheerleaders and the insight you provide for me as a beta reader is crucial to these stories being the best they can be. I'm so incredibly grateful to you.

I have so much appreciation for my dear friend Tanya. Your brain works in ways that mine doesn't and I can't believe that I'm lucky enough to benefit from it! Thank you for obliterating the tasks that are way too scary and overwhelming for me.

Thank you to my communities that have rallied around me. For buying my book, for telling your friends and family about it, for taking the time to read it. I hope you get to see a piece of me in my work and that you are also entertained!

Thank you to my writing group. My fellow grapes, you are so support-ive and encouraging, it's a joy whenever we can meet up, chat, and collaborate!

Thank you to my early readers. You are one of the firsts to see the story and I appreciate your perspective, thoughts, and detailed feedback.

Thank you to my editor – Bobbi Beatty of Silver Scroll Services. I'm so grateful to be working with you and so grateful these stories get your special touch added to them too.

Thank you to Lorna Stuber, proofreader extraordinaire! This book, I learned about the words I use way too much and a LOT about runts...It's also such a special thing to have a fellow author friend to go along this journey with.

I'm grateful to the very talented artists at MiblArt. Your group puts the most beautiful covers together for me and I appreciate working with you!

These books are possible because of the amazing support I have from my family. Thank you to my husband, who reads out of his usual genre for me and is my voluntold employee for all things in this crazy adventure.

Special thanks to my mom for telling everyone she knows and selling my book to all her friends and acquaintances.

To my steadfast furry friends, Truffle & Udon, thanks for reminding me to get up every few hours and keeping my toes warm and keeping me company as I tip-tap away. To Kali, thank you for making sure I get outside for some fresh air and get dirt under my nails once in awhile.

About the Author

Camilla is a lover of many mediums of storytelling. She loves to write strong heroines with animal sidekicks, who can triumph and find the love of their life. She always has projects on the go and loves to consume stories of all kinds—books, shows, movies, plays, amongst many others.

When she is not writing, Camilla is often found exploring animal behavior, crafting, drinking a hot beverage, and clicker training her animals.

Come visit her at CamillaTracy.com or on instagram @camilla_tracy. Sign up for her newsletter by visiting: https://geni.us/CamillaTracynewsletteror by scanning the QR code below:

www.ingramcontent.com/pod-product-compliance
Lightning Source LLC
Chambersburg PA
CBHW051123190726
48290CB00006B/1658